SCORNED

SCORNED

by

GINNA MORAN

Cover design by Silver Starlight Designs
Cover images copyright 123RF

For Inquiries Contact:
Sunny Palms Press
9663 Santa Monica Blvd Suite 1158
Beverly Hills, CA 90210, USA
www.sunnypalmspress.com
www.GinnaMoran.com

To Malory, Ten years ago, you re-introduced me to YA books. With that, you had ignited a passion in me that has only grown over the years, which led me to where I am today. I can't thank you enough for your friendship. No matter how long we go without talking or how far we live from each other, we always pick up right where we left off. You're a friend through all of life's stages. A true friend forever.

PROLOGUE

RULE THE WORLD

HOLDING MY HEAD high, I peer around the crowded room of demons from the safety of my father's side. His cinnamon and clove scent overpowers the rest of the headache-inducing stench of demons, and I watch as he grins at his inferiors.

"Don't let them fool you, Camilla," Malicevile says, shifting to gaze at me. "The only thing stopping them from trying to send you home is that they want something. Remember, treat them like the demons they are." *Home.* I'd like to see them try.

"Beneath us," I say, repeating the words he's ingrained in my mind a million times.

A few demons size me up, and I narrow my eyes as I expose the true demonic body that lies within my human skin. Dainty black horns jet from my forehead in a small crown around my head, and an energy orb bursts between my palms. A red haze tints my vision, turning the dimly lit room almost completely dark.

"Exactly." He reaches up and runs his hand along my horns before pushing my curls behind my ear. "Now, stop letting them intimidate you. You don't have to prove anything to them. If they need proof, they'll find it in their demise."

Clenching my jaw, I say, "I'm not intimidated. I'm bored. Can we get out of here?"

"Whatever you want, my sweet Camilla."

What I really want is to wipe the mocking look off a demonic woman's face, who has been smugly leering at me from her place at a tall table. If Malicevile wouldn't stop me, I'd send a burst of power at her to show her exactly who she's dealing with.

Guiding me to the door, Malicevile keeps his hand locked around my arm like someone might attempt to snatch me away. And they might try. There's no better way to get to Malicevile than through me. It's always a power struggle for demons. They admire and loathe my father, craving to have even a morsel of his power. Power they'll never obtain. Not if my father has a say. They have no choice but to stand with him and hope he finds them useful.

Because times are changing. The world is evolving for the

better. Humans are finally losing the battle. They're losing their souls. And me? I'm standing at the top as the beginning of a new demonic race. One not fit for Hell. One Heaven is terrified to believe. If only they knew that I was created when a nephilim's good grace ripped me from the gates of Hell to save my soul. But I didn't want to be saved. I wanted to live. And now I can—forever.

Pulling myself from my thoughts, I gaze around the room of demons once more. As we pass through the crowd, a woman reaches out her hand and runs it along my forearm, surprising me. In one swift motion, I raise my hand, summoning hot electricity, and I chuck it right at her chest. Her eyes widen as she stumbles back.

I bare my teeth. "Do you know who I am?" I ask.

She doesn't respond. She doesn't need to. Everyone knows who I am.

I'm Cami Hellshire, daughter of Malicevile, and I'm ready to rule the world.

PRICELESS POSSESSION

"YOU CAN'T RUN forever!" I yell.

A man with blond hair cropped short against his head knocks over a trashcan as he rushes toward the entrance of the alley. He peers over his shoulder, fear lining his eyes, the scent potent enough to make me smile.

I launch over the barricade he tried to create to slow me down. "Did you really think you could best my father?" I ask, touching down on the ground. My boots thud against the concrete the faster I move. "You're lucky it's me who has come to collect."

Electricity erupts in my fingers as I follow the man just far enough back to give him enough hope to think he could actual-ly outrun me. It's more fun this way, and a good chase is exactly what I needed to start my night with.

Spending every day in the most boring place in the entire universe is enough to make anyone a little crazy. Especially spending long hours with Malicevile, my demonic father, be-cause my choices of companions in the daylight prison realm are pretty slim. Good company as a demon is hard to find when the one person who doesn't bore me to death can't follow me there.

Speaking of my favorite person. A flash of firelight erupts at the mouth of the alley as Evan comes into view. His face lights up in the darkness as he tosses a fireball in front of him. And he looks so dang sexy. Sexy enough that I slow my steps to admire him. His golden blond hair sparkles orange in his firelight, and his eyebrows wag as he meets my gaze. He dazzles me with a smile wide enough to make me want to end this chase so I can spend the rest of the night pressed against his hot body.

If Malicevile wasn't so insistent that I need a babysitter in this demon-fight-demon world he wants me to embrace yet stay on the fringes of, I probably would put up more of a fight for doing his lowly soul collecting work. Having Evan around is the only reason I agreed to help in the first place. It usually means I get some alone time with the boy who makes me feel more alive than ever, even without my humanity.

"Help!" the man screams, spinning in a circle.

I toss a small energy orb at him. It's just enough electricity to make him squeal from the low voltage shock. His eyes widen as he drops to his knees. His expression is priceless as his hope dwindles before disappearing altogether. Tears rim his eyes, and I hear him mumble a prayer as a last effort to be saved.

I laugh, the sound echoing above the city noise. "You think someone is listening to *you*? That by some miracle, you'll manage to escape *me*?"

The man squeezes his eyes closed without answering me.

"Let me tell you now. No one's coming for you. No one can hear you. You know how I know this? Because I see your soul, and I don't even want to touch that disgusting thing." I close my eyes for a split second to gather my focus. When I open them, the man's soul appears for me to see. Black streaks nearly cover him, with only a tiny fissure of light—what's left of his humanity—shining through.

A tear rolls down the man's cheek. He quickly wipes it away with the back of his hand. "I've asked for forgiveness," he says as he opens his eyes.

I smirk. "No, you've asked to be found not guilty to a slew of crimes. And my father saw to it. He held up his end of the bargain. Now, it's time you do the same. Get up."

With a shuddering sigh, the man climbs to his feet. "This is too soon. I just got released."

I shrug. "You never specified when you were willing to pay. That's your fault. Luckily for you, my father has only asked that I bring you to him." So many people make terribly careless deals with my father. It's almost ridiculous what desperation can do to someone's thought process. I'd pity this man if he totally didn't deserve his crappy deal—actually, I wouldn't pity him. Serves him right for making a deal with a demon.

The man's shoulders shake as he sobs. "Please, there has to be something you want. I can make a deal with you. Please, just tell Malicevile that you couldn't find me. I need a few days."

Evan waggles his eyebrows when I lift my gaze to him. He stands quietly behind the man, a small flame cupped between his hands. "What's a few days, babe?" Evan asks with a smile hot enough to melt my already fiery heart.

I tap my finger to my chin. "Hmmm. Let me think about this." It's the same game as always. Evan gives hope while I steal it away all over again.

The man sucks in another breath. There it is. A spark of hope in his eyes. He's incredibly foolish to think that I'd make a deal with him. I don't make deals—not yet at least—and I'd never risk going against Malicevile. Not now. Not when I need him. Plus, I've learned my lesson when it comes to demonic affairs. I'll steer clear of any and all of them if possible. Though my meddling did get me something I desperately wanted. It got me my boyfriend back.

"Anything. I'll give you anything," the man says. "How about another soul? My sister, she's—"

I cross my arms. "Are you serious? You can't offer a soul that doesn't belong to you. You're pathetic."

The man grimaces. "But I can—"

I raise my hand. "I don't want to hear it. Now you're just

wasting my time." This collection has turned boring fast. I prefer those who fight and this man is a blubbering mess. Why my father wants him in his entirety, I have no idea. He'd be better off just adding him to his shelf of collectibles and calling it a day. Those souls give him a different kind of power. Power strong enough to make him invincible. At least, that's what he told me.

Evan steps forward and grabs the back of the man's shirt, pulling him to his feet. The man yells out as he thrashes. He jerks away from Evan before sucker punching him in the nose. Blood drips from Evan's face when he reaches for the man again, but I launch forward and knock the man off his feet.

He sprawls across the concrete as I land on his back. In one quick motion, I turn the man over and jab my sharp nail into his chest, tearing a hole in the fabric of his shirt. I glare into the man's brown eyes, anger running hotter than the electricity racing through my veins. I can't believe he drew blood from my boyfriend. I can't believe he still has some fight left in him.

Instead of saying anything, I yell into the man's face. The color drains from his skin, and I catch my reflection in his watery eyes. He brought out the demon that lurks just under my skin. And now that my true body is showing for the world to see, I can't control myself.

Gathering my power, I slam my hands into his chest and unleash in it a smoldering jolt of electricity. The man's eyes widen before they roll back into his head. A moment later, I watch as his tainted soul rises from his body.

"Ugh! Where's my bag? Get my bag!" I run my hand over the man's soul, coaxing it toward me. A wave of nausea rolls over me as every bad deed he's ever committed rushes over me while I hold his soul in place. I wouldn't be affected by his sinful life if I didn't have my own soul. It's the one thing that sets me apart from other demons. I have my own humanity and soul. One I can shut off, the other—well, it's my most priceless possession, and I'd never give it away.

Cringing, I force myself to hold onto the soul. He wasn't just a man who made a bad deal with my father. He was a monster, a murderer, and now I have to feel his soul against mine. *Gag.*

Evan drops my backpack at my feet, and I dig through the front pocket and yank out a glass cylindrical vial the size of my finger. Popping the top, I concentrate on moving the soul toward the opening until the soul container activates and sucks the soul inside for safe keeping.

A scream rips from the cylindrical vial, and I cork it, muting most of the noise. Without a second glance, I shove the soul into my backpack before falling back to the concrete. My chest heaves as I force the disgusting images from my mind. The man—who I now know was named Howard Wiles—deserves his fate. I used to think that demons stole so many innocent souls. I used to cry, thinking about all the lives my father collected, but he has very few innocent souls in his possession. They're mostly souls already heading to Hell.

Evan kneels at my side and takes my hand in his. "We were

supposed to bring him in alive."

I blow out a breath. "He hit you." At the time, it seemed really important to hurt Howard when I saw him make Evan bleed, but now that my head is clear, I'm pretty sure I went overboard. It's not like Evan can't handle himself. He's still a better combat fighter than me, which says something since I *am* a fully fledged demon. With my transformation, I got a few new tricks, including a lot more strength than what I had as a half-human.

He chuckles. "I hope you come up with a better excuse than that when you hand that soul over to Malicevile. He's not going to let us out alone if he thinks you're going to kill every-one who raises their hand at me." Leaning over, he kisses my lips, sending a rush of desire through me. "Though you're sexy as hell when you're protective."

I wrap my arms around his neck and let him pull me from the ground. He doesn't set me on my feet right away. Instead, he holds me against him as I bury my face in the crook of his neck. His patchouli and amber scent calms my nerves and slows my heavy breathing while I think about what I've done.

I killed a man. It's the first time this has happened as a de-mon, and the only thing I feel is annoyance. Because now I have to bring back a soul and a body separate from each other to face my father. Howard's death is an inconvenience.

I imagine that the old Cami, the one who made deals with demons to help even the vilest of people, would be broken up about this. But that Cami is long gone now that I bury my humanity away.

After a long moment of silence, Evan asks, "You okay?"

I pull away so he sets me back on my feet. "Yup, just not looking forward to moving the body."

"How about I move the body and you thank me later?" he asks, leaning in for another kiss.

I smile. "I think I can manage that."

⁓ ❧ ⁓

Malicevile taps his foot, his arms crossed over his chest, as he looks between the body Evan set on the floor and the glass cylinder in my hands.

"You're being dramatic," I say, batting my eyelashes a few times. "And honestly, I think you're letting your humanity get the best of you. The world is better off without Howard Wiles."

Even though Malicevile encouraged me to shut off my humanity—because I'm in much better control without it—he still possesses the humanity he acquired from me. As my father, we share demonic blood and a bond unlike anything anyone could ever experience. It doesn't make us closer, but it does mean that he gets part of my humanity. I used to wonder why he'd want such a silly thing, but humanity gives him the ability to work with other demons on a higher level. He also understands the human world in ways lower-level demons could never process.

He thrusts his arms wide, proving my point about his dramatics. "Camilla! This isn't about making the world a better place. This is about what Howard had to offer me. Serial killers of his caliber are hard to come by."

"I think you misjudged him. The man cried at my feet," I say, glancing at Evan who stands behind my father. He presses his lips together when Malicevile follows my gaze. "He wasn't exactly warrior material."

"So you killed him?" he asks.

I roll my eyes. "It was an accident. I lost control, okay?"

"Now what could he have possibly done to make you lose control?" He studies me for a long moment, like I'll break under his gaze. I'm immune to his charm, though. I don't even fear him most days.

I can't think of an excuse fast enough. "It was nothing. I overreacted. I'm sorry." Overreacting and losing control are the result of holding Malicevile's power within me. It's like a ticking time bomb, just waiting to explode. But I can't go without it. Not in a world I don't trust.

Malicevile rubs the back of his neck as he thinks to himself. I hate when he does this, drawing things out longer than necessary. It was one stupid soul, and it's not like I let it get away.

"Evan," Malicevile says, turning to my boyfriend. "Why did Camilla overreact?"

Oh, crap. Seriously? "Hello? I'm standing right here." I reach out and grab my father by his sleeve. Evan never lies to my father no matter what the consequences are. He can't. It has to do with the fact that Malicevile owns his soul. It's part of the reason Malicevile won't give Evan's soul to me. He uses it as a way to control me. He said so himself.

I hold my finger up to Evan. "Don't answer that. This is between me and my dad."

Malicevile brushes my hand away. "Tell me, Evan."

Evan shrugs at me. "She lost control when the guy hit—"

Without thinking, I raise my hand and thrust a small energy ball at Evan, knocking him back, cutting off his words. The moment Malicevile thinks something—or someone in this case—is interfering with my life, he'll do something drastic. I wouldn't put it past him to punish Evan for my mistake, because punishing him would be like punishing me.

"Dad!" I yell. "Leave Evan out of it. It was my fault."

Fire glows in my father's eyes as he directs his anger at me. Raising his hands, he blasts me with a surge of white-hot energy. I don't have time to react. His power knocks me back into the wall, sending sparks through my vision. Malicevile might be my father, and he might care about me in his own twisted way, but he's still a demon. He still loves to punish people. Me especially.

I grind my teeth while he shoots more power at me until I focus enough to absorb it. My hair rises around my face as static clings to me. My soul fills, expanding to the point that I'm pretty sure I'll combust if he continues, but I won't give him the satisfaction of asking for mercy.

Standing over me, he smiles. "Had enough, Daughter?"

Kicking my leg out, I knock his feet out from under him, stopping him from blasting me with another wave of power. If he expects anything less of me, then he doesn't know me as well as I thought he did.

I levitate from my spot on the floor and land just next to him. "Have you?"

He laughs as his eyes narrow. Without answering me, he handsprings to his feet and removes his suit jacket. It gives me the chance to ready myself for his next move. As he rolls up his sleeves, I shrug from my leather jacket and toss it to Evan.

I roll my shoulders, stepping backwards, not touching the floor as I levitate high enough to be at the same level as my father. Malicevile cracks his knuckles like he can somehow intimidate me. It works a little.

Power ignites in my father's fingers, and it doesn't take him long to thrust an energy orb at me. As I catch it, he charges forward, slamming his hands into my chest, pushing me back into the wall. His sharp nails dig into my collarbone, stabbing into my skin.

Jerking my leg up, I knee him in the stomach. He doesn't back down though. He never does. I could fight him all I want, but he only reacts like I'm a pesky fly.

"You're boring me, Camilla," he says, sending another bout of energy into me.

I don't respond. I can't. His energy comes in faster and hotter than usual. It sinks deep into my soul, threatening to consume me. He's testing me, making a point. Showing me that even though I might be a demon, I'm nothing compared to him. It'll take me years to ever measure up to him.

"Have you had enough?" he asks again, smiling at my obvious pain.

"No," I manage to spit out.

"Good." He drops his hands and steps back to give me a chance to try to best him again. "Now stop thinking and just react."

Without waiting for him to strike first, I shoot a fireball from my hands instead of the energy he expects. The fire singes the fabric, smoldering his dress shirt. There's no point in trying to use his power against him.

As he pats the burning fabric with his hand, I rush forward. Another fireball erupts in my fingers, and I chuck it at him again. He's prepared this time though and drops to the ground before propelling from the floor to knock into me. His arms circle my waist, and he flips me up and over his shoulder. He spins me through the air and launches another bout of energy at me.

I can't absorb the power and stop my fall at the same time, so when my back hits the hardwood floor of his office, air bursts from my lungs. I skid across the floor, hitting my back on the door. It shakes on its hinges from my force but doesn't crack like the last time I egged my father on.

I shift, peering at Evan's boots as he stands over me. Glancing up, I meet his serious eyes. His jaw tenses, and we watch each other for a split second. It's long enough for Malicevile to shock me again.

I scream out in frustration and thrust my hands out, sending the power I've been saving for a special occasion at my dad.

The lava bomb flies through the air and hits Malicevile in the stomach. Surprise crosses his face, and he rips his shirt off before the acid-like power melts into his skin. He wasn't quick enough though. His abs glow bright pink.

"Get up, Cami," Evan whispers.

Malicevile's already crossing the room before I have a chance to get to my feet. Fire burns in his eyes as he closes the distance. Energy swirls in his hands, and he comes at me with furrowed brows, a look of revenge on his face.

I raise my hands. "I've had enough."

He hovers over me. "I'll tell you when you've had enough." With those words, he sends a stream of electricity straight into my chest.

The edges of my vision darken as exhaustion consumes me. He hasn't pushed me like this in weeks. I'm pretty sure I'm being punished for Howard.

An angry tear escapes my eye. "Stop!"

"Make me," Malicevile says with a smile.

But I can't. All I can do is succumb to the darkness that drags me away from the world.

SILLY EMOTIONS

"DON'T COME ANY closer," I say.

A shadow crawls across the dead grass under my feet. The scent of apple and rain showers wafts around me, stirring something deep within me that I haven't felt since the last time Malicevile thought I could use a good nap. It's been weeks since I've seen Dylan, and the last time I didn't even give him the chance to talk before reality swept me back.

"I'm not going to try anything. I told you I respect your decision. If this is what you want from life, then I'm not going to intervene," he says from behind me. "But I am here for you."

Swiveling on my feet, I turn to face him. "You make it

sound like I've made the worst decision ever."

He doesn't respond. Of course he thinks I made a poor choice when I refused to let him try to get near my soul. He wanted to fix something that wasn't broken. I'm better now, better than ever, and I don't need some half-angel to make me feel bad about myself.

"I'm not going to say it was the right decision," he says. "I just wish you'd have given me more of a chance."

"A chance to do what?" I ask, looking into his chocolate-brown eyes.

I'd be blind if I didn't notice how attractive he looks in this moment, all dark and brooding, completely opposite than what I think a nephilim should look like. His hands remain clenched at his sides, and I can tell that I'm getting under his skin. So I reach out and touch his face, running my fingers along his jaw.

He reaches up and covers my hand with his instead of pulling away from me. "A chance to figure this out. A chance to be with you. God, Cami. I miss you."

I don't react even though a cruel, immobilizing feeling—regret—sneaks into my heart. I'm vulnerable to my humanity in this dream state. "Be together? Don't be ridiculous. I'm a demon, Dylan. Just the sight of you makes me uneasy."

He sighs. "It's this world. It's because here, I'm close to your soul."

"And you think meeting me in person will change that? Do you know how crazy you sound? If Malicevile were to find out that I let you anywhere near me, he'd kill you." I pause. "Actually, he'd expect me to kill you."

"But you wouldn't," he says.

I shrug. "I don't want to. I still remember that you used to mean something to me."

He flinches at my words. "Just meet me."

I stand on my tiptoes, closing the distance between us until my lips are an inch away from his. He sucks in a small breath, shuddering under my warm grip. I breathe against his lips, remembering what they were like to kiss. But I don't kiss him. I wouldn't. Not now. Not again. Toying with him is much more fun.

"I'll think about it," I whisper. "But I still don't understand why you want to. What do you get out of it? I'm with who I want to be with."

He remains utterly still. "Maybe I'm a glutton for punishment."

I smirk. "Do you regret turning me down now?" In a moment of wild hurt and desire, I wanted nothing more than to be with Dylan when I had thought Evan had changed for the worse. I wanted to use him to forget. He helped ease the pain. That pain is no longer there, though.

He leans closer, so close that his bottom lip brushes mine. But still, we don't kiss. We just feel each other's closeness. "No, love," he finally says.

I pull away. "That's too bad. It didn't stop Evan, you know. He was relentless. Tried everything to get to me."

His jaw clenches as he puts more space between us. "He

did get to you."

I roll my eyes. "He gave up his soul for me, Dylan."

He sighs. "Is that what this is about now? Who can offer you more?" He doesn't say it, but I know he's thinking about how he risked everything for me by stealing me from the gates of Hell before it had a chance to draw me in. It was my last chance at redemption, but by some—I hate saying this word—*miracle,* I transformed into a demon. I wasn't ready to die. I don't think I'll ever truly be ready. It's a good thing I don't plan on it.

"Don't be stupid. I love Evan." At least I know I love Evan. Feeling it is another story. Love is one of the silly emotions that make you weak. People do crazy things in the name of love. I should know. The only emotions I allow myself to feel now are the fun ones. And love definitely isn't fun.

"And you love me, too," he says like he's so sure that I still love him now in this moment. A second later, his wings spread out wide on his back, flashing a blinding light. They've changed—I've changed—and they're so hard to even look at. His wings cause me physical pain, the same pain that all blessed things do.

He notices that I flinch back, and his wings disappear as quickly as they came.

Seeing him in his angelic glory digs deep into my soul, threatening to break through the steel wall I've built around my soul to lock it away and keep everyone else out. It's what protects me from feeling every sharp edge of my broken spirit. It protects me from feeling so terrible in my own skin. A memory that doesn't bother me now, but one I'll never forget.

Covering my eyes, I turn away. "Dylan, please."

"I just want you to remember," he says. He doesn't come any closer, though.

"I can't. Not yet. Not now."

The ground beneath our feet quivers as reality calls me back. A large crack breaks through the dead grass, and a black streak of nothingness threatens to swallow this dream world.

"Please, Cami. Tell me you'll meet me," Dylan says as the ground opens between us.

I brace myself against a stone bench. "Tomorrow night," I say reluctantly. "I'll call you."

He closes his eyes in relief. "I'll meet you anywhere."

"Okay." I hold onto my dream for a moment longer. "But if this is a trap, don't think I won't hurt you."

He nods. "I'd never do that. And, love? Come alone."

Before I can respond, the world explodes around me. Dylan disappears, leaving me feeling slightly sad, an emotion I haven't felt in weeks. But the moment light breaks through the darkness, the feeling is gone—it's nothing but a fleeting memory.

～৶৶～

The bed smolders beneath me when I open my eyes. Smoke stings my nostrils, and I blink, staring at the ceiling without moving. The heat doesn't bother me, but I can't shake the image of Dylan from my mind.

A flash of firelight catches my attention, and I sit up on my bed. My hellhound anxiously runs laps around my room, leaving a black trail across my white carpet. I frown, looking at the mess he created in my room. I'm surprised Malicevile even allowed him in. Pets usually stay outside in the kennel.

I clap my hands, leaning down. "Come here, Greg." Malicevile hates that I call my hellhound by his human name, but it's the least I can do for my guard dog. He did turn on his pack of werewolves to protect me. It's not my fault that standing with a demon was enough to break him. The Greg I knew is gone though. His coal eyes prove it. He's happy to stand by my side, and I'm happy to have him here. Loyalty, since it's hard to come by, goes a long way with a demon.

The hellhound dashes over to me, his black tongue slurping from his mouth to lick my arm. Running my hand over his fiery head, I slide my fingers into the black sludge beneath the fire to rub behind his ears.

"Were you worried?" I ask.

He whimpers a response.

"Well, don't worry now. I'm fine," I say, getting to my feet.

A soft knock sounds on my door, drawing my attention away from the hellhound. Without waiting for my answer, the door swings open and Evan strolls in. He's covered in sweat, and a few black lines run across his arms and the torso of his now ripped and burned tank top.

"How was your nap, Sleeping Beauty?" Evan asks, smiling

as he shuts the door behind him. He crosses the room and slides his arms around my waist despite the low growl from Greg.

"I hate getting knocked out, but it was probably a lot more pleasant than the time you've had," I say, pulling away to inspect him more closely. I'd recognize the burn marks anywhere. Fire doesn't hurt Evan so I know they're from Malicevile, created by his bolts of electricity. "What happened?"

Evan lowers his eyebrows when he looks down at me. His startling blue eyes bore into mine as he tries to decide how to answer. He's torn between protecting me and my father. It's always a battle for him. "It's nothing to worry about," he finally says.

I guess he's trying to protect us both. His loyalty will always lie with Malicevile over me no matter how much I hate it, but he sometimes surprises me.

"I see." I let the subject drop. It doesn't really matter anyway. What am I going to do? Stand up to my father again and cause more problems? Evan belongs to him, not me. That might change one day, but only when I have something worthy enough to trade.

Evan's hand moves from my waist, sliding up my body where the bare skin of my side peeks through the burned fabric of my shirt. My top barely hangs on by threads, and my pants aren't any better. My skin tingles as a small flame erupts in his fingers. He touches the strap of my tank top, and it smolders before snapping, leaving my shoulder bare.

Leaning over, he kisses my shoulder before trailing his lips up my neck. His golden amber and earthy patchouli scent washes away the lingering smells of apples and rain. I lose myself in his heated touch, forgetting about the events of the night. Nothing seems to matter when I'm with Evan.

My heart hammers against my ribcage, banging against his as he pulls me close before kissing me deeply. His tongue slips into my mouth, and he tastes sweet like dessert. I run my hands around his taut shoulders. When he bites my bottom lip, I dig my nails into his back.

He spins me around and pushes me toward the bed. I don't even care that it crunches under me when I fall back and let Evan lie on top of me. It's rare to have a moment alone with him where we're not doing something for Malicevile. I'll take any time I can get—because he's the one who reminds me of what it's like to feel human without all the messy emotions. It's lust and desire and need—the emotions that can distract me from the world—that I enjoy the most. I don't have to care to enjoy Evan's touch.

"I want you so badly," Evan whispers into my mouth.

I flick my tongue over his bottom lip. "I do owe you a thanks for moving that stupid body, don't I?"

"You read my mind," he says, kissing me again.

A tiny spark shocks him as he awakens the power flowing through my veins. It only makes him kiss me harder, desperately, and I wonder if I stir the same feelings in him as he does me.

The first time I saw Evan after he had traded his soul to Malicevile to save my life, I thought he was so cold. I thought he wasn't the same boy I fell in love with. It doesn't matter if he's that boy anymore. Because I'm not that girl. I don't even know if I'm capable of truly loving. It feels different—more calculated. I only know that I love Evan because human habits are hard to break—even without my humanity.

The spicy scent of cinnamon and clove cuts through Evan's scent, and I stiffen in his arms. Of course Malicevile would choose this exact moment to interrupt.

"Malicevile's coming down the hall," I whisper.

"The door's locked," he says, trailing his lips along my jaw.

I smile. He's right. Malicevile will have to break down the door if he really wants to come in.

As soon as I think that thought, loud banging sounds out on my door. It quivers on its hinges but doesn't fly open.

"Camilla! Camilla, open the door!" my father yells from the other side.

"I'm busy!" I yell back.

"Doing what? Open the door."

Seriously?

Evan chuckles but doesn't say anything. He continues to explore every inch of me.

"That's none of your business." I lean up to kiss Evan again.

The door shakes again as Malicevile slams something into it. I should just get up and answer it, but I'm not in the mood to deal with him. He'll have all day to bother me. He knows that.

"Camilla!"

This time, I don't answer him. I just smirk into Evan's lips as he continues to kiss me. There's nothing more fun than making out with Evan all while annoying my father. Serves him right for all the years of torment.

Malicevile curses a few times before falling silent. I tilt my head back and laugh. I knew he'd give up sooner or later. He's lost his persistence now that I'm by his side. I'm sure I'll get Hell for this later, but it'll totally be worth it.

"He's gone," I whisper, tugging at the hem of Evan's shirt before pulling it over his head. "Let's make this worth it."

As the words come out of my mouth, the door flies open, startling me. Evan rolls off me and hops to his feet. Malicevile stands in the doorway with wild eyes, holding a set of keys in his hand.

His eyes shift from green to glowing red as he rushes in and peers around. "Evan, go check the property. There has been an intruder," my father says, ignoring the fact that Evan stands shirtless by my bed.

My brows furrow as his words sink in. "What do you mean an intruder? Who in their right mind would come into a demon's lair uninvited?" *You. You've done it before.*

Evan doesn't linger to listen. He races from the room, leaving me alone with Malicevile. My father crosses the room in a few swift strides and reaches out to grab me. He yanks me from my blackened bed. I cry out as his sharp nails cut into the skin on my wrists.

Holding me in front of him, he sucks in a long breath. "Where is he? I smell him all over you." I'm not the only one with a keen sense of smell. I didn't inherit it from werewolves.

I jerk away. "I have no idea what you're talking about. I've been with Evan."

He shakes his head. "Last time I checked, Evan doesn't smell like—like *Heaven*."

"Have you smelled him lately?" I ask with a smirk. *His scent is damn intoxicating.*

He swings his arms around in agitation. "That's not what I meant."

I force myself to laugh. It's the most ridiculous thing I've ever heard come out of his mouth, and I can't believe we're discussing how someone—my boyfriend—smells. I consider asking him how he knows what Heaven even smells like, but the wildness in his gaze holds me back.

And then it dawns on me. He smells Dylan's scent. It's the only explanation. When Dylan came into my dream, he wasn't physically with me, but his essence would linger. He's left marks on my body before, ones I managed to hide from my father, when he tried to touch me with his wings. I allowed him to stay a lot longer than the last few times.

"This is serious, Camilla. Too many people know about you. Word can travel."

"Like the alliance can do anything to us," I say.

"It's not the alliance I'm concerned about."

"Then who?"

He scratches his neck. "Camilla, I don't have the patience to answer the obvious."

Way to make me feel dumb. I'll just assume he's talking about some mysterious angelic army. From what I know, angels don't interfere often. They merely watch. Dylan's never gotten into it, and Malicevile is too concerned with our own kind to get into it either. It's starting to feel like I'm living with Alana, my old guardian, again.

I push the thought from my mind. She doesn't deserve a second thought from me—not after she abandoned me when I needed her the most.

"Pull yourself together," Malicevile says, shaking my shoulder. "I asked you if you had any contact with the nephilim."

I shake my head, causing my hair to veil my face. "No. I want nothing to do with him." The words come easily enough, partly because they're true. Dylan just makes my world messy. I don't like what he does to me. I wish I had never allowed him to get as close as he did. I should've kept my soul guarded from him from the beginning, but my silly human self thought there was something wrong with being a demi-demon.

He nods, satisfied with my answer. "Good. Now stay here."

"But—"

"Please," he says.

"No. You know I have dibs."

"Then get dressed. We're running out of night."

DESPERATION

"THIS IS POINTLESS," I say, knowing my words to be true. Dylan is nowhere nearby. Even if he was, he'd be safely tucked away behind some annoying blessed barrier this time of night. He might've grown braver since we both left the Hunter's Academy, but it doesn't mean he's reckless. He couldn't find me here either. He lost that ability the moment I transformed.

Since I've become a full demon, we've moved hours away from the academy as Malicevile no longer has a need to have an estate near there. Not like he'd want to go back after the alliance burned the place to the ground—one of the few instances where my father chose not to fight.

"Being cautious is not pointless. Scents don't just magically appear out of nowhere." Malicevile pulls his Maserati to the curb before cutting off the engine.

Evan appears from the shadows between a liquor store and a nail salon. A man in dirty clothes sits slumped against the side of the building, waving a Styrofoam cup in his hand. Evan stops to talk to the man briefly before pulling a few bills from his pocket. The man shakes his head, jerking his cup away. He breaks it between his fingers and lets the pieces scatter across the dirty sidewalk.

Evan drops the money anyway before striding to us. Even in desperate times, there are people who refuse to accept help from the tainted ones. The man must not know that Evan will never be able to steal his soul.

"If the bastard was here, he's gone now," Evan says, leaning his elbow on my open window.

I reach my hand out and trail my fingers along his muscular arms even though his attention focuses on my father.

Malicevile smacks his fists on the steering wheel. "If you were lying to me, Camilla—"

"I wasn't," I snap, cutting him off. I give him a death glare to keep him from arguing. "Maybe you were mistaken."

"Maybe," he finally says after a long moment. "Either way, I hope that if he ever shows his face you'll do what has to be done. Your life depends on it. You're vulnerable with your soul. If you allow him access to it, he—" He pauses. "Just be careful."

I rest my hand on his knee. "I won't do anything to jeopardize myself." I'm not sure if I'm lying or not. I promised to meet with Dylan tomorrow night, but I don't think being in his presence puts me at risk. He doesn't want to see me dead. If I die, I'll go to Hell. I don't think even he could bring me back a second time.

"Good." He starts the car again. Turning his gaze to Evan, he says, "Why don't you take Camilla home? I have an associate I need to meet with before dawn. You two will just get in the way."

Hey now. I open my mouth to argue, but Evan's already pulling me from my seat and wrapping his arms around me. I laugh as he lifts me off my feet before tossing me over his shoulder like he's going to carry me the entire way home.

"See you at dawn, my dear," Malicevile calls from the car.

I don't have a chance to respond before he peels from the curb, leaving a white cloud of smoke as he burns rubber, driving like a maniac. The world spins as Evan swings me around, making me squeal, and heads toward the busier part of our small downtown.

Slaughter Creek is probably the most fitting name for a town inhabited by my father, and I wonder if he chose it based on the name alone. Not surprisingly, the town is as rundown as most places are where demons reside. Our estate, stationed alone at the top of Devil's Peak Road, is the only nice thing for miles.

When Evan reaches the corner of Hollow Drive and Convict Lane, he sets me back on my feet. I slide my hand around his lower back, squeezing my fingers into the curve of his hip, and he makes a deep sound in the back of his throat before he kisses me.

"Keep doing that, and I'll steal that car to get us home faster," he says, nodding his head toward a woman as she packs some boxes into her SUV.

I consider letting him. My father interrupted us in the middle of something I'd really like to finish. Biting my lip, I say, "I bet I wouldn't even have to steal it."

"Loser gets whatever they want," Evan says, tugging me forward.

I grin. "You're counting on losing."

"Don't disappoint me."

I kiss him once more before pulling away to walk diagonally across the cracked street. Evan saunters to the light to watch me from the corner, his face lit up by the red light. My boots glide soundlessly over the pavement, and the woman doesn't even hear me coming. She senses me, though, because when I get within five feet of her, she jerks her head up and jumps, letting out a small yelp as she clutches her chest.

"You scared me to death!" The woman drops her hands to her sides.

I force my lip to pout. "I'm so sorry. I hope I'm not bothering you. It's just you're the first person I've seen tonight, and I don't know what to do." Fake tears burn my eyes as I rub the back of my hand over my cheek.

"Are you okay?" She moves closer. *Brave, naïve woman.*

"Your face."

I turn my head slightly to give her a view of the purpling bruise I got while sparring with Malicevile. It'll be gone before the sun even rises, but she doesn't know that. By the way her eyes sparkle with empathy, I doubt she knows anything.

"It doesn't hurt."

"Is there someone I can call? Somewhere I can take you? This isn't the best place to be this time of night." At least she's right about one thing.

"You wouldn't mind giving me a ride?"

"Of course not." She opens the passenger's side door for me.

I glance over my shoulder. "Mind if my boyfriend joins us?"

The woman's brows lift in surprise.

"Please, he's the only one protect—" Before the words can even escape my lips, a gunshot rings out in the night and a burning pain explodes through my back. The surprise and force of the blessed bullet sends me reeling forward into the woman. Her ear-piercing scream echoes through the air as we hit the ground.

Hot blood drips down my back where the bullet remains lodged. My insides burn as the fragments eat away at me. At least if I'm stabbed, the burning doesn't last long. I'll have to wait until sunrise unless Evan can remove the pieces. *Evan? Where is he?*

"Oh, my God. You're hurt," the woman cries. As she presses her hands into the pavement, my nearly black blood coats them.

I growl. "Looks like it."

Without waiting a moment longer, I propel myself to my feet and summon white-hot energy into my palms. The woman remains on the ground, a mixture of surprise, fear, and shock on her face. Another gunshot booms through the air, and a bullet sinks into the side of the SUV. I dart my gaze around until I spot a figure standing on the opposite corner from where Evan should've been. He's gone though. Blessed bullets, while an annoyance to me, could kill Evan. I know he hasn't gone far, though. He never would.

The figure raises the gun again, and I launch my power in its direction. The hunter drops to the ground as my electricity collides with a tree and sets it ablaze. I don't stop there. I summon more power and chuck it to stop the pest from getting up.

"You've messed with the wrong girl!" I yell, shooting yet another stream of electricity.

A moment later, a fireball erupts at the end of the block, drawing my focus away from the hunter. Evan didn't disappear. He's in his own fighting match, probably with this hunter's partner. Hunters aren't stupid enough to try to attack an upper-level demon alone unless they're desperate, cornered, or have a death wish. From the looks of it, both the hunters are human, so they clearly have a death wish.

The glint of a dagger sparkles under the streetlamp as the hunter before me jumps up. All it took was a second of distraction to allow this hunter a chance.

I grin as electricity sparkles in my palms. "You really think that dagger will be of any use to you against me? The alliance is getting sloppy."

The hunter doesn't make a comment about my observation.

"What? You know it's true."

"Cami?" a masculine voice asks, surprising me.

I freeze in my tracks, stopping a good ten feet away. The hunter pulls his hood down, and I recognize one of my former classmates from the academy. While I wasn't there long, every hunter's face I came across there has been imprinted on my brain.

I don't extinguish my electricity. The boy did shoot me. I narrow my eyes. "What are you doing here, Sebastian? I'm surprised they even let you in the field."

He presses his lips into a thin line. "Early graduation."

Speaks to the alliance's desperation. I can't stop the grin from forming on my lips. "Interesting."

"Why?"

"I never really saw you as hunter material."

His eyes narrow as my words sink in. Anger flashes across his face, and it's like he's suddenly come to his senses.

I step a foot closer. "Come on. I mean, look at you. You've already let your guard down. If I weren't so interested in catching up, you'd be—"

Sebastian lunges forward, dagger pointed. He's faster than I expected him to be, and his blade catches the side of my jacket. Swinging my arm, I sucker punch him before he can yank his dagger free. I smile as he stumbles back, reaching for the gun he dropped when I first tried to fry him with my power.

"Seriously?" I ask. "What's with the gun? It's not going to kill me. Neither are you."

He raises it anyway. "Just leave," he says.

"Why? My father would love to meet you. Maybe he'll make you a killer deal."

Sebastian flinches, the gun shaking in his grip. I almost feel badly for him—almost. Mostly, I feel amused.

"I'd rather die."

"Oh, I can arrange that, too."

He lets out what I can only describe as a whimper.

"Cami, do you really want to waste the rest of our night toying with this kid?" Evan strides up behind Sebastian, a fireball glowing in his hand. "I think we have better things to do."

I lick my bottom lip. "We do, don't we?"

A small click sounds through the air, drawing my attention back to Sebastian. The jerk tried to shoot me again, but it looks like he needs to reload. His wide eyes show his surprise at the realization.

"Seriously, Sebastian," I say. "Are you sure you didn't flunk out?"

Evan laughs, his deep voice echoing over the night. "Come on, babe. Want me to do the honors?"

I shake my head. "No, I think I'm going to let him go."

"You are?" Both Evan and Sebastian ask in unison.

I shrug. "What? I'm feeling generous. Plus, I want Sebastian to deliver a message."

"To who?" Evan asks.

"Who do you think?" As much as I try not to think about Alana, I can't help it. I think about Cadence, too. She's probably trying to track me down the same way we both tried to track down Evan. Even after everything, Cadence stood by my side. But life by a demon's side? I want to spare her from that, even if it means we'll never be on the same side. Dumb human memories. "This might be my one opportunity."

Evan shakes his head. "Alana tried to kill you."

"I know." I ignore his pleading eyes and turn to Sebastian. "Tell Alana that I spared your life. Tell her that I haven't forgotten her, and that the world is changing. If she plans on surviving, she's going to have to accept me for who I am."

"As a demon?" Sebastian asks.

"As her family. The alliance is going to fall, and I'll be the only one who can save her."

With those words, I blast Sebastian with just enough power to knock him out. The last thing I need is to be stalked by a hunter who might see me as weak since I let him go.

Evan takes my hand. As we walk forward, he leans over and kisses the top of my head. We stroll past a body lying in the gutter of the street—the hunter who tried to take on Evan. I don't take a close look. I don't really care who it was.

"Your father's not going to be happy," Evan says, breaking

the silence.

Definitely won't be. "I know. I let a hunter who shot me go."

"He actually hit you?"

I motion to my back, and he lifts my shirt. I can't see the damage, but I can feel it. I've just grown so used to pain that I know how to function through it. Another lovely gift from my father.

He swears. "Stay here. I'm going to kill him."

I reach out and grab him by the back of the shirt. "No you're not. He has a message to deliver."

"Cami."

I wrap my arms around his neck and look in his eyes. "We've wasted enough time as it is." I point at the sky. "The sun will rise soon. So, please. Let it go this once."

He frowns. "Just this once."

I know I won't have to hold him to it. The next person who tries to mess with me is in trouble. I look forward to it.

"You're hot when you're mad," I say teasingly.

"Oh, I can show you hot."

JUST A PHASE

"KEEP UP, CAMILLA," Malicevile says, speaking to me over his shoulder. He's still slightly annoyed that I battled with hunters and didn't bring home anyone or anything apart from the blessed bullet that fell out the moment the sunlight prison realm sucked me into it.

The sun moves across the sky overhead as we walk down a cracked, black path that winds through a forest of gnarled trees. The air hangs heavy around us, hot enough for me to feel, though it isn't uncomfortable. Time moves faster here than on the human plane, which I'm thankful for. I don't think I could handle half a day of human hours with my father.

Getting trapped in the daylight prison realm is one of many annoyances that come with my new life. First of all, the place sucks. It's dead and ugly and lacks the conveniences of the human realm. It's like getting stuck back in time, except the only life we ever stumble upon are other demons—well, lower-level, animalistic demons. My father knows this world even better than the earth plane, and he makes sure we never come across other demons who might bother me. And they love to. Everyone wants to know the secret to my transformation.

But Malicevile says those answers come with a price, and he hasn't thought of one yet. He just assumes that someday I'm going to tell him how it happened, because I never did get into the details. He has no clue that Dylan was involved. But I'm not so sure I'll tell him. At first, I had the need to protect demi-demons from my fate. But now, I actually like being an oh-so-special demon. I love the power I hold with this information.

After another few miles of walking, I say, "I don't see why we can't wait until sundown so we can just take the car."

Malicevile slows his pace until I catch up with him. "And waste the few precious hours we have? I know you enjoy sitting in a car with your boyfriend for long periods of time, but I find being trapped in a metal box with the both of you to be quite unpleasant."

I laugh. "You knew what you were getting into when you made that deal for Evan's soul."

"I just look forward to when this phase passes." He eyes me in his peripheral vision.

"You think my love for him is a phase?"

"Camilla, what else can it be? He's going to grow old and die."

I frown at the thought of my eternity. I never thought of existing in this world as a demon without Evan.

"Now, don't give me that look. There are a million other ways to occupy your time." He glances at me again, gauging my reaction.

I don't give him one though. The daylight realm numbs everything in me. I'm sure once I return to the earth plane, all sorts of unbidden emotions will try to sneak under the wall protecting me. But now, all I can do is hold onto the idea.

I consider telling him that Evan isn't merely a distraction. He's so much more. But what's the point? I rarely see a point to anything these days. I'm just living day by day as they blur by. My life might not be normal, but it sure is boring. Last night was the most excitement I've had in a while. I would have killed for a boring life before, but not now. I'll kill just so it isn't boring.

"What? No snarky comment?" he asks after a long moment of silence.

I ignore him, strolling a bit faster so I don't have to see him at all. One of these days, when I'm brave enough, I might just sneak away before sunrise so I don't have to suffer through the day listening to Malicevile's opinions, thoughts, and demonic lessons. As long as I'm far enough away, he won't be able to reach me in time before night falls again. Because his blood runs through me, I can never truly hide. Maybe just stay a few steps ahead of him. *Not like you're going to run. He makes life easy.*

"Camilla?"

"Oh, my God! Can we not do this?" I just want him to shut up. Just because we're trekking through the daylight realm together doesn't mean I want to talk about life or my future. I can still be his daughter and not actually enjoy his company. My humanity might be gone, and he might have changed—sort of—but I didn't just forget my human life. He has a lot to make up for.

He reaches out and yanks me to a stop. "That kind of language is unnecessary. And yes, we do have to do this. Your reckless actions and out of control temper will get you into trouble. You let a hunter—one who tried to murder you, if I might add—go last night."

"Do you think I really care? Come on, Dad. You're the one who wanted me to turn off my humanity in the first place. It's not my fault I want to do everything I can to feel things again. Taking risks does that." Just not all the grief, regret, and fear—the stuff that threatened to ruin me. That can stay far away from me. "You understand, don't you? You know what it was like to have humanity and then lose it. It's why I'm alive. When Melanie died, all that was stolen from you, but you were left with the memories."

We haven't talked about my dead sister much. I haven't really felt the need since I'm clearly not like her. I'm beyond comparison. She fell at the hands of the Hunter's Alliance, but she died with a good soul. Unfortunately for her, it didn't stop Malicevile from keeping it. Melanie didn't have Dylan to save her. Malicevile murdered her Demon Watcher, just like he murdered his own, who was much more powerful than a silly nephilim.

He motions for me to start walking again. "So you want to release your humanity again?" he asks without commenting on my statement.

"No, I just want you to give me a break." I don't like caring about things that are far beyond my control. It's agony to care about people who think the best thing for you is death. And, it's especially painful to relive the moments when I was at my weakest—to relive the horrors inflicted on others because of me.

"Fair enough. I guess I was a little hard on you," he admits.

My mouth falls open. "Who are you and what have you done with my unforgiving, demonic father?"

He chuckles. "Don't tell anyone I said that. I have a reputation to maintain."

I hate admitting it, but it's moments like these that I feel a real connection to Malicevile, and not just because I'm his daughter. When we don't have to deal with the complexities of the human world, things feel normal. I wonder how different things would've been had the Hunter's Alliance never interfered with us or had my parents held up their end of the bargain. It might've saved me a whole lot of pain and heartache. My soul would've never shifted for Hell. I'd still be half human. *You don't know that...*

"Oh, I'm telling everyone you're just a big soft—"

Malicevile covers my mouth before I can finish my sentence all while pulling me to a stop again. He steps in front of me, power glowing in his hands, and he chucks it at a nearby tree, setting it ablaze.

The hint of nutmeg and sugar wafts through the air, and I step out from behind Malicevile. "Hear anything good, Raphael?" I ask. I'd know the demon's scent anywhere.

As Raphael steps out from behind a gnarled tree, Malicevile throws another energy ball at him. Raphael easily sidesteps it, and the power sets another tree ablaze. He smiles as he meets my gaze. His short blond hair is styled slightly to the side, and his cerulean eyes, the same shade as his demi-demon daughter's, sparkle in the soon-to-be setting sun.

"Could never sneak up on your father, Cami," he says, closing the distance between us.

Raphael offers his hand to me, and I allow him to take my fingers in his. He brings my hand to his mouth to kiss it. He's come a long way since trying to kill me for breaking into his lair to kidnap his daughter, Faith, when I thought she was in trouble.

After a moment, he turns to my father to greet him.

Malicevile shakes Raphael's hand. "I'd deserve whatever you had to offer if you did surprise me."

The two demons, who were previous competitors, have come together for the simple fact that they have similar interests. They're both upper-level demons with daughters. Without Raphael having to say so, I know he'd like Faith to have the same fate as me. Unlike me and Malicevile, they have a deep-seated relationship that isn't based on convenience and need. I'd compare it to what Malicevile shared with Melanie.

The air shimmers with an orange glow as the sun starts to set, falling into the horizon much faster than it does on the earth plane. Malicevile and Raphael look at each other before Malicevile takes me by the elbow and pulls me along, forcing me to practically jog to keep up with him.

When the sun disappears and the earth plane flickers into view, I suck in a deep breath of ocean air. We stand on the porch of Raphael's beach fortress, a magnificent house made of concrete and bulletproof glass.

A second later, the front door flies open as a petite blond girl charges out and wraps her arms around me, knocking me back. I levitate to stop us from hitting the stone pathway. Faith's vanilla scent, similar but slightly different from her dad's, engulfs me as her blond hair veils over us. She doesn't let go of me until Raphael pulls her back and gives her a hug. He looks slightly jealous, and I'm pretty sure she never greets her dad like that.

"I'm so excited you're spending the night. Evan's already here. Are you hungry? Evan brought pizza. Cheese, just like you like." If Raphael wasn't holding Faith, she looks like she'd rush me again.

I turn to Malicevile. "I'm spending the night here? What

are you doing?"

"We have some business to attend to," he says.

"The Hunter's Alliance?"

He pats my shoulder. "We're not going on a killing spree if that's what you're thinking."

I shrug. "I don't care."

Faith audibly gasps, but I don't look at her.

"I mean, that's good," I say, correcting myself. "I could use a break from you anyway."

Malicevile chuckles. "Something we can both agree on."

Raphael whispers a few words to Faith, who nods in agreement before strolling back inside her house. The two demons turn to me, and I feel myself shrink under their gazes. Even though I'm a demon myself, I still recognize the power they possess. Together, they're doubly intimidating.

"I expect you to be on your best behavior, Camilla," Malicevile says.

"Faith is not to leave the house, understood?" Raphael adds.

"Same goes for you. If you need something, send Evan." Malicevile studies my face for a reaction to see if he can trust me. I've grown exceptionally good at hiding all my expressions unless I want him to really know how I feel. One of the benefits of actually getting to think things over without my emotions instantly taking control.

I roll my eyes. "Fine, whatever. It's not like I had plans." But I do. It's why I'm not putting up more of a fight. With

Malicevile busy with Raphael, my chances of not getting caught meeting Dylan are a million times better. I considered canceling after last night, but something stopped me. *Because you want to see him.* I push the thought away.

"Good," Malicevile says, pulling me into a hug.

Raphael looks at him for a moment before they both turn to go. They don't waste any time when it comes to business. I'll have at least until midnight. That is, if I can sneak away from Evan. With Faith it might be easier. He won't be glued to me in front of her. Even I have boundaries as a demon. Corrupting a sweet, tween demi-demon isn't on my to-do list.

"Hey, Dad," I call out as they head toward the open garage to get into Raphael's Ferrari. He turns and glances at me over his shoulder. "You run into any of *them,* remember that they're mine." I don't have to say who. He knows I'm talking about Alana, Cadence, and even Dylan.

"Of course, my dear." He waves once before disappearing into the garage. I stand on the porch and watch Raphael race down the street faster than really necessary. Demons love to show off.

The scent of patchouli breaks through the smell of the salty air, and I spin on my feet in time to face Evan as he wraps his arms around me. He kisses my forehead before my lips and then pulls me inside the beach mansion.

"I missed you," he says as he breathes into my ear.

"It's been an utterly boring day with my dad. You try walking here from home," I say.

"No, thanks," he says, laughing.

"Cami!" Faith calls from down the hallway that's full of the weapons Raphael kept from the hunters who faced him and failed. "Evan said we could work on some combat training tonight."

I frown. "Really?"

He kisses me. "Gotta occupy our time with something. Didn't think you wanted to play games."

"Depends on the game," I say with a smile.

He grins as he shakes his head. "Come on before we get into more trouble."

Faith waits for us in the kitchen. She stands at the counter, eating a piece of pizza, and shakes the box until I cross the room and take a slice. She rambles on about her day and how Raphael actually hired a nanny to watch over her instead of using one of his tainted minions. She also tells me how annoyed she is because she feels old enough to stay alone. I have to agree with her. No one will mess with someone who could melt them with lava bombs.

"If it makes you feel better, I have a babysitter, too," I say, tilting my head toward Evan. "He doesn't let me get away with anything."

Evan scratches his neck. "That's what you think."

I toss the crust of my pizza at him, and he catches it before taking a bite. Faith crinkles her nose but doesn't say anything for a long moment.

The landline rings from its spot on the marble countertop,

and I glide to answer it. I knew it wouldn't be long before someone called to check on us.

"We're fine and the house isn't on fire," I say as I answer.

"Faith told me you were going to be there," a familiar voice says through the line.

I stiffen, hearing Dylan's voice. He's out of his mind for calling here, especially after dark, but that's not what concerns me the most. He just said he talked to Faith.

I clear my throat so my voice doesn't break when I say, "You know I'd call you if I needed anything. Faith and Evan were about to practice some combat." Hopefully Evan believes that I'm talking to my father, and hopefully he doesn't ask him about it later.

"Please, tell me you're still willing to meet me. I just—I have to see you, love," Dylan says.

I ignore my suddenly racing heart. "Yeah."

"He's standing right there, isn't he?"

"Yeah," I repeat.

Turning my head, I peek over my shoulder at Evan as he watches me. I shrug my shoulders and smile at him. Faith looks quietly between us. I'm going to have to corner her alone later to ask about Dylan visiting her.

"I'll pick you up out back in ten minutes, okay?" he asks.

I want to tell him no, to tell him that he's risking a lot coming so close to a demon's lair, especially the house of one I have no influence over. But the words stick in my throat. Just the idea of sneaking out makes me feel alive. It's the rush I crave every second of the day.

"Okay," I manage to say. I hang up without saying good-bye. Turning on my heels, I face Evan and Faith. "You know, I'm not really feeling up to sparring right this second. Why don't you two go ahead while I sit down for a while? I've been walking all day."

My body actually feels awesome since demons heal and re-fresh in the daylight realm, but I don't mention that. I can't think of another excuse to keep Evan occupied.

"We can wait," Evan says, closing the empty box of pizza.

Ugh. I knew he'd be considerate. "Really, it's okay. I kind of just want a few minutes alone if you don't mind."

Evan closes the space between us and leans down to whis-per in my ear. "Everything okay?"

I shrug. "Yeah, I can't get a few things Malicevile said to me out of my mind. You know how it goes. I just need to sort things out. I'll tell you about it later, okay?" I push my father's conversation about Evan from my mind before I do start to process it. I can't. Not now. I need a clear head for whatever comes next.

I don't know what to expect with Dylan. He could be set-ting me up for all I know. *He wouldn't.*

Evan kisses my cheek. "Okay, come find us when you're ready."

Faith watches me, and I have a feeling she knows a lot more than she lets on. She doesn't even question or argue my desire to sit a fight out—especially because I love combat fighting with someone that won't knock me out.

"Take it easy on him," I say to Faith, making her smile.

"Enjoy your *rest*," she says with a lot more meaning to her words. It's in this moment that I know she definitely knows something I don't. But I can't ask her.

Evan follows Faith down the hallway, and I wait for their scents to disappear before I rush to the recreation room that leads out to the back patio and beach. As I step out of the house, excitement courses through me.

And then fear.

It's the first time I've felt it in weeks. But there's no turning back.

Wind whips through my hair, the scent of apple and rain showers cutting through the scent of the sea. Without time to prepare, a light shines over me as I'm swept off my feet and blinded by achingly beautiful wings.

TRUST WORKS BOTH WAYS

THE BLACK OCEAN churns far below as Dylan flies us into the night. I have no choice but to hide my face in his shirt because the icy wind stings my eyes even more than the ethereal light that emanates from his wings.

"Where are you taking me?" I ask as the beach house disappears along with the shore. This was a huge mistake. He's kidnapping me, and there's nothing I can do about it. If I fight him, I'll fall into the ocean and get swept away. I can't levitate over water if it's too deep. I can't drown, either, but the experience isn't something I want to go through. *It might be your only chance.*

He doesn't respond as he nosedives, descending a few feet, sending my stomach into my throat. I dig my sharp nails into his neck, tightening my hold. It's not the first time he's flown with me in his arms, but this time is ten times more unpleasant. It's awkward. His heartbeat thrums in my ear sending my own heart racing.

"Dylan, please. Take me back. I can't be away when dawn comes. I need Malicevile's protection." I haven't felt so powerless since my transformation. I hate it. "Was this your plan all along? To break me?"

"When have I ever wanted you broken, love? What happened to trusting me?" The softness of his voice helps me relax. It crawls under my skin and burrows into my fiery heart, cooling the flames of mistrust and paranoia.

"You ally with people who think I'm going to destroy the world," I say. "You're probably going to report back to them with an update on my existence. It's what you do." I focus on all the secrets Dylan had kept from me before to keep the wall protecting my soul firmly in place.

He descends lower, swooping just above the dark ocean. Seawater sprays across us, steaming when it hits my skin. I cling to him tighter, and I'm pretty sure he's flying like a maniac to get a reaction out of me.

"I'm no longer your watcher, love. So no, I won't be reporting to anyone," he finally says. "I'm only half angel. We don't look after full-blooded demons. We're not even supposed to engage."

"Then why are you?"

"Why do you even ask?"

"I like to hear it," I say.

"You do, do you?" he says, a smile playing on his lips.

I tilt my head up so my lips linger an inch from his neck. His apple and rain scent swirls around me, and I inhale a deep breath, making him shiver. I like tormenting him. I hope being so close makes him question everything he thought he knew. He's playing a dangerous game, and I'll make sure it's at least fun before everything starts crashing down around him.

"Yeah, tell me," I say into his neck.

The world rushes around me, sending my stomach into my chest, as Dylan lets go of me. We're just high enough that I'm sure hitting the ocean will hurt, but all I can do is scream.

Just as a wave swells to meet me, strong arms wrap around me as Dylan pulls me against him. I smack the palm of my hand against his chest hard enough to feel a stinging sensation in my own hand.

"What the hell?" I ask, half-yelling, though my voice gets lost on the wind. "Did you just drop me on purpose?"

"Yeah," he says without looking at me. "Because that's how you're making me feel, Cami. Like you're pulling me to you just to push me over the edge to watch me fall. This isn't a game."

"Then what is it? What is even the point? You're trying so hard to get to me, to get to my soul and my humanity, and for what? You're eventually going to die like everyone else I know in this life. Is this how you want to spend your life, setting me up for a whole lot of pain and heartache? Because that's what this feels like to me." A surprise tear drips onto my lower lashes, and I grimace when it gets caught on the wind.

The only time I've shed tears since I've turned off my humanity was when I felt physical pain. It was my body reacting. Now, it's my heart. I'd be worried if I actually felt anything through the numbness. The disconnection between my mind and soul is more obvious than ever. My humanity isn't gone; it's just buried deep within me. Now Dylan is waving an imaginary shovel.

"Don't you get it, Cami? I want to spend my life making sure you're okay in the end."

"And what about you?"

Dylan doesn't respond as he navigates through the air, ascending when we come to an enormous cliff. If it weren't for the light of the moon, I'd have never even noticed it. I cringe when he flies awfully close to the black rocks, close enough that I could reach out and touch them if I wanted to.

When we reach the top, Dylan flies up into the air a good fifty feet, like he's considering flying higher until we're just another sparkle in the star-studded sky. But he slows down, and then descends, landing a few feet from the cliff's edge.

When his feet touch the ground, I scramble out of his arms and put some much needed distance between us. Crossing an arm over my chest, I hug myself. Cool air wraps around me as the ocean breeze blows through my wild, dark hair.

He tries to close the distance, but I step back out of his

reach. "Dylan, please. It hurts to be close to you."

Rubbing his hands over his face and into his hair, he brushes black locks from his forehead. His wings disappear a moment later. We're standing just a few feet apart without saying anything. It feels familiar, reminding me of one of the first times we hung out when I first arrived at the Hunter's Academy—when we didn't even know what to say but were both okay with not saying anything at all.

The silence doesn't last though. The space between us doesn't either. He reaches out and pushes my hair behind my ear. "Does it still hurt?"

I slowly shake my head. "You know, I could kill you. Not because I'm a demon, either. Bringing me here was stupid and dangerous. Malicevile went absolutely crazy last night because he smelled you on me from when you dream walked."

He smiles, flashing his irresistible dimples. "He's scared."

I raise an eyebrow. "My father isn't afraid of you."

"That's what you think," he says.

It's my turn to laugh. "Whatever you say, Angel Boy."

"There's my Cami." He holds my gaze for a long minute, his chocolaty eyes staring into mine. I don't shift my gaze away. If he wants to study me, he can. Maybe it'll awaken some sense in him.

When he doesn't say anything else, I clear my throat and say, "So, is this all you wanted to do? Stand next to me and stare into my eyes, or did you steal me away for something more fun?" He stiffens when I reach out and rub my fingers across his cheek, feeling the prickle of day old stubble on my fingertips. "Maybe you wanted to argue some more and tell me how I'm playing with your heart? I seem to recall telling you I'd break it. You had fair warning."

"You're right about that. You did break my heart. But this isn't about my heart."

"Then what is this about?"

"I wanted to make sure you were okay." He takes a breath. "And I thought I should tell you myself that I've been reassigned to Faith."

My forehead crinkles. He's answered at least a few of my questions with that one sentence. "This isn't good, Dylan. The alliance has no business getting involved. Look what happened to me because of them."

"How many times do I have to tell you this has nothing to do with the alliance? They're struggling to keep themselves together because of Malicevile, and you know I've only ever helped the alliance as a messenger. I don't work for them." He takes my hand and links our fingers together.

I smirk as I think about how far the alliance has fallen. I used to think they were so powerful and intimidating. As a whole, maybe. But my father has been taking it apart hunter by hunter. Humans are so easy to break. "So you're with the angelic army my father talks about. Figures." I tilt my head back to peer up into the night sky like I'll somehow see something I haven't seen before. "Should I blame them for this?" I ask, waving my hand down my body.

"If anyone is to blame, it's you and me. What we did…"

I'd like to blame the entire universe for my transformation, but the fact is I let Dylan into my Hell-bound soul. He used his angelic influence to rip my soul from the gates of Hell, and then I let go before he could redeem me. A trip to Hell and back destroyed my mortal body at the perfect time, and I ended up in the daylight prison world. It was hard to understand at first, but here I am, alive because of him but a demon because of me.

I close my eyes for a second. "Is this why you were assigned to Faith? Are you supposed to make sure it doesn't happen again?"

He tightens his jaw. "It's not going to happen again, and especially not to Faith. She doesn't want to be like you, Cami. She told me so herself."

I'm not sure whether I should be relieved or offended by Faith's decision. "Raphael's going to be disappointed."

"You can't tell anyone."

"So, are you going to steal Faith away?"

He shakes his head. "Of course not. Her soul isn't at risk. Only the alliance would ever try to intervene anyway."

"And what if it starts to sway?"

"I can't talk about this anymore, Cami," Dylan says instead of answering my question. "You have to understand why. You're under your father's influence, and I've told you too much already."

I narrow my eyes. "Trust works both ways, you know." But I know he can't trust me. Trusting a demon is a huge mistake.

"I want to trust you, love."

I tug my hand away. "I get it."

My cell phone rings from my pocket, startling me. I didn't even know I could get cell reception on this cliff top and of course I have no idea where I am. Pulling it from my pocket, I see my father's number flash across the screen.

I consider not answering it, and Dylan shakes his head at me not to, but I tap the glowing screen anyway. "Hey, Dad. What's up?"

"You didn't pick up Raphael's landline," he says.

I tense. "Sorry. Had the music up loud. I'm just watching Evan and Faith spar."

"You should be the one working with her," he says.

I let out a small breath. "Didn't feel like it. So, why are you calling? Hopefully not to check up on me."

He clears his throat. "I can check in to see if you're following the rules any time I want, but no, that's not the reason. I had a run in with a special hunter tonight. She belongs to you."

My heart thuds in my chest. "Who is it?"

"It's a surprise. I'll text you the address. Leave Faith at home with Evan. Raphael doesn't want her involved in our matters." Without another word, the line goes dead.

I clench my phone, staring at the dark screen until it lights up with an address one town over from Moonlight Shores.

"I have to go," I say.

His eyebrows furrow as he looks at me. "What's wrong?"

"Malicevile caught someone for me," I say.

He reaches out and locks his fingers onto my shoulders. "You can't be serious, Cami."

But I am. I've been waiting a long time for this. I bet Alana got the message loud and clear. Maybe being alone all this time has given her a change of heart.

I don't react to his accusatory stare. "Just take me home."

"Fine, but I'm going with you."

I don't argue. "Suit yourself."

After being dropped off on the beach, I enter Raphael's beach fortress only to crash right into Evan. Hitting his solid body knocks me back, and I thump against the glass door. Faith stands in the doorway behind him, and they both look at me with emotions I can only decipher to be curiosity—on Faith's face—and suspicion on Evan's.

"Where were you?" Evan asks, pulling me forward to steady me.

"On the beach." I hold his gaze so he believes my half lie. I was technically on the beach, just not for very long.

"I didn't see you," he says. The boy in front of me isn't my usual sexy, can't-keep-his-hands-off-me Evan. This is Malicevile's servant Evan. And I don't like this version of my boyfriend.

Clenching my fingers at my side, I say, "Well, you didn't look hard enough. Anything else you want to question me about, Mr. Nanny?" I don't mean to snap, but I don't need this. I need to get out of here before Malicevile realizes I wasn't here when he called. He's so in tune with time and distance that I'll already have to make an excuse for not dropping everything to rush to his side.

He steps back, his expression softening. "I'm sorry, Cami. I didn't mean to accuse you of anything."

I release a breath, letting my anger go. "It doesn't matter." My phone chimes again from my pocket, and I know it's another text from Malicevile. I'm taking too long. Without checking my phone, I say, "I have to go. Give me my keys."

He doesn't ask me where or why.

"And my father told me to tell you to stay here with Faith," I add without an explanation.

Before he hands me the keys to my Mustang, he grabs my wrist and pulls me to him. Sliding his hands down my sides, he locks his fingers on my hips, squeezing just enough to send tingles through me. As I look into his eyes, it's easy to forget that Dylan is lurking somewhere nearby.

I kiss him before I force myself to pull away. "I'll be back soon, okay?"

He nods. "Stay out of trouble."

I smile. "But trouble is so much fun."

With a quick hug to Faith, and a whisper that we'll talk later, I rush out the front door to my Mustang parked in the driveway with the top down. I wait only a minute to warm up the engine before I reverse and stomp the accelerator, squealing the tires as I peel down the street.

I peer into my rearview mirror to glimpse Evan standing in

the driveway before I skid around the corner that'll take me to a main street. A bright flash startles me, and I jerk the wheel when Dylan drops in the seat next to me.

"Get out of my car," I say, smacking his arm. "Malicevile will know you were here."

He pulls the seatbelt across his chest. "The top's down. You can drop me off before we get there."

Ugh. Dylan's changed from the boy who'd do whatever I'd say. He's also braver than before, like he's testing his limits. He used to be so uneasy leaving a safe house after dark. Now, he's riding shotgun in a demon's Mustang. I might've underestimated him all along.

"You have no business meddling in demonic affairs. Look where it got us last time. I can't protect you from Malicevile, Dylan. He'll rip your wings off and hang them on the wall as a trophy." The thought of Malicevile even laying a finger on Dylan stirs anger within me. I'd fight my father over it, but I'd lose like always.

"Then I'll walk," he says. His jaw twitches, and I can smell the fear emanating from him for the first time.

I slap my hands on the steering wheel. "Seriously, Dylan!" Slamming the brakes, I stop my Mustang in the middle of the empty street. "I don't want you to get hurt."

He shifts in the seat and brushes his fingers along my cheek. "Why?"

And he said I was the one playing games. "It's not in my little demonic heart to say it."

"Liar."

"What do you want from me? You know I'm with Evan. It's like you love to torture yourself." My cell phone chirps, and I dig into my pocket and see two text messages from Malicevile. I ignore them and accelerate forward. I don't have time for this.

"I want you to admit how you feel," Dylan says.

I heave a big breath. "I don't feel *anything*."

I flick my gaze to him as he watches me. I don't meet his eyes. Instead, I train them on the road and floor the gas pedal, speeding well over the speed limit. I dare any human to try to stop me. All I want is to get to Malicevile so that Dylan will leave me alone and stop whatever he thinks he's doing.

But he doesn't stop. He unhooks his seatbelt, reaches over to grab my chin, and then he kisses me. The car shakes as I hit the reflector lights in the center of the road, but I don't stop kissing Dylan. I can't.

The rush of my life spiraling out of control pierces deep into my soul, cracking the wall protecting me from my humanity. Unlike the pain and anguish I felt the last time I kissed Dylan, all I feel is a tidal wave of emotions I forgot I was even capable of truly having. Love, excitement, joy—emotions I want to hold onto—crash through me more powerful than ever. The numbness releases me, and I feel like I've woken up from a long slumber. I feel powerful. I feel *everything*.

Dylan smiles into my lips, the wind blowing around us. I'm not even afraid of crashing my car. I dare anything to get in my way.

"Now tell me you don't feel anything," he whispers, kissing me again.

I open my mouth to say something, anything, but the scent of cinnamon wafts into my car, caught on a breeze. It's enough to jolt me back to reality and to get my senses together. I push Dylan back, straightening my car on the empty, straight stretch of road.

"Dylan, he's here!" I scream.

Without waiting a second, Dylan launches from the car, disappearing into the night sky. My heart races as I try to pull myself together. I suck in a few deep breaths until the scent of Dylan fades, and I'm left feeling empty. His kiss put a crack in the wall imprisoning my humanity and soul, and I'm not sure I can fill it. He's rocked me to my core, disturbing my very foundation.

I'm so lost in my own world that I don't see Malicevile standing in the street in front of me until it's almost too late to stop. I stomp the brake pedal, clenching the steering wheel as my brakes squeal, sending the smell of hot rubber through the air. The putrid smell is enough to hide the lingering scent of Dylan. At least I hope.

Malicevile propels into the air before I run him over and lands effortlessly on the hood with enough power to dent the metal. Firelight flashes in his eyes as he grips the top of my windshield and leans down to peer at me behind the wheel.

I force myself to laugh. I can't let him see how distracted I am by the rising emotions threatening to leave me weak. "You didn't have to dent my hood."

"You should've been paying attention. What took you so long?" Malicevile hops from my car and opens my door.

"I hit every light," I say as I slide from behind the wheel.

"You should've run them." He places his hand on my back and guides me toward a decrepit bungalow with dead grass and a broken path.

The house smells foul, like death and decay, and I can't ignore the streak of blood coating the porch. Crinkling my nose, I bring my hand to my face to protect myself from the stink with my sleeve. A tiny hint of apple lingers on my jacket, and I force my heart to stop racing. I should feel guilty about kissing Dylan, but I stopped regretting things I enjoy when I saw Hell.

"You said you wouldn't go on a killing spree," I comment, motioning to the blood.

"Who says I did that?"

Doubt trickles into my mind, but then a loud, ear-piercing nose sounds through the quiet night. I jump as a demon appears from the side of the porch. Like a cross between a monkey and small deer, the hairy beast taps across the porch, clicking its hooves as it stands on its hind legs. Its humanoid hands hang well past its torso, nearly dragging on the ground. Suddenly, they reach out for me, causing me to automatically step back. It curves its mouth into an eerie smile, revealing blunt orange teeth better suited to grind than bite.

I glance between my father and the animalistic demon, unsure of what I'm supposed to do. My first instinct is to kill the thing. I reach for a weapon that hasn't been on my hip in weeks. So instead, I summon an energy ball.

The demon latches its fingers onto my arm, pulling me to it. The stench of rotting eggs nearly knocks me off my feet. I gag, jerking away, before chucking my energy ball at the thing. It screams as the power shocks it. It comes at me again, wrapping its arms around my waist. It doesn't squeeze or hurt me but embraces me.

"Stop it!" I yell.

Malicevile laughs but doesn't intervene.

"My lady," the demon says, its throaty voice sending goose bumps over my arms. "I have a gift for you."

It's not until this moment that I see the body lying on the ground in the shadows.

"A soul." The demon finally releases me and taps toward the figure on the ground. It locks its long fingers around the ankles of the body and drags it closer. Blood streaks behind it, and when the demon pulls the body into the porch light, I meet the wide eyes of a man—and not just any man—another hunter from the alliance.

And he's still alive.

BRANDED

"YOU DON'T LIKE it, Camilla?" Malicevile asks, coming up to my side to peer down at the dying man. His dark clothing is so soaked in blood that I have no idea where his wounds are.

What the? Is he joking? I like the finer things in life. This is definitely something I was not prepared to receive as a gift.

I mask my expression by covering my mouth and nose with my sleeve again, pretending that the stench is overpowering me. The crack Dylan created in my façade made it impossible not to react.

"I'm sorry. It's just—it smells disgusting here." I compose myself, forcing my eyes away from the hunter. He doesn't speak or fight. All he does is stare at me with a look that pleads for me to save him. But I'm no angel. I can't save him. I can put him out of his mortal misery, but it won't save his soul. "Plus, I don't have the same hobbies as you. I don't need a worthless soul collecting dust on a shelf."

With the expression my father makes, you'd think I smacked him. He's clearly insulted but whatever.

"Camilla, souls, even this one, give you power. Take it," my father demands.

But I really don't want to. "Why? To appease that *thing*," I say, pointing at the unsettling demon I wish would stop looking at me. "No, thank you."

"Camilla," Malicevile says with a hiss to his voice. "You're being rude." Hah. Funny. Where are my soul-taking manners?

I crouch down in front of the dying man, touching my hands to his chest. Trailing my fingers down his torso, I concentrate on seeing his soul. It shines brightly within him, though black streaks mar the golden color. He's far from pure.

Instead of taking the man's soul, I touch my fingers to the hilt of his blessed dagger. My skin sizzles from the contact, but I don't pull away. The pain stops me from doing what I desire— to take his soul now that I can see it, feel it, hear it whisper to me. In one quick motion, I slide the dagger free and throw it, hitting the demon in the chest with it.

It explodes in a fountain of black slime, pouring over me and the hunter. Malicevile sighs as the demon blood splatters across his slacks and shiny dress shoes. He doesn't yell at me though. He doesn't do anything I expect him to.

Using the sleeve of my leather jacket, I wipe the black slime from my face and peer up at my father. "You put me in an awkward position, and you can't force me to take a soul I have no interest in taking."

He lowers his eyebrows. "This is why I can't take you any-where or introduce you to anyone. Raftikan doesn't often give away souls, and you had to go and send him home. He'd have made a good ally to you, Camilla." Malicevile kicks the blessed dagger I used to kill the demon, Raftikan, toward me. "And you did it in the most humiliating way possible. I hope it hurts."

I hold out my blistering hand. "Feels *great*," I say, smiling.

He only sighs. "Come on. We'll take care of the hunter lat-er. Raphael's waiting inside. I don't want him to get too tempt-ed with our catch. Your deal was with me, not him."

With one more glance, I step over the hunter and follow Malicevile to the door of the house. It squeaks at its hinges when he swings it open. I peer around the messy living room, taking in the dusty furniture, trash scattered across the coffee table, and the black-stained carpet. It smells of mildew and damp soil but doesn't stink as badly as the dead demon outside.

Reaching down, I pick up a stuffed kitten from the floor and hold it to my chest. Malicevile watches me but doesn't say anything. I wonder if he can tell that something is off with me. I don't feel like being under his scrutiny. He'll push me to my breaking point and cause me to close myself off again. If that's even possible.

Raphael grins at me from his spot in the hallway. "She's a feisty one. Would you consider changing your mind so I can have her?"

Alana would never go down without a fight. Last I heard, she'd taken up active hunting again instead of hiding in the safety of the research center at the Hunter's Academy. Funny how easy it is to keep tabs on someone. Malicevile only had to pay off a few demons to keep a look out for me. All the demons in the state know she's off limits.

I place my hands on my hips. "Depends what you have to offer," I say in true demon fashion.

"Name it."

Malicevile glances between us with surprise in his eyes, any doubt he had about me before clearly gone. I know how to act the part of a demon—I've had many weeks to learn without the messiness of emotions—and every demon can be bought for the right price. It'd serve Alana right for trying to murder me. I would've fought with my last dying breath for her. If she had stuck by me, I might not have allied with Malicevile. I could've figured out how to be a demon—probably not a very good one—without him.

I push the flare of emotions away. When I usually think about Alana, it pisses me off, but now, sorrow sneaks up on me. *Stupid Dylan. I'm not a fairytale princess. He can't just kiss me and change my life.*

Raphael taps his foot on the grimy carpet, waiting for my answer. I twist my lips to the side. What could I ask him for that I know he won't give up? Almost everything's replaceable. It just depends how much worth he puts on someone.

"I want your beach house...and your Ferrari," I say.

He tips his head back and laughs. "Maybe if she was an alliance leader."

My eyes widen. Alana *is* an alliance leader, which means... "You mean?"

"It's not Alana," Malicevile says from behind me.

Someone bangs on the closed door at the end of the hallway. "Cami, I swear to God if you're really negotiating with Raphael over me you better get something better than a stupid house and car! I'm worth at least his first born, too!" A familiar feminine voice yells through the door. One I'd recognize anywhere.

Without looking at either Raphael or Malicevile, I rush to the closed door where I heard the voice. I thrust it open and find Cadence standing near the wall with her dagger drawn. Her purple hair shines in the light of a lamp that sits atop the nightstand next to an unmade, disgustingly dirty bed. Bars cover the open window, and a mirror lies shattered against the wall.

On the floor lies another body. This one's clearly human and dead. Cadence follows my eyes to the body.

"I didn't kill her if that's what you're thinking," she says, looking past me.

I peer over my shoulder to see both Malicevile and Raphael standing in the hallway listening.

"Can't I have some privacy?" I ask. "Cadence was the only

one who didn't turn her back on me when I transformed into a demon. She's not out to free my soul or send me to Hell or whatever."

Cadence lowers her dagger. "I told them that. They don't understand the concept of a best friend, though. And best friends don't let best friends go to Hell unless they're going together and going down doing something awesome."

A smile creeps onto my face, but I hide it when I turn back to Malicevile. "Are you going to make me fight for a moment alone with *my* human?"

"If you think Faith is bad now," Malicevile mutters to Raphael as he shuts the door. I'm sure they're about to bond over raising demon teenagers like that's worse than having demons for fathers. If Evan wasn't already in my life, I'm pretty sure Malicevile would try to murder any boy who showed interest in me.

"I'm *your* human, huh?" Cadence asks, strolling up next to me. "I don't recall ever selling you my soul." She looks me over before pulling the stuffed animal from my hands. "I thought you'd look different, but you don't. Is that demon blood?"

"I don't deal with souls, but yes, you're mine. I've claimed you," I say, ignoring her last remarks.

"Could be worse, I guess." Cadence reaches out and touches my arm on the only clean spot. "You don't know how much I've missed you."

A million questions circle through my mind. I want nothing more than to yell at her and knock some sense into her, but all I can think about is how much I've missed her, too. I didn't feel it until the moment I heard her voice. Now, all I want to do is spend the remaining hours until dawn talking with her, catching up like old times.

But that's impossible. Not only is it dangerous for her, but it's absurd. How can she even forgive me for how things were left between us? I turned my back on her when I shut my humanity off. I left her grieving for me. I didn't even care. I'd still do it over again, too.

"What are you even doing here? What would your dad think?" I ask. Cadence's dad, like Alana, is an alliance leader. He's the one who had the Moonlight Shores werewolf pack go after me. He's the reason Greg stood up for me in the first place, triggering his hellhound transformation. The anger runs hot through my blood. This is why it's dangerous for Cadence to be here. I'd like to kill her dad. Best friends aren't supposed to do that. *Best friends aren't supposed to be demons, either.*

"I haven't talked to my dad since—" She snaps her mouth shut. "That isn't important. I'm here because Grams sent me."

"The storyteller sent you? Why? What did she see?"

I haven't seen Vivian since the day the alliance sentenced me to death. I haven't thought much about her either.

Cadence licks her lips. "She didn't say anything. All she did was tell me how to find you."

"Well, she shouldn't have."

Hurt flashes across her face. "I didn't have a choice. I need to make a deal with you."

I hold my hands up, shaking my head hard enough that my hair hits my face. "Stop it. I don't make deals."

"Then I'll make it with your father."

Cold dread seeps down my back. In any other situation with any other person, I'd gladly hand them over. "Are you insane? Just because I'm going to Hell, doesn't mean I'm going to let you do it, too."

"Let me? You act like that's something you control." She balls her hands in front of her while blowing her hair from her face. "Cami, you're so selfish, you know. I've been here for you through everything. I even turned my back on basically my life for you. And now, when I want—need—something, you're telling me no because you're worried about me? I didn't even think that was possible."

"Human habits die hard," I say, straightening my shoulders. "But that doesn't mean I won't help you. What's so bad that you've tracked down my father to get to me?"

"Did you see that hunter outside?" she asks.

I slowly nod. "What about him."

"The alliance sent him after me. Guess who had an unfair trial and was sentenced to death for associating with demons?" She wags her eyebrows with a smirk.

My mouth falls open. "But you—"

"I was planning to run away with you. The Moonlight Shores pack took that information to the leaders in return for their own personal hunters to protect them since you know where they reside. My father's hands were tied. All he did was manage to buy me time until now."

Dylan mentioned that he was no longer working for the Hunter's Alliance. I wonder if his reason is the same as Cadence's and why they didn't stick together.

I close my eyes for a second. I'm going to regret this. "Okay, I'll help you. But I'm not making any deals. I'm doing this because you're my best friend."

She nods, tears shining in her honey-brown eyes. "This is why you're the only demon I trust. Thank you, Cami."

"So, you're absolutely sure about this?"

She shrugs. "Might as well earn that stupid death sentence."

I hook my arm with hers. "I guess it's time to formally introduce you to my father."

She audibly swallows. "I guess so."

<hr>

"If I even suspect she's still working for the alliance, I will kill her," Malicevile says, jabbing his finger into my shoulder. Firelight shines in his eyes. "And Evan."

I levitate to get in his face. "She isn't and leave Evan out of this. I swear, Dad. You'll regret it." My emotions run hot and out of control. It takes all my willpower to rein them in. "You have to trust me."

"This might actually be a good thing," Raphael says from behind me. I never in my wildest dreams thought he'd ever stand up for me. "A human willingly on our side? This could be interesting."

Malicevile peers over his shoulder at Cadence sitting in the front seat of my Mustang. "She's going to have to earn her keep. I don't give out things for free."

I roll my eyes. "Yeah, I'm well aware of that."

Malicevile strides to my car and towers over Cadence. "Because of my daughter's annoying attachment to you, I'll provide the protection you need and the means to live. But don't think it doesn't come without a price."

She straightens her shoulders. "I don't kill, cook, or clean houses."

I smirk. "She's good at body removal."

Cadence narrows her eyes but doesn't argue.

Malicevile glances back at the house. "Good idea, Camilla. We can't leave a trail for hunters to follow now, can we?" He turns to face me. "You two stay here and take care of this mess and then head back to Raphael's. I want you by my side an hour before sunrise. Raphael and I still have business to attend to."

I grimace. "But—"

"She's your responsibility, so don't argue." Malicevile turns and nods at Raphael. "Are you okay with the girl returning to your house or shall I get a hotel?"

Raphael turns to me. "The weapons have to go."

I nod. "Sure."

Without another word, the two demons head to the red Ferrari and climb in, leaving me alone in front of the decrepit house. Cadence waits until the taillights disappear down the street before she moves to get out of my car. She holds herself as she peers around, and then comes to my side.

"We just need to squeeze the bodies into my trunk. I'll have Evan get rid of them." I turn toward the front porch where the hunter lies where we left him to die on his own. Waving my hand, I ask, "Did you do that?"

She presses her lips into a thin line. "He interrupted my interrogation with the freaky animal demon. I might've pushed him into the demon's arms. Not my fault the alliance sent an inept hunter after me."

"And I thought Raftikan went through a lot of work to give me that present. He totally deserved his fate," I say more to myself.

"You killed it? I thought it was against some demon law."

I hold out my blistered hand. "Demons kill each other all the time."

"Oh."

I motion for her to stroll next to me back to the porch. When my eyes fall on the hunter, I release a long sigh. I thought by now that he'd be dead or that maybe Malicevile or Raphael would've taken care of him. But of course not. He was my gift after all.

Lifting my hands up, I hold a ball of energy over the hunter. He blinks as he stares into the white light powerful enough to stop his heart. Cadence turns her back on me. It's enough to send a sliver of guilt into my chest.

"I'm showing him mercy," I say, like I have to defend my

actions.

"I'm not judging you," Cadence says softly. "It's just—I haven't seen you use your power to kill someone on purpose before. It makes this much more real."

"You're going to be disappointed if you don't recognize that I'm not the same Cami you knew."

The scent of dewy apples wafts through the air. A brilliant flash of light blinds me, causing me to take an automatic step back. A soft thud sounds on the path when Dylan lands. He flaps his wings once before they disappear from view, leaving shadows in my eyes.

"That's where you're wrong, love," he says, sauntering closer.

"Eavesdropping is rude, Dylan," I snap.

Cadence rushes from the porch and meets him halfway, throwing her arms around him. He laughs as she nearly knocks him off his feet. Watching them reminds me of our time at the Hunter's Academy. Dylan and Cadence lived in apartments next to each other. They spent a lot of time together. Not in a romantic way, but in a friendly way—how it was supposed to be between me and Dylan. Not this complicated relationship I don't even know how to define.

The moment Dylan lets go of Cadence, she swings her arm out and smacks him on the shoulder. "Where have you been, Angel Boy?"

"Around."

His answer isn't good enough for Cadence, so she smacks

him again. "How convenient that you show up after I've already agreed to work for demons."

I glance between them and then back to the hunter. While they argue, I can use the distraction to kill him without them watching me. Raising my hands again, I ignite an energy globe.

"Cami, stop!" Dylan yells. Something hits me hard, knocking me back.

I struggle as Dylan lies on top of me, pressing me into the concrete. His body jerks as my power shocks him. After a second, his heavy weight squishes me when he falls on me completely. He breathes into my hair as he composes himself, and I lie utterly still. I'm afraid to move an inch because he might look me in the eyes. Being this close to him sends my heart ramming against my ribcage. If he lies on me any longer, I'm sure it'll break through.

I push my restricted hands against his cool chest. "Dylan, get off me. That hunter is suffering. There's no saving him."

"I'm not saving him. I'm saving you," he whispers. "His soul isn't yours."

"Well, technically it is. He was a gift to me from a demon." I shouldn't have to explain myself to him. Now would be a good time to prove to him that Cami Anders, the demi-demon, died at the gates of Hell.

"I wish you didn't say that," he whispers.

"Why?"

"Close your eyes."

"What? No. Dylan, just get off me."

"Close your eyes," he repeats.

Struggling under him, I thrash until he eases some of his weight off me. But he doesn't let me go. Anger courses through me as he ignores my pleas. I dig my nails into his chest, ripping the fabric until they bite into his skin. He squeezes his eyes shut for a moment and asks me to close my eyes once more.

I don't. Instead, I wriggle my hand free and reach up to grab his neck. He doesn't let me go though. Blinding light flashes in front of me as he unfurls his wings. My eyes burn as they come down, hitting the ground on both sides of me.

I freeze.

A moment later, Dylan flies away from me to the dying hunter before shielding him with the heavenly light of his wings. I've never seen anything like it. Not from Dylan, at least. His wings fill out into a corporeal form as they extend out far enough to touch me. He hasn't changed. I'm just seeing him for what he truly is for the first time.

As I sit up to get a better view of Dylan redeeming the hunter's soul before my eyes, the tip of his right wing brushes across my chest. Searing pain blisters along my collarbone. Had I remained on the ground, they'd have never touched me. Now, it feels like I've been branded with a red-hot poker.

A scream rips from me as the fabric on my shirt smolders from my burning skin. The pain is bad enough that shadows edge my vision, threatening to knock me out. I always believed that Dylan was defenseless to demons, but he can send me to my knees without even laying a finger on me. He doesn't even need to be a fighter.

After what feels like eternity, the blinding light flashes off. My chest heaves as I cry. It's the last thing I wanted either Dylan or Cadence to see, but I can't help it. Every inch of me hurts. These wounds run deeper than a simple touch of the wings. Dylan burned more than my skin. He seared right through me to my soul.

Lifting my hands from my sides, I summon my father's power. The demonic light pushes the haze away. In one swift motion, I thrust an energy orb at Dylan, hitting him in the chest. He jumps back when I throw another one. I'm so angry and hurt; all I want is for him to feel my pain—to regret ever coming back into my life.

"Cami, stop!" Cadence yells.

But I can't.

They need to see who I've become.

They need to see what I'm really capable of.

FEEL AGAIN

"CADENCE, GET IN the car," I say, throwing another energy orb at Dylan.

His blindingly brilliant wings expand from his back as he launches into the sky to put distance between us, but he doesn't fly away like he should. Instead, he circles the sky above, making it hard for me to get a good aim.

"Cami, stop. Please," Cadence begs. She keeps her distance between us, and the tears in her honey-brown eyes cause me to pause.

Clenching my fingers at my sides, I say, "Do you believe me now?" I sink to the ground and curl my knees to my chest, resting my head on them. I need to figure out how to fill in the crack Dylan opened on my humanity. I still don't feel human, but I hate that I'm actually starting to care. It's like I'm caught on a wave as it throws me to shore before dragging me back to sea. I have nothing to anchor me. That's what shutting off my humanity did. It kept me from drifting on the rough current.

"I've never doubted that you were a demon, Cami," Cadence says. "What I doubt is that it's all that you are."

When Dylan lands in front of me, a gentle breeze tosses my hair. The night darkens as he returns to his normal self. I can't bring my gaze to look at him. He knows he's won whatever game he's playing.

Holding myself tighter, I say, "I think you should go with Dylan, Cadence. I'm sure he can take care of you."

Dylan plops down next to me and stretches his legs out. "She can't come with me."

I force myself to look up at him. "You owe me. I trusted you and look what you did." I pull down the front of my shirt and show off the blackened skin in the perfect shape of a feather. "You acted like putting the hunter out of his misery was bad. It's not like I was going to keep his soul. That's not my thing."

"You said—"

I push him, cutting him off. "You assumed. I'm not my father, Dylan. I might do some of the collections, but those souls are his."

"Cami, I'm sorry," he says.

"Forget it. You claim that you care about me and that you

love me, but how can you really? The second I act like the monster I've become, you flash your wings. Now, please. Take Cadence and leave. I'll figure out what I'm going to tell my father." I get to my feet and dust myself off. I head toward the house to take care of the bodies. Malicevile's right about not leaving them here.

Cadence peers between me and Dylan before she heads in his direction. He shakes his head, motioning for her to follow me. She doesn't argue when she joins my side. The last few years, I had always thought I was in Purgatory when I was closer to Hell. Cadence is the one who's really in Purgatory. Neither a demon nor half-angel wants her. Maybe that's a good thing.

Dylan crosses his arms. "I know you won't believe me now, but I have to say it. I love you, Cami. I've loved you for a long time, and I love you now, even at your worst. It kills me that I hurt you, but I had good intentions."

"Then take Cadence." I don't respond to his confession. I can't. Not now.

His jaw tightens. "I can't. You might not realize it, but you need her right now since I can't be with you."

"This was your plan all along." He doesn't have to say it. He knew exactly what he was doing when I let him get close enough to kiss me. He knows he cracked my foundation. And he thinks Cadence will help me through. But I don't want to go through anything. I just want it to stop. "Break me and leave me."

"I don't understand," Cadence says.

"He's trying to get to my soul. He's not taking you because he knows you'll help him. He knows you'll be a constant reminder."

"You're using me? I love Cami, but are you crazy? I'm not some game piece to be manipulated to fit whatever the hell it is you're doing. This is my life, and you've taken advantage of my desperation! You abandoned me when I needed you, Angel Boy. I could've been killed!" Cadence's voice echoes through the night. Angry tears brand pink streaks on her cheeks. I reach out and touch my best friend's shoulder, and she turns and hugs me.

Dylan watches us, some indecipherable glint in his chocolate eyes. "I didn't abandon you, Cadence. I can't explain, but you have to believe me when I say that you were never at risk. Even now, going to a house of demons, you'll be safe, okay? Trust me."

Her shoulders relax. "Okay."

Okay? That's it? Cadence might buy his explanation, but I don't.

Something snaps in me at his words. How can he even guarantee her safety? Whatever he's not saying unsettles me. Rushing toward him, I grab his shirt in my hands, shaking him. "What are you up to, Dylan?"

"Love, I can't answer that."

I slide my hands to his cheeks and cup his face. "Please, tell me. Haven't you kept enough secrets from me? I can't just blindly trust you anymore."

"Have faith in me, Cami." He brings his hands up to hold my hands under his, pressing my fingers deeper into his skin.

"Faith isn't what I need," I say, pulling away from him.

He doesn't let me go. Instead, he leans forward and presses his lips against mine. It's enough to stop me in my tracks as his love seeps into the crack he created and fills me up until I'm overflowing with emotions I didn't know I missed until this moment. It's far beyond need and desire. It's like he's taken everything good within him and poured it into me, soaking my soul with his very essence. It doesn't just numb the pain and anger and fear—it takes it away completely.

I'm left standing in shock when he pulls away.

He smiles as he hugs me. Whispering in my ear, he says, "I have to go, love. Remember what I said. Hold onto that, okay?"

He pulls away, bends his knees, and then launches into the air, leaving me frazzled and lost. I cover my face before his wings can sting my eyes. As he disappears into the night, everything that had touched me seconds earlier disappears. I feel emptier than ever. Because how can I hold onto something that threatens to tear down the only thing that protects me? How can I even let him try?

"So, the bodies..." Cadence's voice trails off as she shifts on her feet next to me.

I laugh. I can't help it. "Yeah, we better hurry before there are more interruptions." I try to push Dylan from my mind, but the coolness of his lips lingers on mine.

"And what an interruption that was," she says, lightly

punching my arm.

I shake my head, sighing. "An unwanted one."

"You sure about that?"

I don't answer because I don't know. Hell has me, and it's like Heaven is trying to rip me away through Dylan. In the end, I think both will end up just tearing me apart.

The moment I step into the beach fortress with Cadence on my heels, Evan emerges from the hallway with Faith trailing behind him.

"Cadence!" Faith squeals as she rushes toward us. She stops in her tracks a foot before touching either of us. "My dad called and said you were going to be staying here with us while Cami was in town," she says, crinkling her nose. We both look disgusting.

"Why don't you show Cadence to her room?" I ask Faith.

"Sure." She motions to Cadence to follow her, and my best friend only glances at me once before leaving me to go deeper into the house. I know I should stay by her side until she feels comfortable, but I just want to climb into the shower and think.

Evan grabs the back of my jacket before I can stroll away from him. He hugs me from behind, kissing my neck, and I reach up and run my fingers over his cheek. He stiffens at the sight of my blistering hand.

"You're hurt," he says.

"Yeah," is all I say. I'm hurting more than just physically.

I'm drowning in guilt, too.

"Come on. Let me help you get cleaned up." He pushes me forward, still holding me from behind, and I let him. His patchouli and amber scent helps wash away the smells of the rest of my night, including one I just want to forget altogether.

He guides me to his room, which is right next to Faith's, and across the house from the guest rooms. Placing Evan next to Faith's room wasn't accidental. He's to protect her at all costs while we're in town, because trouble likes to follow me. If Raphael knew about Dylan becoming Faith's Demon Watcher, I'm sure he'd take even more precautions.

Evan kicks the door closed and then spins me around in his arms to look into my face. His aqua eyes bore into mine for a second before they trail down my neck. He stiffens a second later.

I knew this moment was coming. There's no point in trying to hide it. If he didn't see the brand mark from Dylan's wings, I'd have told him myself anyway. He has a right to know that I kissed someone else. He knows my history with Dylan after he traded his soul.

He runs his fingers over the burned fabric where my own sizzling skin set it on fire. "Is that?" Before I can answer, he brings his other hand up and rips my shirt open, revealing the perfect imprint of a feather tip now seared black into the skin just above my bra.

"I saw Dylan tonight," I whisper, not sure if I even said the words out loud.

"*He* did this?" His deep voice reverberates through the room. "Your father was right about him coming around. We have to call him."

I reach out and grab his hand. "I agreed to meet him."

His brows crinkle. "Why? You know what he's capable of, Cami."

I shrug. "I don't know, honestly. But that's not all. He kissed me—I mean, we kissed."

Jealousy crosses his face for a split second before he composes himself. He doesn't say anything for a long while, and I wish he'd say something, do anything, so I know what's going through his mind.

"I'm sorry," I say when I'm certain he's not going to respond at all. "I didn't mean for it to happen. I didn't want it to happen. It just did."

"Okay," he says after a moment.

"That's all?" I expected a whole lot more from Evan, not just "okay." He should be screaming at me, making me feel guilty for my actions. He should turn his back on me, freeze me out, something—anything.

He shrugs. "I'm annoyed that you let him get that close to you but whatever. You're here with me."

I let out a breath of relief, but then something dawns on me. Evan isn't reacting because he doesn't care. How can he when he shut his humanity off? He's demon tainted. He lives on the same emotions I do when we're together—lust, desire. But not love. Not in the same sense as before when we were both far from Hell.

Turning away, I grimace toward the wall. "He doesn't care that I'm a demon, you know. He doesn't want to change me." I know I'm being petty, but I want to get a reaction out of him. I want to feel like he'd fight for me and not just assume that because I'm by Malicevile's side that I'll automatically be with him. I want to feel like he'd give up his soul for me all over again.

"Why are you telling me this?" Warmth crawls over on my bare arms when Evan closes the space between us, pressing into my back.

"He makes me feel alive." I reach up behind me and lock my fingers on his neck, arching my back to glimpse his face.

He tenses under my fingers. "Cami, stop," he whispers.

"He told me he loves me," I continue, my own heart breaking at my words. I hate myself a little for trying to get under Evan's skin. I'm letting my demonic self take over, putting a bandage on the crack Dylan left on me. *Excuses. Excuses.*

"Cami..."

I spin in his arms, placing my hands on his taut chest. "What, Evan? Am I bothering you? Because I thought you didn't care."

He swallows, his Adam's apple bobbing in his throat. "This isn't like you."

"Like me? It *is* me." I levitate a few inches higher until my lips hover an inch from his. "This is who I've become."

He shakes his head. "No, you'd never purposely try to hurt

me."

"Hurt you? Is that even possible?" I lean forward and kiss him deeply before pulling back again. "I didn't think you could feel anything that messy."

He jerks away. "Cami, stop. Just stop. What did I do to you to piss you off?" Furrowing his brows, he glares at me with fire in his eyes. It's what I was looking for, but now that it's here, I want to run away and hide. *What the Hell is wrong with me?*

"You—" I pause, taking a deep breath. "You didn't do anything."

"I can't deal with this right now," he says. "I get treated like this enough from your father."

Ouch. He's right, though. "Evan, wait."

He strolls toward the door.

I rush after him and lock my fingers to his shoulder. "I'm acting like this *because* you didn't do anything. I just told you I kissed Dylan, and you acted like it wasn't a big deal."

"So, it *is* a big deal to you," he mutters.

A tear escapes and rolls down my cheek. I guess it is. "Evan, I'm sorry. I'm so, so sorry."

He studies me for a minute as I silently cry. It's the first time I've broken down since the night Greg transformed into a hellhound before I turned off my humanity.

"I'm a terrible person," I say, wiping my cheeks with my hands. "I just miss you. I miss who you were."

"The nephilim got to you," he says, his voice low. "I'm going to hunt him down and kill him myself."

My hair sticks to my cheeks when I shake my head. "No, please. It's not about Dylan."

He reaches out and cups my face in his hands. "You're hurting. Turn it back off, Cami." His frustration and anger shifts to worry. "This isn't about you kissing Dylan at all."

I suck in a shaky breath. "Isn't it? Please, just be mad at me. Yell at me. Do anything. Feel something!"

Pulling away, he rubs his hand down his face. "Why do you want me to hurt so badly? You know what will happen if I turn my humanity back on. You know how devastated and betrayed I'd feel. I traded my soul for you. I gave up my eternity so you could live."

"Not like this!" Turning toward the wall, I throw a bolt of energy hard enough to make the lights flicker out, leaving the room in darkness. "It wasn't supposed to be like this."

Evan closes the space between us and wraps his arms around me, kissing my temple and hair. He holds me tightly, just hugging me, letting me bury my face into his shirt. The crack in my wall is slowly growing, threatening to break it apart.

He rests his forehead against mine. "You're right. It wasn't supposed to be like this, but it is. I still wouldn't change my decision to trade my soul for your life."

I never deserved such a gift. If I could go back in time, I'd have just accepted my fate. Then everything would be the way it should be. I wouldn't have hurt everyone in my life. I wouldn't have caused so much fear and pain. Dylan could've saved my soul and that would've been that.

But Evan's right. It is what it is.

And it kills me.

If this was Dylan's plan all along, to slowly break me to get to my soul, then it worked. My humanity—the good and bad—leaks out. There was a reason I turned it off. I couldn't live with myself otherwise. I can barely live with me now.

I sniffle, trying to compose myself, but it's impossible. "I'm losing control," I admit after a long moment.

"We have to tell Malicevile that he got to you," he says. "You shouldn't have to feel this way. Dylan should've never done this to you. If he loves you like he claims, he wouldn't want you to hurt. He'd do anything to make the pain stop." Something about his words cuts deep into me. He's right in a way.

I shake my head. "Please, Evan. I don't want him to know. It's my fault. I shouldn't have agreed to meet Dylan. I just—I need the sun to rise. I need to disappear from here for a while."

"Cami..."

"Promise me, Evan."

He's silent for a long moment. "I promise," he finally says. "But I swear on my life, Cami. If I ever see him again, I'll cut those wings from his back for doing this to you."

I don't argue. I don't even know if I'd protect Dylan.

Instead, I let Evan hold me while I feel every jagged, broken piece of my soul.

RELOCATED

THE SCENT OF cinnamon and clove swirls through the ocean air. The sky lightens in front of me as the moon disappears, and I wait for the sun to rise behind me. Cadence sits next to me in the sand, digging her bare feet deeper, watching me watch as the seconds tick by before the sun will steal me away for another dozen earth hours.

"You're late," I say, tilting my head up as Malicevile strolls behind me. "You were supposed to be here an hour ago."

"Something came up," he says offering his hand to pull me from the sand. "We'll discuss it later." He gives me The Look before shifting his gaze to Cadence who now stares at the sea.

He won't say anything around her—probably never will.

I dust the sand off my clean jeans. I've washed away the remnants of the night along with my tears. The only things that remain are the blisters on my hand and the brand over my heart, now covered with a fresh shirt.

Malicevile pulls a piece of folded paper from his pants pocket and tosses it on the ground in front of Cadence. "I've created a list of errands I need done for tonight. Evan will escort you."

Cadence only nods as she picks up the paper from the sand. I can't help but think about Dylan's words and how her being here was part of some "help Cami" game, which I don't even believe. There's more. Always is with Dylan.

I reach down and squeeze her shoulder. "Evan will take care of you. He promised me."

She smiles up at me with tears in her eyes. "I know."

Turning away, I catch sight of Evan hovering on the back patio. He watches me with serious eyes. He doesn't agree with my decision not to clue in Malicevile on the state of my humanity and soul, but I know he won't say anything. It'll come down to whether or not I can hide it from my father.

I cross the space between us and slide my arms around his neck, pulling him to me. He relaxes under my touch as I brush my lips against his. He locks his fingers on my hips, pressing against me as he kisses me deeper.

"We'll figure this out," I whisper into his lips. "And remember, I'm with you."

He breathes against my lips. "Always."

A second later, the world shimmers around me, and Evan disappears as the sun steals me away to lock me up in the daylight prison. Relief washes over me as all my emotions and pain numb. The ache in my hand subsides as I heal from touching the blessed dagger. A coolness washes over my chest as well, but I don't look into my shirt with Malicevile strolling to my side. I close my eyes for a second, just taking in the sweet nothing.

"You look happy to be here," Malicevile says, forcing me to open my eyes. I don't see Raphael anywhere. I'm not surprised though. This is the only time Malicevile gets me where I have to listen and talk with him.

"You think this is my happy face?" I run my fingers through my messy curls.

He hooks his arm through mine as he heads in the direction of the familiar gnarled trees. "I know it is. It's so rare to see that I'd recognize it anywhere."

"Does that bother you?"

He shrugs. "It's never been one of my priorities."

Of course not. "Yeah, mine either." It's true in a way. Happiness wasn't exactly on the top of my list of things I wanted before I turned into a demon. Surviving and basic necessities, sure. I never thought about my happiness, though. *Because it was natural.* I didn't have to think about my happiness because despite everything, I *was* happy. "But I'd like it to be." I don't know why I say it.

"Is this because of the human? I know memories can be

difficult sometimes. You know, there are ways to keep her out of harm's way without having her around. I don't want these silly relationships to get in the way of how you live your life, Camilla," he says.

I tug away from him. "What life? Parading around by your side? Doing what I'm told?" My words are even when they come out of my mouth. It's easy to talk to Malicevile here without the intensity of emotions from the earth realm.

"You're unsatisfied," he says.

"I wouldn't say that. I'm just—I want Evan's soul." There. I said it. I haven't ever asked before because I knew he'd never give it to me. He probably still won't, not unless I have something good enough to offer, but I have to try.

Malicevile laughs, tipping his head toward the hazy sky. I'd be angry if we were anywhere else but here. Instead, all I can think about is how much the disappointment will hurt tonight. Maybe I shouldn't have asked after all—not with how out of control I'm becoming.

I cross my arms. "What do you want for it?"

"Camilla, you said it yourself. You're not into collecting souls."

"I said I wasn't into collecting souls that didn't interest me."

His smile wipes away with my words. "You really think I'm going to give up your little boyfriend's loyalty to me?"

"You want to risk losing my loyalty to you?"

He stops in his tracks. "Don't think for a second that I'm

not willing to start over with another child. I'm a very patient man, and who knows, the third time might be a charm."

He's bluffing, and he knows I know it. "Good luck with that."

I stride forward to put space between us. Maybe today will be the day I venture off on my own. Maybe he needs to be put to the test. He's gone through so much effort to keep me out of things that I can't imagine him throwing it all away to make a point. But I might.

I get fifty feet ahead before I hear him sigh.

"Camilla, stop."

I wave my hand over my shoulder. "Leave me alone. You need time to plan the birth of your third child anyway."

"Will you stop if I make a deal with you in regards to your boyfriend's soul?"

I stop and turn around. "Don't lead me on."

He raises his hands up. "Hear me out."

"I'm listening."

"I'll give you Evan's soul when his mortal life ends." Malicevile doesn't move from his spot as he watches me.

It's not the deal I wanted, but I can't refuse the offer either. "In exchange for what?"

"Consider it a gift for your loyalty."

I blink a few times in surprise. "Okay. I accept your offer."

A smile crosses Malicevile's face as he strides forward to close the distance between us. The scent of jasmine flowers drifts through the air, drawing my attention away from

Malicevile. He's still twenty feet away as the sweet, strong smell tickles my nose, coming from the direction behind me.

I don't even have a chance to turn to look before Malicevile raises his hands, an energy orb ready. He thrusts the orb in my direction, and instead of catching it, I duck. A small groan echoes from within the trees, but the scent doesn't go away. It gets stronger.

I scramble to my feet to run back to Malicevile's side, but it's too late. Hands wrap around my waist and yank me away. I hit the hard chest of another demon, but I can't even see it. All I can do is watch Malicevile disappear from view as the demon drags me away.

<hr>

"Let me go!" I scream, elbowing the demon as hard as I can in the stomach.

The world spins as I'm thrown to the ground next to a black lake that bubbles and smokes with fiery heat. A metallic head with two beady eyes emerges from the surface of the lake to peer at me before sinking back under.

The demon can't send me to Hell here, but if it manages to keep me away from Malicevile until sunset, it could do so the moment we enter the earth plane. And unfortunately, this demon has enormous wings. It's the only part of it I've seen.

Without waiting, I push to my feet and dash toward the forest. The trees are so close together that the demon will have to go by foot. It won't be able to take flight from within the dead forest either.

"Cami," a masculine voice calls. "Don't run. I'm not going to hurt you."

Rule number whatever: Demons lie. We lie so well that even we might believe we're telling the truth. So I don't stop. I pound my boots hard against the dead ground, and slide between two narrow trees. Something hits the trunk near my head, but I don't pause to find out what this demon's power is.

Footsteps sound behind me. This guy's not going to give up. And why would he? I'm the daughter of one the most powerful demons. Malicevile was right about the world. They could use me against him. I wasn't serious when I told Malicevile to think about having a third child. I really do want to live. I'm not ready to face the fiery pits of Hell. I don't even think Dylan could save me from that fate. *Stop thinking about Dylan and run faster!*

But running faster is nearly impossible with how sporadic the trees are. I can't even jog in a straight line for more than two steps.

A screeching noise echoes in front of me, and I bend my knees and levitate into the air just as a lower-level demon comes into view, trapped by invisible boundaries that keep it from moving in this realm. The demon looks like a warped rabbit with two giant spikes for ears, glowing red eyes, and a body covered in shimmering scales. It hops up, using tiny fingers like hamster paws to latch onto my boot.

The air whooshes from my lungs when I slam straight into a white-barked tree. Flying back, I smack into another tree before colliding to the ground. The creepy rabbit demon squeals as it claws up my legs. It's a lot heavier than it looks, and strong, because when I bat it with my hand, it doesn't budge. It just sits on my stomach and stares at me with its glowing eyes.

And then it smiles. "My lady."

Raising my hands, I summon a burst of energy in my palms. Before I can thrust it at the rabbit demon, a black boot kicks it right off me, sending it into the nearest tree with a loud crack. I take the opportunity to shock my stalker. The demon drops to his knees with a heaving breath.

I raise my hands again.

"Wait!"

It's not until this moment that I actually get a good look at my demon kidnapper. And he's gorgeous. He holds up his hands, covering his face protectively. Definitely not trying to attack me.

"For what? You kidnapped me!" I don't attack him though.

"No, I relocated you."

I clench my fingers, shaking my hands in front of me in frustration. But I still don't blast him. He's a lot less scary now that I can see him.

After a second, he realizes I'm not going to blast him with energy again and lowers his hands to the dead ground. His hazel eyes glow against his deep tan, and his walnut brown hair is styled with product, the sides shorter than the top that looks like he ran a comb through it once and let it stay where it stood. He's wearing what I can only describe as a ridiculous screen-printed T-shirt with palm tree silhouettes stamped a dozen times over a red sun. His dark washed jeans fit him well, and his boots look more stylish than work-ready. And he's young-looking, like he's in his early twenties. But you can never tell with demons. He's probably as old as my father.

"Relocated me? What the heck for? If this is some kind of demonic power play, I swear to God you're going to regret it the moment the sun sets." I dig my fingers into the dry grass before I push myself to my feet. "I might not look like much, but I've sent way scarier demons home without using any power."

"Swearing to God," he says, smirking. "You must be serious. Why do you think this is a power play anyway?"

"Do you even know who you took me from?"

He wags his eyebrows. "Malicevile. He sure looked pissed, too."

The simple gesture irritates me enough that I toss a small energy orb at his chest. It wipes the smirk right off his face. "Of course he was mad! And you interrupted an important conversation."

"What about?"

My mouth falls open. "You think I'm going to tell you?"

The demon doesn't push to his feet. He remains sitting on the ground, crossing his legs to get comfortable. I hope Malicevile comes soon. I'd love to see the look on this guy's cocky face when he has to face the wrath of my father.

"Why not? It's as boring as Hell here, and Malicevile won't

find you anytime soon," he says.

I turn my back on him and stroll between two trees. "That's what you think. If Malicevile wants to find me, he will."

"So the rumors are true." The demon's jasmine scent circles around me as his shadow cuts across the ground. Now he's following me because I've said too much.

"What rumors?" I ask instead of confirming anything.

"That he has a daughter—a full-blooded demon daughter to be more specific," he says.

I stop in my tracks and turn to face the guy. A lot of demons know about me, but I'm never in the center of things. I'm not surprised he didn't believe I existed until he saw me. "You must be new here. I can show you just how demonic I am if you'd like."

He takes a step back before I can jab my fingernail into his shirt. I'd definitely rip the fabric if I could. "I'd love that, Cami. I didn't come all this way for nothing." He says my name for the second time, and if I were on the earth plane, I'd probably be freaking out.

Which leaves me with the question of why. While the demon world is large, it's still miniscule compared to the number of humans. Malicevile really does know every demon, at least in our area. This guy has to be on top somewhere else.

"You know what? I don't have to prove myself to you. If you'd like to request my presence from my father, be my guest—that is, if he allows you to live." I stride faster so the demon doesn't stroll next to me.

"Empty threats don't scare me, and I'm sure Malicevile has his reasons for keeping you to himself. Must be embarrassing for him that you allow all that humanity to mess with you. Not to mention that soul. I'm surprised you even got to keep it."

I frown as I spin. "First, you have no idea what you're talking about when it comes to my humanity. Second, why would I not get to keep my soul?"

"I thought he'd take it."

"Who?"

I expect him to say the Almighty or Lucifer or something, but he doesn't. Instead, he says, "Your father."

Oh. "Well, it does belong to *me*. I wasn't going to just let him have it. I'm not a piece of his property despite what he sometimes thinks."

I don't know what this demon wants or why he's making all these speculations, but something about him isn't threatening. He's much more easy-going than my father—Raphael, too. It doesn't help that he wears casual well. He's not exactly dressed how I'd expect a demon who was planning to conquer the world would. But demons are tricky. I don't exactly dress the part either.

He jogs in front of me to look at me. Without even looking over his shoulder, he manages to miss every single tree we pass. "You're not what I expected."

That's creepy. "Thanks, I guess."

He laughs. "You're welcome."

We stroll for another few minutes. I breathe deeper than

necessary, because I hope to catch my father's scent. I'm not against screaming for his help. This demon might be acting friendly, but demons don't just kidnap or kill other demons without reason. He's up to something.

I heave a long sigh when all I continue to smell is his jasmine fragrance. "So I know you didn't kidnap me from my father to stroll in the forest."

"I like long walks," he says, smiling.

I roll my eyes. "I hate walking, especially with demons like you."

"You've met a lot of demons like me?"

No. "Yeah."

He lifts an eyebrow. "You're a terrible liar. Shouldn't you be better at deception?"

"Well, get used to it. I haven't had forever to practice."

"You don't have to lie to me."

Um. "You're some psycho demon who thinks taking me from my father is hilarious. I'm not going to tell you anything," I snap, clenching my teeth with my words.

He chuckles. "His face was quite amusing. He didn't even see me coming...or going."

I throw my hands up. I can't deal with this right now. This demon really is insane. He's unlike any demon I've ever met, and I'm more annoyed by his presence than I realized. He's too unpredictable. I like to know my enemy, and all I know about this guy is that he likes making fun of everything. He's as scary as a kitten, which means something fierce lies within him.

"You're so serious, Cami," he says after a moment.

I ignore him and sit down. I'm not walking anymore. Not with him. "Stop saying my name."

"Why? Do you hate it?"

"Oh, my God. Just shut up."

"Would it make you feel better if I told you my name?" he asks.

I sigh. "No, but if you do at least my father will know who to hunt down."

"You won't tell your father," he says.

"How do you know?"

"You might be a bad liar but you're good at keeping secrets."

The more I talk to this demon, the more unsettled I get. He knows a lot more than I do, and he knows it.

"You don't know that."

"Well, how about we make a deal. I'll tell you my name if you promise to keep it secret."

I shake my head. "I don't make deals."

He links his fingers together. "Interesting. I'm Zach by the way."

"What kind of name is that?" I ask, surprised he even told me. I have a feeling he wants me to tell Malicevile. He's just playing some stupid game with me.

"What kind of name is Cami?"

"Whatever. I'm done talking to you. You're welcome to sit here until sundown, but just know that I won't hesitate to kill you if I'm so far from where I want to be that I miss the few hours a day I get with my boyfriend." I stretch my legs out in front of me while leaning my back on a tree trunk.

I expect him to ask about Evan, but he doesn't. Instead, he holds up his hand at me. "I guess this is goodbye then."

I frown and raise my hands up to blast him with an energy ball, but it's too late. A dark haze erupts from his fingers, stealing the world from me. The last thing I see is the sun as I fall over and lose consciousness.

MIND GAMES

"TWO TIMES IN a week. I like this new habit of yours, love. Feels like old times." Dylan stands with his arms crossed over his chest in front of a broken angel fountain. The dead world around us is nothing like the dreams he used to create for me before—the ones full of blue skies and flowers. This one is just plain sad.

"Well, enjoy it while you can. I might be going to Hell any second now." A small blip of sadness grips my heart. I turn toward Dylan to meet his gaze. "Think you can do me a favor?"

He tilts his head to the side but doesn't comment about my revelation. "Anything."

It's about to get awkward, but I don't care. "Will you make sure Evan's okay? Cadence, too?"

"You really think you're about to die?"

"I was knocked out in the daylight prison realm by the most ridiculous demon in existence. So yeah, I'm pretty sure that the moment the sun sets, I'm as good as dead." I shift on my feet. "Which is stupid." I kind of knew I'd die by the hands of a demon, but I always thought it would be Malicevile, not some guy named Zach in a palm tree shirt. I didn't even have a chance to go down with a fight. How lame.

Before he can respond, I close the distance between us and embrace him, burying my face into his chest. He's not who I should be spending my last moments with, but I'm just thankful I'm not alone. "It wasn't supposed to end like this, Dylan."

He rests his hands on my shoulders. "It doesn't have to."

The world shakes, causing me to stumble away from him. I don't even have the chance to ask him what he means before the ground cracks between us, and I'm swallowed back into darkness.

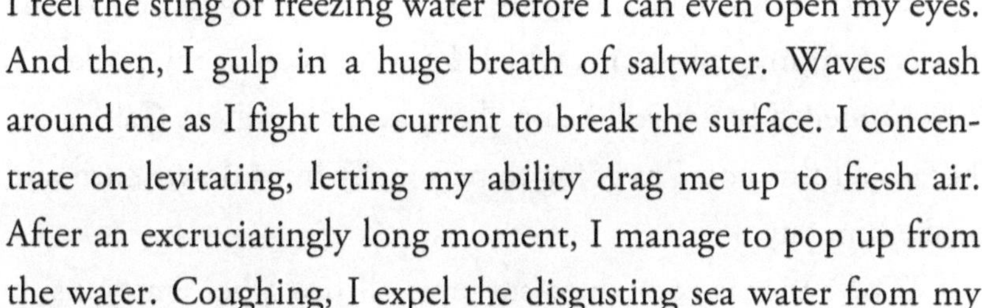

I feel the sting of freezing water before I can even open my eyes. And then, I gulp in a huge breath of saltwater. Waves crash around me as I fight the current to break the surface. I concentrate on levitating, letting my ability drag me up to fresh air. After an excruciatingly long moment, I manage to pop up from the water. Coughing, I expel the disgusting sea water from my lungs and suck in a burning breath of air.

I emerge halfway from the ocean and spin around, power already radiating in my hands. Confusion washes over me as I peer around the empty ocean. Lights shine on the shore, close enough that I can swim without a problem.

But why am I here? What was the point of taking me from Malicevile to leave me unharmed come sunset? *Maybe you're still dreaming?*

"Dylan?" I whisper.

Only the roaring hum of the ocean responds. I'm definitely awake and back in the earth realm, which means a lot of time has passed. I bet Malicevile is either freaking out or really planning on procreating again. *Ugh. Don't think about that.*

A swell lifts me higher in the water, and I half-swim, half-levitate toward the lights on the beach. It's a lot harder to swim in a leather jacket and boots, but somehow I manage to make it to the sand.

I lie on the beach for a few minutes, staring up at the star-studded sky, catching my breath. I inhale and exhale, expecting to catch the scent of jasmine, but all I smell is the fresh air. Zach is long gone. *Stupid, annoying demon.*

Sand clings to me, coating me from my soggy hair to my boots. And my cell phone, which I always keep in my pocket, is now ruined. I better still be on the coast of Southern California, because if I'm not, I'm going to personally hunt down Zach and make him pay.

The anger is enough to suppress all my other emotions. It helps that the iciness of the water numbs the rest of me.

The low sound of voices invades my quiet night, sending me to my feet. It's just my luck to go from one threat to another. I thought I was past this since I'm no longer half-human or torn between sides. But I guess I was wrong.

"You sure this is the place?" a feminine voice asks. Two shadowy figures walk the stretch of beach near the bike path. Luckily, they haven't seen me yet.

"Galvin said eight. We still have a few minutes."

The two people walk under a streetlamp that lights the walking path, and my heart sinks into my stomach at the sight of the two hunters. The alliance really has put all hunters on deck like it could even make a difference. They're lucky I'm not in the mood for a fight because if I was, they'd be in trouble.

A low whistling sound echoes through the air, causing me to tense. A moment later, something hits me hard in the chest before thumping into the sand. A smooth, black rock rests near my sand-covered boots, surprising me.

Then another rock hits me right in the middle of my forehead. I yell out, covering my face just long enough to get myself together to realize that the hunters have spotted me, and one of them is chucking rocks at me. Like, seriously? Rocks? Have they run out of weapons?

Energy sizzles between my palms, and I launch the orb directly at the rock thrower. It hits the hunter in the shin. A feminine scream pierces my ears as I rush forward to face the hunters in all my demonic glory. I'm in no mood to be messed with. They couldn't just leave well enough alone. Now, I'm going to have to finish what they started.

I stride closer, catching the scent of something spicy—like smoked paprika—on the ocean breeze. One of the hunters isn't entirely human. And I'm guessing it's the rock thrower. I vaguely remember encountering an ability like hers at the academy.

"I'm in no mood for your crap tonight," I say, summoning demonic power into my hands.

The other hunter, the human one who smells like citrus deodorant, flashes her dagger at me. In the dim light, I can see she's not much older than me. I kind of feel badly for her, but the feeling disappears quickly when she waves a metal flask in her other hand.

I stop in my tracks. Not because I'm afraid of her, but because holy water burns like Hell. I don't want to spend the rest of the night covered in oozing blisters. Call me vain, but I don't want to have to hide my face.

"Don't come any closer," she says.

I don't but not because she says so. "Don't worry. I don't have to."

I grow the energy in my fingers until it is the size of a basketball. It's unnecessarily large for such a petite girl, but intimidation is a whole lot of fun.

"Camilla, dear. You've found me a present." Malicevile's voice erupts through the night before I launch the electricity in the hunters' direction to petrify them. I guess you can't terrify someone who has already succumbed to debilitating fear. By the looks on both the hunters' faces, they look like they've died of fear.

A warm hand grips my shoulder. "Where have you been?" It's like my father to question me at the most inconvenient times.

The human hunter takes the opportunity to try to throw her holy water at us. But Evan steps in the way, getting the majority of the spray. It's just like a cool shower to him. Blessed things don't affect him. It allows him to go places that my father and I can't. Not like we'd want to anyway.

Malicevile wipes off a drop of burning water from his cheek with his sleeve. It only leaves a small blister on his smooth face. "Take care of that one, will you?" he asks Evan. "Restrain the other one. I want her alive."

My forehead crinkles. Why on earth would he allow either of them to live?

Evan summons fire in his hands.

The human hunter jerks back. "Wait! Wait! I want to make a deal."

Well, that was easy.

Malicevile smiles as he turns to me. "My questions will wait. I'm just glad you're okay, Camilla." He turns to Evan. "Take her home to prepare. I'll catch up soon enough." He saunters closer to the hunters. "Business awaits."

Evan slides his fingers into mine and pulls me away from Malicevile without a word. I force myself not to glance back at the hunters I left in his merciless presence. Their souls don't stand a chance. *Don't feel guilty. They'd have sent you to Hell the moment they had the opportunity. Get yourself together.*

Once we're out of hearing distance from my father, Evan stops in his tracks and spins to face me. His eyes travel from my sandy, tangled hair to the shirt that clings to my chest. The way he looks at me makes it easy to forget the trauma of the day, of thinking I was about to die. It's easy to lose myself in his aqua eyes. He stares at me so intently that I expect him to devour me in the best way possible.

He pushes my damp hair behind my ear and leans in close, grazing his lips against mine. "You had your father worried. He said you vanished, and he couldn't track you in the daylight realm."

"Is that why he took so long to find me?" I'm not expecting an answer from Evan, but it explains a lot. That stupid demon—Zach—is way more powerful than I thought.

"What happened?"

I open my mouth to spill my soul about how I was kidnapped by the most annoying person in the universe, but the words lodge in my throat. I physically can't say them. My heart races and fear lines my forehead.

"Are you okay?" Evan asks.

I shake my head. "I feel sick."

He scoops me in his arms, unfazed that I could throw up on him any second, and hurries to my Mustang, which he parked against the curb on Ocean Avenue. It takes me a moment to realize it, but we're only the town over from Moonlight Shores. Zach didn't take me very far.

Evan slides me into the front seat and bends down to look into my eyes again. "Did something happen to you?"

I expect to close down, but somehow I manage to say, "Yes. It was a—"

"Another demon?"

I nod. If Evan wasn't good at guessing, I might not have been able to answer. Whatever Zach did, it messed me up on a deeper level. His ability must include mind control or something. The thought makes me uneasy. What else did he do to me? Will I somehow snap and start attacking Evan? My father? What if he set me up to do his evil deeds? And I can't even warn anyone. Mind games are the last thing I need.

Evan swears while pulling his cell phone from his pocket. He hits a button and waits for it to ring. After a second, he says, "You were right. It was a demon." He pauses and looks at me. "She doesn't know. Should I cancel tonight's plan?" More listening. "Okay." A second later, Evan brings his gaze to mine.

"What plans?" I ask.

"We're going out."

I crinkle my nose. "Where?"

"Business meeting with your dad."

"Even after a demon basically kidnapped me?"

"Especially because of that."

SPECIAL

THE LAST THING I want to do tonight is to parade myself around the demons who admire and despise my father. I knew that it was inevitable that I'd be forced to accompany him to one of his boring demonic soirees since we've come all this way to Raphael's, but I was hoping that I could get out of it. My behavior while meeting Raftikan should've made Malicevile hesitant to parade me around for a while.

Evan sits next to me on his bed. "Come on, Cami. Relax. We'll do what we always do. Hang out for a bit and then find somewhere private to—"

"Unless you're about to say somewhere private so we can

all gossip about the most ridiculous demon, you better rethink your plans tonight, Demon Boy," Cadence says, as she finishes painting her nails.

"Scared of a few demons?" Evan asks, goading her on.

She chucks the bottle of nail polish at him, but he easily catches it. "No, but if you two even consider ditching me so I have to hang out with Malicevile, I'll make sure you'll never have any alone time again."

I laugh. "I think she's serious, Evan."

He kisses my cheek. "I'd like to see her try."

Cadence fake glares. "You'll regret it."

A knock sounds on the door, drawing my attention away from my own thoughts. I consider telling Evan not to answer it, but before the words come out of my mouth, he slides off the bed. When he cracks the door open, I catch sight of Faith on the other side. I haven't seen her since yesterday. Raphael had taken her out by the time Malicevile and Evan had found me tonight.

She clutches a dress bag to her chest as she rocks on her feet. It isn't until she holds the bag out that I realize she's wearing a sapphire-colored baby doll dress that brushes her knees and silver flats. Her blond hair is braided in a crown with tendrils falling down her back in soft waves. Diamonds sparkle from her ears and wrist, and she's even wearing makeup.

"Your dad asked me to give you this. You're supposed to get dressed and meet us in the foyer in an hour." She turns to Evan and Cadence. "Malicevile requires your presences now."

I knew this was inevitable. I was just hoping something would come up.

Cadence groans before standing. She grumbles as she heads toward the door. "I should be the one helping you get ready. It's my specialty."

I laugh. "I think I can manage to put on a dress."

"But what about your hair and makeup?"

"I thought I'd skip that."

Cadence grumbles again as she hooks her arm through Evan's and bares her teeth at him but not in a smile. "Your girlfriend drives me crazy sometimes."

"Me too," Evan says, eyeing me on his way out with Cadence.

All I can do is roll my eyes.

Faith enters the room, closing the door behind her. I don't move from my spot on the bed as she carries the dress bag over to me and lays it near my feet. With the way she stares at her polished fingers, I know she has a lot on her mind. Something is holding her back from talking to me, though.

Sitting up, I pat the bed next to me. "Are you afraid of me, Faith?"

She pales at the question. "What? I—no."

"It's okay if you are."

She smoothes her dress over her knees. "Really, Cami. You don't scare me."

"Then what is it?" I shift my legs so that I half face her. She doesn't meet my eyes and continues to stare at her glittering nail polish.

"Dylan's been coming around," she finally spits out. "And today he brought a letter for you." She reaches into her bodice and pulls out a folded piece of paper. "Sorry. I didn't know where to hide it."

I smirk, holding the folded piece of paper in my hands. It smells of vanilla, like Faith, but I can still smell Dylan's lingering scent. I don't open it right away. I'm not even sure I'm going to, not after yesterday. He put me in a vulnerable position—one I can't seem to fix either. This letter could be another attempt to get under my skin. Another one of his games. He might love me, but Evan was right. He shouldn't have wanted to cause me pain. Putting a crack into my armor does just that. Not to mention that I can't allow myself to be in a position to hurt Evan again.

I get angry just thinking about it—angry at Dylan, but also angry at myself.

"You don't have to read it in front of me, but please, Cami. Read it," Faith says.

I clench my teeth at her words. "You should be careful around him, Faith. It's easy to open your soul to a nephilim."

She crinkles her nose. "You don't have to worry about me. He's not going anywhere near my soul. I'm not Hell-bound anyway." Her words actually sting a lot more than they should.

I slowly nod, composing myself so I don't lash out at her for something out of her control. "Okay. I just—" I don't even know what I want to say. I want to protect her. She's so sweet.

Despite Raphael being a demon, he's done an excellent job at protecting her and maintaining her innocence. *Look where that left you when Alana did the same.* "Never mind."

Silence falls between us after a moment, and I do nothing to fill it. I feel badly about wanting to ask her to leave, but I also don't want her to stay. She reminds me too much about everything I lost. Of everything I can't have. It's not her fault that I suddenly feel small bits and pieces of everything again, but I worry that she'll only make it worse. Especially because she's pressuring me on Dylan's behalf. *That jerk.*

"Just give him a chance, Cami. I know it's hard—"

I raise my hand, holding my palm up. "Stop, Faith. You have no idea."

"Dylan said—"

"I said stop!" Anger sneaks up on me, but no matter how hard I try to swallow it back, it begs to take control. Faith has no idea about how hard things are. She's clueless. It's not her fault either. Standing, I move from the bed. "I think you should leave."

"Cami, wait. I'm sorry," she says.

I point to the door. "I said leave."

Tears shine in her eyes as she meanders across the room, dragging her feet. She doesn't say anything as she walks past me.

I purse my lips, too angry to give into her sad blue eyes. "And Faith, tell Dylan that if he tries to use you like this again that I'll tell your father that he's been around. I mean it."

Her bottom lip quivers as she nods without a word. I hold

open the door for her and slam it shut the moment she steps into the hallway. Hot tears burn in the corners of my eyes as I try to process what just happened.

I'm so over the night already. Maybe if I refuse to get dressed, I won't be forced to pretend I'm the perfect, powerful demonic daughter. *Then you'll have to tell Malicevile what's wrong. He'll see right through any of your lies.*

"Damn it, Dylan," I whisper, catching sight of the letter. I snatch it off the bed, squeeze it in my hand, and imagine setting it on fire in my palm. But something stops me. Maybe it's the way he loops the M in my name or because I'm curious—either way, I perch on the end of the bed and unfold the single sheet of white paper.

Love,
Don't be angry that I asked Faith to give you this letter. She's the only messenger I knew you wouldn't try to kill.

Ha-ha. I shake my head. He's lucky.

I just need you to hear me out. I wanted to apologize for kissing you—for putting you in a bad position. I know that you love Evan. I know that you've wanted him all along, and that I never really stood a chance. Especially now. You're a demon after all. That knowledge alone shows how crazy love can make you feel. I never in my wildest dreams believed I could love a demon, but here I am, in love with you. Loving you at what I thought was your worst. Loving you when you could ruin me. Wanting you to ruin me.

I consider stopping. It hurts reading his thoughts.

But I was wrong. So very wrong. It's just hard to think that you no longer want or need my protection. You're strong, powerful, and even though you're Hell-bound, even though you've fallen from grace, you're still Cami. You're still full of good, despite what you think. The fact that you even care an ounce about the people in your life, including Malicevile, proves it. You're different, love. Special. I've always known it. And now, I'm not the only one.

What's that supposed to mean?

I can't explain, not like this, so I hope that you'll meet with me again before sunrise. You have my word that I'll remain in control of my emotions, and I promise to behave as long as that's what you want. I'll be waiting for your call.

Love,
Your Guardian Angel

I mentally insert "self-appointed" because really, what demon needs the protection of a guardian angel? I set the letter on my lap and just stare at the words without reading them. Something in his letter worries me. That some unknown people believe I'm special. But how? I'm not even a very good demon. And I'm being noticed? What. The. Hell. I've been lying low for weeks and guarded like the princess Malicevile teases that I am.

The clock ticks on Evan's nightstand, and it's not until ten minutes until eleven that I force myself to get off the bed. I'll definitely be late meeting my father, but I don't care. He should expect no less from me anyway.

Evan's cell phone sits heavy in my pocket since he gave it to me until he can get me a new one tomorrow. Using it might be a huge mistake, but my mind was set the moment I finished reading Dylan's letter. I have to meet him. Curiosity is my weak spot. He knows this. Anyone who knows me knows this. *Thanks, Alana.*

Taking a deep breath, I tap in Dylan's number and let it ring. He answers after the fourth ring, taking long enough for me to almost lose my nerve.

"I'll meet you," I say. "But under one condition. I get to pick you up this time."

"Come alone."

I stare at the door, half expecting it to fling open. "Give me at least an hour or two."

"I'll be waiting for your call."

HOTTER IN HELL

"CAMILLA, YOU'RE LATE," Malicevile says when I saunter from the hallway to find him waiting alone in the foyer. He narrows his eyes when he sees me. "What are you holding?"

"My boots." I dangle them out from my fingers. "You can't expect me to survive in shoes this ridiculous." Pulling up the hem of my ink-colored gown, I stick out my strappy, four inch stilettos. I drop the soft material, and the gown drapes around my ankles. The laced sleeves and low-cut back makes it impossible to wear a bra. At least the fabric is light, and I can actually move, unlike several of the other gowns he bought for me.

"Leave them here. You'll be neither fighting nor trying to

survive," he says, crossing his arms.

I cross my own arms, letting my boots hit my side. "I don't care."

He sighs. "They stay in the limo."

I twist my lips to the side. "Fine. What's all this about anyway?"

"I have a few associates in from out of town who would like to meet you before we move forward with our mutual business endeavors." He gauges me for a reaction.

Despite my better judgment and all my practice, I give him one. My nose crinkles, and I purse my lips. "This is about my transformation."

"Among other things. We still need to discuss what happened today."

"I told Evan everything. It was just some stupid demon who—" Seriously mouth? It snaps shut against my own willpower. I swear if I see Zach again, the first thing I'm going to do is shove my sharp nails through his heart.

Malicevile's eyebrows peak on his forehead. "Go on."

"I—I don't remember."

"That's hard to believe. You were gone for hours. What aren't you telling me?"

Uh-oh. *Damn you, Zach!* I close my eyes, trying my best to force the words from my mouth. "I—" Nope. Nothing. Not happening.

"Would you recognize the demon if you saw it in person?"

I nod. "I think so. He had—" This is getting annoying.

"He—He was wearing a silly shirt." Whoa. At least that was something. Not much, but it's better than nothing.

"I guess I'll be extending our guest list to include a few more people."

I sigh. "Really? I'm not so sure I can handle any more of us."

His jaw twitches. "Camilla, don't be ridiculous."

"Ridiculous? Look what happened to Raftikan. He was only trying to be nice, and I obliterated him."

He only laughs. "You'll be fine, my dear. Now, come on. The others are waiting. You don't really want to send your human to a demonic gathering alone, do you?"

Ugh. Of course he's using Cadence to get me to do something I don't want to do. He knew all along that I'd protest. If I didn't think Cadence would kill me for bailing, I might still refuse to go.

"You're evil, you know," I say, wrapping my fingers around his outstretched arm.

He smiles. "And you need to work on your insults."

I roll my eyes before letting him lead me out to the stretch limo that idles in the middle of the street outside the beach fortress. My heels click on the concrete path for a second before I levitate just high enough to stop them from making the annoying sound. It also relieves the pain in my feet and guarantees I won't trip.

The driver greets us, and Evan holds his hand out to me, helping me into the limo. Faith and Raphael sit at the front near the closed partition, and I don't meet Faith's gaze.

Cadence sits to Raphael's right wearing her own extravagant gown, a chiffon halter-cut style with a thigh-high slit in a pretty charcoal color that complements her purple hair, which is twisted and pinned off her neck. She raises an eyebrow when I drop my boots on the floor. No one comments.

Evan kisses my cheek and whispers, "Wish we were alone."

Heat crawls up my neck. Normally I wouldn't be embarrassed, but it's another one of the stupid emotions I've lost control of.

Everyone's scents mingle together when the driver closes the door. I haven't been in a space so small with so many people in what feels like forever. Three demons, two demi-demons, and a former demon hunter—not exactly a normal group.

"I almost forgot. Cadence, did you remember to bring the box?" Malicevile asks when the limo lurches forward.

Cadence claps her hands. "Of course!" She reaches into her purse and pulls out a metallic paper wrapped box. She leans over and hands it to me. "This is for you, *princess*."

I sink into the seat. "Don't even start with that crap."

She laughs but doesn't respond. Everyone quietly waits for me to open the box, and when I do, my cheeks burn. I'm pretty sure my whole face just set itself ablaze.

"You couldn't get me a necklace or something? I'm not wearing this," I say, pulling out the diamond and ruby tiara.

"What's the fun in that?" Cadence asks. "You're royalty."

"Not in the sense you think," I argue.

"Just humor me, Camilla," Malicevile says. "All I ask is that you smile and act accordingly for a few hours. If you can manage that, I'll allow you a night out tomorrow to do as you please. I won't even require supervision."

This must be really important if he's willing to negotiate. What are a few hours anyway?

"And I get to take your car," I say, adjusting the glittering tiara on my head. He's never let me drive his Maserati before.

He raises and drops his shoulders. "I suppose."

"Then you have yourself a deal."

⁓ ୧ ⁓

I've never been more uncomfortable in my life. As easy as it was to forget that Malicevile was at one point my worst enemy, meeting a bunch of his demon friends in disguise at what I can only describe as a late night happy hour in a crowded club is harder to swallow. I can't help thinking about all the horrible things these strangers are responsible for—how many people they've manipulated and killed...

I squeeze my eyes shut. Demons punish those who need to be punished. Only the damned truly attract the damned. *What does that say about you?*

"What's wrong?" Evan's warm breath tickles the curls falling around my ear. He slides his hands around my waist, resting his chin on my shoulder. Sucking in a breath of his patchouli and amber scent, I relax the best I can and open my eyes again.

I link my fingers through his so he doesn't try to spin me around to meet my gaze. "Everyone's scrutinizing me. Judging me. I kind of miss all the years I believed I was human. I've never felt so utterly pathetic."

"Nothing about you is pathetic. You have the capability of being the most powerful demon here. Even more so than Malicevile," he says, slowly turning me so I have to peer over the crowd within the VIP area of The Morningstar.

"A demon with a conscience will never be powerful, Evan," I say. "We both know that."

He's silent for a long while. The pulsating music beats to the rhythm of the deep red lights that cast the whole place in a blood-like glow. Coming here wasn't exactly what I expected. I thought for sure Malicevile would parade me around and introduce me to a bunch of people, but so far, he hasn't forced me to greet anyone. My presence is enough. At least this time he left my side. He knows I'm aware that all these demons are beneath us, and I don't have to give them the time of day.

But just because I haven't met any of them personally, doesn't mean that they aren't all talking about me. I can hear my name whispered along with the music. As always, the unfamiliar demons don't believe the rumors. To them, I don't look like a demon.

I should be used to it. I never fit in with humans, and I never fit in with hunters, so why would I fit in with demons?

I scan the room for a minute. Such beautiful people. If only their true forms could compare. I feel bad for all the humans that crowd outside the VIP area, begging for attention. If only they knew how lucky they were that the demons aren't showing them the time of day—I mean night.

Evan squeezes my hips tighter, swaying me to the beat of the alluring music. "You're so tense. Relax, babe. This doesn't have to be a bad time."

I relax a little and spin to face him. "You're right," I say as I flick my tongue across his bottom lip before I suck it between my teeth.

He moans into my lips, sliding his hands lower. If I allowed him, he'd probably pull me off my feet and carry me straight for the exit. The thought alone causes me to pull away. It's too tempting. Evan's too tempting. I can't let my guard down.

"Tomorrow can't come soon enough," I whisper into his ear, causing him to shiver. This night isn't so bad as long as I can tease Evan.

Evan suddenly stiffens, drawing my attention away from him though I don't look around.

"Brace yourself, Cami. Here comes a new friend," Evan says.

I'm afraid to turn around. It's unlike demons to approach uninvited, and all I can think about is how it's probably Zach. Malicevile had instructed me to keep a look out for him, but once I saw he wasn't here, I let myself push thoughts of him to the back of my mind.

Taking in a deep breath, I jerk my head in the direction he motions in, expecting to see Zach's beautifully smug face. Instead, my gaze falls upon a gorgeous auburn-haired woman with eyes so dark that they're basically black in the red-tinted light. She saunters through the crowd, and people move out of her way before she even reaches them. She doesn't smile when her eyes take me in.

"Don't let her intimidate you, Cami," Evan whispers. "Remember what Malicevile taught you."

It's only then that I realize my father is staring at me from his place across the room. Cadence stands slightly behind him with Faith at her side, both of them watching me, too. Actually, now that I have a moment to check my surroundings, everyone is watching the woman approach me. It feels like one of those moments where everyone holds their breath, expecting something huge to happen.

Lifting my chin higher, I straighten my shoulders, keeping my fingers twined through Evan's while letting his other hand linger on my hip as he stands behind me. Unlike normal human social expectations, a handshake isn't necessary. I don't even have to acknowledge her existence if I don't want to. It's up to her to make herself known, to impress me enough to show her the time of night.

"Camilla Hellshire," the woman says, stopping a little too close for comfort. Her cherry scent perfumes the air around us, surprising me. I expected her to smell sultrier—like incense or sandalwood—not like fruit. "I always knew your father would be responsible for accomplishing something no other demon has ever done."

I don't laugh as much as I want to. It's tempting to ask exactly what my transformation has to do with my father. Sure, his blood runs through my veins, but I'm responsible for what I am. He wasn't even there when it happened. He wasn't the one to shove the blade in my stomach. He wasn't the one who went to Hell to intercept my soul. I'm not even sure he remembers what Hell's like. He's been on earth for longer than I can even grasp.

Evan pinches my hip. He doesn't have to be a mind reader to know what I'm thinking.

"I'm impressed by your bravery," I say instead of acknowledging her statement. Flattery goes a long way.

She smiles, but not in a way to show her thanks. She almost leers, like she thinks she's working her way under my skin. She's calculating every action without emotion exactly the way I should be so as to not be surprised. I should be thinking about what this woman can offer me and why I should let her be in my presence. As far as I know, she has absolutely nothing.

"You must impress easily," she remarks. "But why wouldn't you?"

I swear the room suddenly gets quiet despite the blaring music. Even Evan tenses behind me. How am I supposed to respond to that? I'm pretty sure I shouldn't start a fight, especially in my gown. But letting her get away with her insult might leave me open for more potential demonic harassment—and I highly doubt Malicevile would put a stop to it. He'd think I'd deserve it. He'd just make sure no one tried to murder me. But hurt me? Yeah, he'd think it was toughening me up.

Any sort of snarky response sticks in my throat so I do the only thing I can think of. Narrowing my eyes, I give her my most intense glare before swinging my hand out and slapping her hard across the face, hard enough to jerk her head to the side and leave a swelling imprint on her cheek.

There. I don't need my dad swooping in to rescue me anyway. "You know," I say. "I thought you were brave, but I'm sure you're just stupid."

The demon cups her face with her hand. When I look past her, Malicevile subtly nods his head.

"You little brat. Do you even know who I am?" She rolls her shoulders, her body slightly shaking as she prepares to retaliate. Her nails elongate into points sharp enough to impale me if she tried, and her perfectly straight teeth morph into fangs. She doesn't reveal her complete true body, though.

I stand tall with levitation, refusing to show my own demonic form. I don't have to prove that I'm really a demon underneath my skin with my crown of dainty black horns, my gold-hued skin and sharp nails. I don't want Cadence to see me like that. The way she and Faith watch me with worried eyes compared to all the looks of mockery is the only thing that stops me from competing in this game of who's the scarier, more powerful demon.

"Who you are doesn't matter to me." I turn to Evan. "Come on. I'm not about to ruin my gown."

As I push past her, the woman reaches out her arm. She doesn't grab me though. Instead her sight is now on Evan. Her sharp nails slice through the sleeve of his suit jacket, and something in me snaps.

I bend my knees and launch at the demon, using my levitation to carry us a dozen feet into the air. Smiling as I wrap my fingers around her dainty neck, I hang her a foot off the floor while still levitating. Her face turns red, not from the lack of air but because she's livid. If she could grab hold of me, I'm sure she'd attempt to send me to Hell.

I release a burst of energy in my free hand and shove it against her rigid collarbone before dropping her. Her spiked heels slide out from under her, and she hits the floor hard. I don't stop there. I drop to the ground on top of her, stabbing her with my own heel but not enough to do any damage.

My chest heaves as I inhale a few long breaths to stop myself from finishing her off. Killing a demon on behalf of a demi-demon would only put Evan at risk. Other demons will see him as my weak spot, a way to get to me. It'd be like other demons trying to get to Malicevile through me, like Zach, but I'm pretty sure my father will not have to worry about that now. Not with the demons here at least.

I dig my heel in an inch farther, smiling as the woman winces. "Touch my possessions again if you want to test your bravery. I won't be so kind the next time." I slide my foot out of my heel, leaving it in the demon's stomach. The shoes were really uncomfortable anyway.

Evan helps me take off my other heel, and I throw it a few inches from the demon's face. Her eyes burn, shining with hot firelight, but she doesn't say a word. It helps that Malicevile finally crosses the room and slides his arm around my back.

"You make an unforgettable impression, Camilla," Malicevile says, grinning.

I tuck my curls behind my ear. "She embarrassed me."

"You did well returning the favor to Enviana, but now I'm going to have to step in before she tries to send you to Hell. She's nothing if not persistent." Malicevile's words sit heavy on my mind. I don't need his help. That demon, Enviana, can try all she wants to hurt me, but I've been tormented by worse. My pride gets the best of me. In this moment, I welcome my demonic nature. It pushes away all the messy emotions I've been constantly drowning in.

I meet Malicevile's gaze. "I don't need your help. What will people think if you intervene every time trouble comes my way? You might think I'm your precious little princess, but I'm not in distress." Not now at least.

He presses his lips into a thin line. "The only thing they will think about is how not to get sent home."

His answer gets an eye roll from me. "Are you really going to treat me like some porcelain doll for the rest of eternity?"

"No, I'm going to treat you like my daughter," he says, guiding me toward the table where Raphael sits, talking to a few other demons.

They all smile at me as I glide by Malicevile's side with Evan trailing behind us as usual. Cadence and Faith stand near the wall, and Evan joins them.

Before Malicevile has a chance to pull out a chair for me, I shift away from him and place my hands on my hips. The thought of eternity in this constant state in the same battle over and over again suddenly feels suffocating.

"I'm going to get some fresh air." I don't give him the chance to respond. It's not like I'm asking for his permission.

"Camilla," he says.

I step just out of his reach. "I came. I played as nicely as I could. I even smiled a few times. I haven't seen the demon you were hoping to find, so if you don't mind, I kind of feel like leaving."

He narrows his eyes. "Take your human and boyfriend and wait in the limo but do not leave. Understand?"

I shrug. "Whatever." I'm not going to argue. At least in the limo I won't have to fake my regal persona.

I motion for Cadence and Evan to follow me. They leave Faith at her father's side and come up next to me. The other demons don't take their eyes off me, so I don't explain what the plan is. They wouldn't expect me to.

It's not until we're out of the VIP area and almost at the exit that I relax. "I hope you two don't mind if we hang out in the limo for a while."

Cadence releases a long breath. "Thank God. That was torture. When that demon tried to start trouble, all I wanted to do was jump in and cut her heart out with her own dagger nails."

The bouncer holds the door open for us so we can exit into the parking lot. The limo is parked near the back of the lot along the curb that separates the parking lot from the main street. The Morningstar is one of at least a dozen clubs that line the busy downtown street of Tortuga Harbor, a city just north of Moonlight Shores.

"I enjoyed watching Cami," Evan says, squeezing my hand. "She's hot when she's protective."

"She'll be a lot hotter in Hell." The feminine voice comes from behind us.

I don't even have a chance to react when Enviana charges me. Her hands connect with my shoulders, and a wave of power erupts from her. It's enough to knock me through the air, like I was hit by something invisible, then a loud boom pierces my ears. I was hit with some sort of shockwave.

My back scrapes across the asphalt, my skin ripping with my dress, and pain slices through me sharper than any of the alliance's daggers. Cadence screams, drawing my attention to her, and I watch as the demon raises her hands toward my best friend.

In one quick motion, I propel a burst of electricity toward the woman. She quickly draws her gaze to me, expelling her power in my direction instead. I absorb the shockwave enough where it only steals my breath away for a second.

When Enviana realizes that her power didn't affect me like she had expected it to, she races toward me to try to get to me while I'm still on the ground. Her sharp nails catch my attention, and I scramble to my feet as fast as I can.

My throbbing back hits a car, trapping me in place.

Enviana screams as she charges toward me. I don't even summon enough power when she closes the distance between us, determined to send me to Hell.

All I can think is how I'm about to die because of my stupid pride.

I hate that in the end, I needed Malicevile after all.

Except he isn't here.

It's just me and my inner demon.

PRINCESS

THE WORLD SPINS as I'm yanked off my feet. My scalp screams from the pain, but I don't cry out. Instead, I push the shock of the situation away enough to levitate so I'm not dragged through the air by my hair.

Landing on my feet on the other side of the car, I scamper back a few feet half expecting another fight. But no one stands on the roof of the car. A flash of light draws my attention through the window in front of me. Fear crawls up my spine for the first time tonight as I watch Enviana fold in on herself before exploding like a water balloon dropped from a roof.

The scent of jasmine trickles over the car to me, and I stiffen when I see the back of a man with chestnut brown hair. He swivels on his feet, and I swallow as I meet familiar hazel eyes. Zach stands in the puddle of demon with a mischievous grin plastered on his lips. He rubs the goo off his hands on his dark jeans.

"Hello, Cami," he says. "I heard you've been looking for me."

My words stick in my throat, and I peer past him to look for Evan and Cadence. He follows my gaze toward the front of the club, but the sidewalk is empty.

"Your friends ran inside," he adds.

My forehead crinkles. I doubt Evan and Cadence would purposefully leave me at the mercy of Enviana, even if they were planning to get my father. Only one of them would've gone. Not both of them.

I straighten my shoulders in an attempt to compose myself. "I should be heading in myself. I don't trust a bunch of demons around them."

He smirks, a dimple flashing on his cheek. "They'll be fine. I thought we could go for a drive."

It doesn't sound like I have much of a choice.

"Come on, you don't look like you were having a good time anyway," he says, motioning for me to join him on the other side of the car.

He's right about not having a good time, but everything in me tells me to run. I've been taught not to get into cars with strangers, especially demonic strangers. But that was before I transformed into a demon myself. This guy killed Enviana before she even had a chance to hurt me. Why would he do that? He must want something.

I hug my arms over my chest when I reach his side. "I don't know what your motives are, but I don't like playing games. Just tell me what you want."

A smile plays on his lips. "You."

I grimace.

Laughing, he shoves his hands in his pockets. "I didn't mean it like that, Cami. You seem nice and all, but you're just a child."

A child? The guy looks barely a few years older than me. "I assumed age doesn't matter when you're eternal. Plus, why go through all this trouble?" If he's not interested in killing me to get to Malicevile, and he's not interested in me in a grossly romantic way, then I have no idea what the Hell all of this is about. *You could go with him and find out...stupid curiosity.*

"You're special, princess." Not this crap.

I wave his words away. "Can you not call me that?" The only people who can get away with that are the people I care for.

He reaches out and taps the tiara on my head. "I had assumed—"

Heat crawls up my neck. "You assumed wrong."

Voices echo from the club, drawing both our gazes toward the door. Malicevile stomps out with Cadence and Evan behind him. He throws his hands up, yelling. Cadence shrinks back when he points his finger at her, but she doesn't turn away. Instead, she yells right back at him.

My father takes a deep breath of air before rubbing his hands down his face. He turns and stares right at us but doesn't move from his spot. A second later, he says something I can't hear to Evan. Evan takes Cadence's hand and pulls her away.

It's not until this moment that I realize none of them can see us. Zach is one crazy, tricky, powerful demon.

"Ready to go for that ride?" Zach asks.

I'm in trouble now. "I—"

He pulls a key from his pocket and shocks me by opening the door to the beaten up, yellow Toyota Tercel that is parked right next to us. I blink a few times when he opens the passenger's side door for me. The tan seats have seen better days. A few burn holes pepper the seats, and they're covered in grime. My gown and tiara probably cost more than his ride. *Judge much, Cami?*

There was a time in my life that I wouldn't think anything of the car. I didn't even have one before Malicevile bought me one. But demons, especially ones as powerful as Zach, take every opportunity to show off through material items.

"Something wrong?" Zach asks when I don't move to get in.

I place my hands on my hips. "Well, yeah. How do I know you're not going to just send me to Hell the moment I get in?" I cover my surprise with concern so he doesn't know that I'm secretly judging him.

"Because if I wanted you dead I'd have done it already. Now, can you please just get in? We can grab something to eat."

I sigh. "Fine, but I'm calling my boyfriend so he doesn't worry."

"Deal." Just the words I don't want to hear.

I slide into the front seat, wishing I had kept on my shoes when my bare feet touch the dirty floor full of old food wrappers, some dead leaves, and an unidentifiable sticky stain. Zach moves around the car and gets behind the wheel. He watches me in the corner of his eye as he backs out of the spot and navigates through the parking lot to the street.

The Morningstar disappears behind us as he drives at a snail's pace. He even stops at the stoplight despite the lack of cross street traffic. I think he might be humoring me because he knows I used to be half human. What he doesn't know is that I don't follow anyone's laws these days.

"I think we're far enough away that you can call your boyfriend if you want," Zach says after a long minute. "Keep it short though."

He reaches into his glove compartment and pulls out an ancient flip phone that doesn't even have a keyboard. I hold it in my hand and stare at the tiny rectangular screen with actual buttons on the bottom half of the phone.

"You're unlike any demon I've ever met, you know," I say, punching in Evan's phone number.

Zach doesn't have time to answer because Evan picks up on the first ring. He doesn't even have to ask to know it's me.

"Tell me you're safe," he says, breathing heavily into the phone.

"As safe as I can be," I say.

"Where are you?"

I hesitate before I answer. Not because I want to, but because the words refuse to come. "Can you tell my dad that I couldn't wait until tomorrow to have the night off?"

"Yeah, but where are you so I can meet with you?"

I frown. "He told me I didn't need a babysitter." The words fall flat when I say them. Guilt nudges into my mind as I imagine what Evan's thinking. He might not have a lot of feelings, but he can still think I'm being unnecessarily mean.

"Cami..." His voice trails off.

"Don't worry. I'll be back before dawn." I hope. Without waiting for his response, I snap the phone shut and peer out the window into the dark night.

"What was that?" I snap. "You've been messing with my head."

He doesn't answer my question. Instead, he says, "You love him?" He's questioning my relationship with Evan.

"What kind of question is that?" I'm not about to have a heartfelt conversation with another demon. Most demons don't even understand the concept of what love is. Though Malicevile has his humanity now, even he doesn't know or feel what love is. His actions with me come from the sole idea that I'm his blood. We don't share a familial bond. It's possible he had loved my sister, but I'll never know. He wouldn't dare mention it.

"You know what that is, right? I thought since you used to be human and all," he says, making a left turn when we reach the next signal.

"I was never human." It's a way to avoid answering his question.

"But you thought you were."

All the demons I'd ever come across when I thought I was human died by Alana's hands. Most of them were lower-level demons we just happened across. All the demons now, all the ones who know of me have only known me as Malicevile's daughter. And hearing Zach bring something up he couldn't have possibly known unnerves me. The car is suddenly suffocating me. It's not until I reach for the door handle to jump out that I realize it's missing.

I take a few calming breaths that don't help much since every time I breathe, I gulp in his jasmine scent. "Is this an interrogation or something? You ask too many questions."

The demon eases off the gas pedal when we reach a long stretch of road nestled between a cliff and another hillside. The only light comes from the headlights and the moon shining over the black ocean.

Fear trickles down my back when he comes to a complete stop in what's probably the worst spot, right at the beginning of a curve. If someone comes flying around the bend, they'll collide right with us. I might not die, but I can still get hurt.

He shuts off the engine, cutting off the headlights. "I'm only trying to be friendly, Cami. If you don't want to answer something, then just say so."

I scoff at his response, feeling in the dark for a button to roll down the window. There isn't one though. The old car has nothing automatic on it, and the window crank to roll it down with is missing like the door handle. I touch the glass, wondering how quickly I could break it to make an escape.

"I don't want to answer your questions," I say, keeping my voice as even as possible. "I don't even want to be here."

"Why?"

"Why?" The words come out as a yell. I regret the sudden outburst, because terror is so clear in my voice that even an animalistic demon could sense it—taste it even.

Zach reaches over and touches my hand that I have gripping my knee. The gesture startles me enough that I jump under his touch. I jerk my hand away and cross my arms over my chest. My heart pounds in my head as I concentrate on pulling myself together.

"Cami, I'm not going to hurt you. I told you this already. You don't have to be afraid of me." His soft voice wraps around me as if he's talking to a young child, one who's afraid of the imaginary monsters in the closet. I'm no child though, and my monsters aren't imaginary. They're very much real, and one sits right next to me in jeans and a lavender T-shirt with an illustration of a cityscape printed across the front.

"I—I'm not." My voice cracks as I say the words. My own inability to keep myself under control infuriates me. I deserve whatever my fate is tonight because I'm not as tough as I want to be—as tough as I should be. I'm Malicevile's daughter after all. I shouldn't be such a disappointment.

"You're a terrible liar," Zach says, making things worse.

Slowly lowering my hands to my sides, I quietly unbuckle my seatbelt. I can't stay in this car anymore. I don't care if I have to kick out a window. I'm leaving.

"Well, that's better than being a kidnapper," I mutter, pressing my hands against the cold glass before digging my fingers into the seal in hopes of getting some leverage to force it open.

Zach watches me for a second before turning the key over to start the engine back up. "You willingly came with me. I'm not holding you captive."

I shift in the seat, noticing the door handle on his side. "Then why am I trapped in here?"

"Uh, it's an old car. Sorry I couldn't manage to get my hands on something nice. Living among humans isn't easy for everyone, you know. No one greets us with a welcome packet and a ton of cash despite what you probably think, *princess*. We don't all have daddies to buy us the world." He's actually mocking me. I shouldn't be surprised.

The car lurches forward as Zach stomps the accelerator. He doesn't ease up this time, surpassing the slow speed limit at a speed more my pace.

"You're joking, right? I spent the last few years running from my dad. I lived in some gross places with nothing more than a backpack full of stuff most of the time. This—" I run my fingers over my soft gown. "This is my father's way of making sure I stay by his side. Sorry if for once in my life I'm going to enjoy the material things. I've been to Hell and back. I'm not going to let you make me feel guilty." As the words come out, I cringe. I'm overreacting. No demon would even feel the need to justify themselves. I'm failing badly. *What is wrong with you? Don't allow him in your head.* But I'm not allowing anything.

Without waiting for Zach to call me out on my human behavior, I lean over his lap and push the door open. He swerves into the other lane, but luckily there isn't any oncoming traffic. I don't stop though. Raising my elbow, I thrust it back in his face, hitting him squarely in the nose before crawling into the small space on his lap. The horn blares when I grip the steering wheel to pull myself completely onto him.

He locks his fingers into my hair, letting go of the wheel completely, and the car veers right. The headlights flash over the rock side of a hill, and I quickly maneuver the car back into the road to stop us from crashing.

"Are you crazy!" Zach yells, struggling to shove me back onto my seat.

I remain half on his lap as I yank my dress free of the gear shaft. "A little," I respond, locking my fingers on the door, swinging it out again.

Zach stomps the brake pedal, and I hit my side on the steering wheel before bouncing against his hard chest. Reaching his hand over my lower back, he tugs the keys from the ignition. I don't waste a moment. I elbow him in the face again and shimmy the rest of the way out until I somersault onto the hard asphalt without levitating to break my fall.

My elbows bleed, and the lace of my bodice rips, but apart from that, I'm in better shape than Zach, who bleeds from the nose as he thrusts off his seatbelt and hops from the car to chase me.

I scream out for help, but only because human habits really do take forever to get over. It's not like some poor soul will come and fight another demon on my behalf. They'd be stupid to even try.

"Princess, what do you think you're doing?" Zach calls from behind me.

I peer over my shoulder. "Getting away from you."

"Anyone ever tell you that you're the most difficult person in the world?" he asks. He's not chasing me, just walking behind me.

"Malicevile tells me that all the time," I say.

"So *now* you want to answer my questions?"

"No," I mutter, picking up my pace. "I want you to leave me alone."

"I never thought I'd say this, but I'm starting to feel sorry for your dad."

Anger burns under my skin, and I spin on my feet. The edges of my vision shadow in a dark red haze as I lose control. This guy has a lot of nerve. Not only has he ruined my night with my friends, he got under my skin and insulted me. Really insulted me—worse than Enviana.

I blast energy at him, but he dodges out of the way.

"Then feel sorry for him!" I scream. I can't help it. "He has it so tough trying to control someone whose soul doesn't belong to him. He's so damn used to getting his way, it's so hard trying to control me. I'm so impossible with my freewill and desire to be whoever the Hell I want to be. He's just lucky that he currently owns my boyfriend, and there are a whole lot of people who are bent on saving me from these horrible, demonic ways. 'Cause, if you haven't heard, being a demon turned me evil. I'm just a servant to dear old Uncle Lucifer."

Zach blinks a few times before bursting out laughing. His eyes water as he waves his hand in front of him like I've said the most hilarious thing in the world.

I place my hands on my hips. If I were wearing my shoes, I'd tap my foot for good measure. "You think this is funny?"

He swipes the back of his hand under his eyes. "Don't you?"

It is so absurd that I can't help cracking a smile even though I want nothing more than to fling another burst of energy at him. I heave a sigh. "God, my life is ridiculous."

"At least it's not boring, right?"

I thought my life was boring for a few weeks now, but I take it all back. I'd give up all this for a boring life where all I had to worry about is deciding what I was going to wear or what I was going to eat for dinner.

Silence falls between us for a long moment. We just stare at each other, studying each other like it'll somehow give us the answers we need but neither one of us are willing to give.

It takes the low murmur of voices to draw our attention away from one another and to the road behind me. It curves around another corner, and whoever the voices belong to are just around the bend.

But the voices don't belong to just anyone. I recognize them.

Zach rushes forward to grab me, but I side step him and dash in the direction of the people whispering in the night. My feet don't touch the ground as I levitate over it, my ability taking on a mind of its own. Power erupts in my fingertips when I reach the beginning of the bend as the voices sound out more clearly.

And then I freeze.

BETRAYAL

I DON'T BELIEVE my eyes. Less than twenty feet away, Alana wipes a bloody dagger against a yellow rag. At her feet lies what I know is the remnants left of a demon, one who reeks of gasoline.

Her blond hair hangs around her chin, a streak of blood staining a few strands. Shadows from her position under a streetlamp create dark circles under her steely gray eyes. She's wearing her normal jeans and a leather jacket, and apart from the strange seriousness in her expression, she looks exactly as I remember her.

I recognize the person she's talking to as well. Aston Dubois stands a good foot taller than Alana. They must've taken up a partnership after I left. It's strange though, considering that it's more common to pair a human with a halfie. It makes them stronger that way. But Alana is used to fighting demons alone—she had done so for years.

With his back facing me, I stare at the black head of hair I'd know anywhere. Dylan quietly talks to the two hunters, waving his hand out as he speaks. Seeing him here is enough to send me charging forward. He lied to me. He told me he was no longer with the Hunter's Alliance. He swore he was working with a greater power.

I'm livid.

I can't stop myself from yelling out. Dylan slowly swivels his waist to glance behind him. Strong hands grab me from behind, one pulling me back while the other slaps over my mouth. The scent of jasmine nearly chokes me as Zach stops me in my tracks.

Alana and Aston follow Dylan's gaze but they quickly avert their attention. Only Dylan remains staring at me. His dark eyes line with surprise, but he doesn't acknowledge my existence. Whatever Zach's doing, he blocks us from Alana and Aston but his powers don't seem to work on Dylan. And to think I was going to meet him tonight. He was totally planning to betray me, and to the Hunter's Alliance no less.

I bite Zach's palm, forcing him to remove his hand from my face. "Let me go!"

Dylan glances behind him again but doesn't react like he

should. If he loved me, he'd see that I was in trouble and try to rescue me.

"As long as you promise not to do anything stupid. Those hunters can't see us," Zach says.

"What? You don't want to destroy them? They just killed a demon," I say.

"You want vengeance for a demon you don't even know?" he asks.

Oh, jeez. I don't even know how to deal with this guy. He's so strange. I wave my hand out. "Of course not."

"Then why were you trying to go after them?" Zach's breath tickles my neck as he holds me in place.

"I wasn't going after the hunters. I was going after the nephilim," I say.

Zach hums under his breath, holding me slightly tighter like he's afraid if he lets me go, I'll rush forward. I might. "Don't you have better things to put your energy toward? He's a powerless half-breed."

I throw my hands up. "Oh, I have plenty of energy to spare. And I'm going to use it to pluck his pretty little wings from his back." I say it loud enough that Dylan turns to grimace at me. "He lied to me."

In one quick motion, I jerk my arm back and elbow Zach in the stomach. He grumbles as he loses his grip on me. I don't make it far though. He tackles me from behind, shoving me into the asphalt, holding me down with his weight.

I scream out again, and he covers my mouth once more.

Zach shakes me once. "If you don't stop, I'm going to knock you out, princess. All I wanted was to grab something to eat and go for a drive, not get in the middle of a battle because some kid hurt your feelings."

"I don't have any feelings!" I thrash, using my levitation to push from the ground. All I need is to get a few feet in the air before I can knock the annoying demon off me.

The weight on my back suddenly lifts, and the scent of jasmine disappears. I levitate back to my feet and spin to look behind me, but Zach is nowhere in sight.

"Cami, love." Dylan's words hang heavy in the air. It's enough to make me stop to look at him as he stands in front of me. Alana and Aston are nowhere in sight, and I wonder where they went and if Dylan sent them away to protect them from me, like I'd do something impulsive to hurt them. "You were supposed to call me."

"Zach!" I yell. "Zach! You can't just drag me out here and leave. This is your fault!" As the words escape my mouth, I realize that I've actually said them out loud. It's the first time his name has managed to escape my lips. "Seriously! Are you doing this to make me look like I've lost it?"

"Cami? You look disoriented. Come on, I'm parked nearby." Dylan tries to grab my arm, but I pull away.

"You didn't see him? You were looking right at us," I say.

His brows scrunch together. "I don't know what I saw. I wasn't exactly expecting you to show up here so I wasn't on the lookout. If you didn't notice, I was in the middle of a meeting."

I swear I'm going to blast that demon to bits. "Zach!" I yell. "Show yourself."

"Cami..."

I push Dylan in the chest. "I know I'm not crazy. I'm being stalked by a demon. He kidnapped me in the daylight prison realm. Then, he killed a psycho demon on my behalf. He brought me here. His name is Zach. He drives an ugly yellow car and wears silly T-shirts." And why can I say all this to Dylan?

"Will you calm down if I say I believe you?"

I squeeze my eyes shut for a second. "But do you really? I need you to believe me. You're the first person I've been able to talk about him to. He has some crazy mind altering power. One I don't know how to steal."

"Could be his influence has no effect on me because of my angelic heritage. I can't fall under demonic charm."

That gets a smirk out of me. "Is that so?"

He chuckles. It's enough to take my mind off the current situation. "Want to try?"

Yes. No. "Mayb—" My words are cut off when a hint of jasmine trickles into my senses. I swivel on my feet. "Zach! Eavesdropping is not cool, you jerk!"

The demon doesn't show himself though.

Dylan links his fingers to my shoulder. "Let's get out of here. He might be waiting for an opportunity to attack. I don't like demonic surprises, and the way he has you freaking out, I don't want to chance it."

I rake my fingers through my wild curls. "That's the thing. He's not even scary. Not even close. And that's what scares me. I don't understand what he wants from me."

"Probably what everyone wants from you, love. To figure out how to use you to their advantage."

"Is that what this is about?" I wave my finger between us.

"Come on, Cami. We'll talk in the car." Dylan slides his arm around my shoulders, pulling me with him.

I shrug away from him. I suddenly don't even want him touching me. "You can't really expect me to get in another car with someone I don't trust. I don't make the same mistake twice. I'm not in the mood to be messed with."

"Cami, I can explain. I swear I'm not using you," he says.

"But you were with *her*." I can't even manage to say Alana's name out loud. "You told me you didn't work with the Hunter's Alliance."

"I don't."

"But you were here with them."

"It was only because they called me to pass on a message," he says.

I stop in place and cross my arms over my chest. "About what?"

He sighs. "Really?"

I narrow my eyes. "Yeah, if you want me to believe you, you'll tell me."

"Well, it won't be any news to you."

What's that supposed to mean? How on earth would I

know? "That's cryptic."

"You can't honestly say that you had no idea that demi-demons are being taken by demons. Your father's behind the whole thing according to that pile of goo on the ground." Dylan waves his hand toward the rotting demon left behind by Alana and Aston. "That hunter that went after Cadence wasn't alone. Jacie was with him. Two others have gone missing as well. Just this evening."

Shock washes over me hearing about Jacie. Cadence never even mentioned it. Maybe she didn't know. Maybe she assumed Jacie got away. She was locked in a guarded room when I showed up. As for the other two...I know only one. I had just assumed the worst.

"I didn't know he was taking them," I say quietly.

"Yeah, sure," he accuses.

I flinch like he hit me. It's enough to soften the expression on his face.

What I want to know is why would Malicevile show interest in demi-demons that aren't his blood? The only reason Evan's at his side is because he had something to offer. Why take Jacie though? She's not Hell-bound, and she's the type of person that would die before she even considered selling her soul. Why take other demi-demons at all? To weaken the already broken alliance? Probably. Whatever Malicevile's reasoning, he's kept me out of it.

Dylan reaches out and touches my chin, lifting my head so I have to look at him. His apple and rain scent washes over me, stirring something deep within my soul. It takes everything in me to push my emotions for him aside.

"You really didn't know," he whispers, tilting his head slightly to the side.

"No. I had no idea. If I did I'd—" I snap my mouth shut.

"You'd what?"

"I don't know." I wouldn't have done anything yesterday. I'm not even sure I'd do anything now. "I'll talk to him, though."

"And how will you explain that you found out?"

He has a point. The only way to approach my father about what he's been up to is find the proof myself to confront him. Otherwise, he'll think I'm secretly going behind his back. I'll already have a hard time explaining my sudden absence.

I press my lips together in a thin line. "I'll figure it out, okay?"

"The alliance will be relieved to know that someone's looking into it."

I blink a few times. "The alliance can go to Hell. I'm not doing this for them."

"Then why? You've been doing your father's dirty work. Why do you suddenly care?" His dark eyes bore into mine as he searches for answers in my soul. "I need to hear you say it."

I take an automatic step back, afraid he'll try to get to my soul again. "Because of you, Dylan."

"It's more than that."

How do I even explain? Last week I wouldn't have cared.

This week—well—I suck at being demonic. "Why do you want me to admit how much you got to me? You know you destroyed me in the worst way possible, forcing me to open myself up. I can't even act like I'm supposed to. It's endangering me."

"I'm sorry, love. I had to. I had to try."

I should be angry. I should scream and yell at him for what he's done. For splitting my protective wall wide open. But I can't. Because now that I've had time to process and adjust, I remember why I didn't want to turn off my humanity in the first place. I've missed feeling things, despite how messy it is.

"I know," I whisper. "It hurts thinking about everything."

"It won't always feel this way," he says.

A tear prickles in my eye. "I'm afraid it is. I'm afraid it's just going to get worse. Thinking about being like this for all eternity makes me wish I didn't have to live forever. But I don't want to go back to Hell either. I might be a demon and Hellbound, but I don't belong there. Everything is so twisted."

He closes the distance and wraps his arms around me but not in a romantic way. It feels like it used to when we were only friends. It feels like it did before we knew we had feelings for each other. Before we had ever kissed after Evan was lost to me.

"No, you don't. You don't even belong with Malicevile, Cami. I know you think you do, but it doesn't have to be this way." He sounds so sure of it, like he could somehow just take me away from it all and spare me my suffering. But the truth is, he can't, and it does have to be this way. Every time the sun rises, I'm reminded why I can never escape.

"Dylan," I say with a sigh. "We can't do this. You know I won't leave Evan."

"What happens when he finds out?"

I grimace. "He knows. He knows everything."

"Cami, why? I know you love him, but he's not loyal to you. He's not even yours." Dylan pulls away from me and turns to look at the dark ocean in the distance before bringing his eyes back to me. He doesn't really look at me though.

"You're wrong."

A light cuts across his face. "Then why are they coming here right now?"

My heart falls into my stomach when I peer over my shoulder to spot my Mustang racing toward us. I can't believe they're here. I told Evan that I was taking my night off, and I didn't want anyone coming around.

"Dylan, you need to leave," I whisper. If Malicevile sees him—that is, if he hasn't already—he'll do everything in his power to hurt him. He swore to me he would. Even Dylan's scent is enough to send Malicevile into a rage. "They'll kill you."

"And what about you, Cami?"

I honestly don't know.

And then I remember the reason I ended up on this road in the first place. There's no way that Zach just abandoned me. I've been so distracted with Dylan that I had forgotten he has weird shielding powers. Maybe I can make a deal with him to block Dylan. It'll save us both.

"Zach!" I yell, spinning around, my gown flying around my ankles. "Zach! I know you're here. You're too curious to leave me alone."

"You're right," the demon says, shimmering into view. "And I found your conversation with the nephilim quite compelling. I knew you were a softy, princess."

"Please, will you shield him or whatever it is you do?"

"I thought you wanted to pluck his wings from his back? I can assist."

I pale at his words.

"Lighten up. I'm teasing you. You're fun when you're desperate."

I groan. "Please. I don't usually make deals, but if you do this for me, I'll make a deal with you. Within reason, that is."

A car door slams, and I glance behind me to see Malicevile step from my Mustang where Alana and Aston had killed the demon. He bends down and runs his fingers through the guts before peering around.

It's in this moment that I realize that Zach's already blocking the three of us. I side eye Dylan who just stands quietly, staring at my demonic acquaintance.

Zach offers his hand out to me. "Okay, princess. We can make a deal. I'll find you when I'm ready."

And with the words, he and Dylan shimmer out of my view, leaving me standing in the middle of the road to face my father.

The moment I inhale a deep breath, Malicevile jerks his attention to me. "Camilla?" he asks like he's unsure if it's really me. "What are you doing here? Did you do this?" He's referring to the demon guts on the ground.

"What am I doing here? You followed me. I told Evan to tell you this was my night off," I say.

"I was concerned. Your presence keeps disappearing. I thought the nephilim might've gotten to you," he says.

I clench my teeth as I peer past him at Evan sitting in the front seat of my Mustang. "Why would you even think that?"

"Because you saw him."

I can't believe Dylan was right. I knew all along where Evan's loyalty lay, but it's hard to swallow his betrayal, especially after he promised me he wouldn't tell my father. It hurts me deeply, straight to my soul.

"So? I told him to leave me alone."

"Then why can I smell him all over you now?"

I curse under my breath. I forgot he'd be able to smell Dylan. "I don't know."

Malicevile raises his eyebrows. "You don't know?"

I shake my head. "No."

"I guess I'll have to jog your memory."

PRISONER

THE WORLD SLOWS as Malicevile glides forward, a sadistic look in his eyes that wouldn't usually scare me. But now, standing in my tattered gown with my emotions all over the place, I can't help the terror gripping my soul. Not only does he look angry, he looks out to hurt me—to break me. We've only gotten along these last few weeks because I've been cooperative. I've been who he wanted me to be despite my stubbornness.

In this moment, as he closes the distance, I'm reminded of the first time I laid my eyes on him after he murdered my parents and burned my house to the ground. His eyes light with fire, and his lips curve into a smile.

I'm caught in his demonic charm and can't find the will to move, to fight. To do anything I can to protect myself from the monster that is my father.

My bottom lip trembles as much as I try to show a brave face. "Dad, please." My voice cracks. "I didn't come here to meet with Dylan."

Malicevile closes the distance and grabs me by the shoulder, digging his sharp nails into my skin. I cry out as pain rushes down my arm. As much as I want to fight back, I don't. He likes fighting. He likes showing me how powerful he is and how he can destroy me if he wanted to. A few days ago, I'd have fought back, and we'd have worked through our issues. This is different though. This isn't fighting over a stupid mistake. This isn't even fighting to protect Evan. Meeting Dylan, even unintentionally, and lying about it is a huge betrayal. My father kills for less. I might have his blood running through my veins, but now that I'm no longer just a measly demi-demon, I am a threat. Like Evan told me at The Morningstar, I have the potential of being the most powerful demon on earth. Malicevile would never allow it.

He digs his fingers deep enough that shadows edge my vision. Hot blood drips down my shoulder, soaking into my inky gown. "Then why are you here, Camilla?"

I open my mouth to offer an explanation, to tell him that Zach was responsible, but the words stick in my throat. The truth just won't come. And because of that, I'm going to have to face Malicevile's wrath.

When I'm not quick enough to answer, Malicevile jerks his arm out and slaps me across the face. Pain swells in my cheek as my head snaps to the side, tears exploding from my eyes. It's enough of a shock to slam some sense into me.

I block his next attempt to hurt me by ripping away and levitating a few feet to put distance between us. He follows suit, propelling from the ground to collide into me. He shocks me with a bout of power that I don't absorb.

"Why are you here, Camilla?" he asks again.

"I—" I take a deep breath. "I don't know! Something's wrong with me." Tears spill from my eyes as the words escape my lips. I slide to the ground before he can lock his fingers around me and curl my legs to my chest.

He freezes, a weird look crossing his face. Surprise? Confusion? I'm not sure. "What are you doing?"

I swipe the back of my hand across my face. "Isn't it obvious? I'm freaking crying!"

A car door slams, drawing my attention away from Malicevile as he stands there, energy glowing between his palms, without doing anything. Evan strolls in our direction away from my Mustang. He keeps his hands in the pockets of his slacks, his suit jacket probably left in the car. Cadence peeks out the back window. Her bottom lip pouts as she watches me.

"Cami," Evan's soft voice drifts through the air.

I expect Malicevile to yell at him, to put him in his place, but he just turns his back on me and strolls a few feet away, linking his fingers together on the back of his head. I drop my gaze to the dirt. Dust coats my dark dress, and I start laughing through my tears. Because this is ridiculous. I can't ever wear anything nice without ruining it.

Evan stops in front of me, stirring up more dirt into the air. His warm scent trickles over me, but it doesn't do anything to calm me. Not in this moment when I'm upset. But I'm not even sure who I should be angry at. Evan? My father? No, myself. I've been ignoring so much over the last weeks. Tonight, when Dylan pointed out that I was stupid for trusting my own boyfriend, it was a huge reminder about what has come of my life. And I did this all myself. I chose to join the demon who had broken me to pieces so he could rebuild me the way he saw fit.

"Get off the ground, Cami," Evan says, holding out his hands to me. "We can talk about all this at home. I'm sure there's a good explanation."

I crinkle my nose. "I'm not going with you."

"Cami, please. You're not yourself," he says. He bends down to try to pull me off the ground, but I swing my arm out to bat him away.

"This is me. Don't you remember?"

"It's not."

I dig my fingers into the ground. "Then you don't even know me."

"Cami, that's not fair."

"None of this is fair!" My voice echoes through the night. "And I'm done. I'm done with everything." I turn my gaze to

Malicevile. "I'm not going back with you. I'll figure things out on my own."

A flicker of anger crosses his face. "Carry her to the car, Evan."

Before Evan can get his hands on me, I summon energy in my fingers and hold it out. It's enough to make him hesitate and look back at my father. Malicevile lifts an eyebrow, the corner of his mouth tilting up. With a nod of his head, he motions for Evan to continue.

Evan squeezes his eyes shut for a second before locking his fingers under my arms. I don't shock him though. Malicevile knew I wouldn't either. It's why he asked him to do it. Even though Evan betrayed me by telling my father about Dylan, I still can't find it in me to hurt him. I hurt enough for the both of us.

He gently cradles me in his arms as he strolls back to the car. Tears stream down my face, and I'm so, so angry. But what can I honestly do? I need to suck it up and accept that nothing good will ever come out of trying to run. Malicevile will always find me. At least when I'm by his side, I know where he is. I'm facing my demon head on.

Evan slides onto the front seat with me on his lap, but I don't stay in his arms for long. I shift in the tight space until I manage to crawl into the backseat over the center console and between the seats. The black leather feels icy against my warm skin, and I shiver as I settle next to Cadence.

My lip quivers as I meet her watery eyes. She blinks away

her tears, straightening in the seat, and then she reaches out and pulls me against her, hugging me. I squeeze my eyes shut so I don't have to meet Malicevile's gaze as he slams his door shut. I just let my best friend hold me and whisper in my ear that everything's going to be okay.

When we jolt forward, I slowly draw my gaze behind us. In the shadows of the hillside, I spot two figures moving into the road to watch us leave. One launches into the air, brilliant wings blinding me. No one can see them but me, because if my father could, he'd have turned around.

"I'm sorry I bailed on you," I whisper to Cadence when I can no longer see Zach or Dylan. "I didn't mean to."

She pats my knee. "Never worry about me, Cami. I can take care of myself. I was just worried about you."

I swallow as I nod. "I was too."

Still am.

Probably always will be.

◈

"Are you sure?" Cadence asks from her spot next to me.

The moment we returned to Raphael's beach fortress, I locked myself with Cadence in her room. The scent of patchouli drifts in from under her door as Evan stands on the other side. I can't face him right now. I have nothing good to say. So, I've ignored his pleas until he gave up and positioned himself outside the door. He'll stay there until the sun rises and takes me away.

I'm dreading the moment.

I lean close to Cadence. I doubt Raphael has bugged the room with listening devices, but I can't be too careful. I wouldn't put anything past a demon. "Dylan told me. They took Jacie and who knows how many others."

"I had no idea. She wasn't with her partner when he came after me," she whispers. "Had I known, I'd have told you."

I knew Cadence couldn't have known about Malicevile kidnapping demi-demons. But now that she does, she can keep a look out during the day. Demi-demons don't get stuck in the daylight prison. Malicevile would have to be keeping them somewhere. I hate the idea of putting Cadence's life in danger by even suggesting she look into it, but I have no idea what else to do.

"Think Evan knows?" she adds, peering at the locked door like she can see through it.

"I'm afraid to ask him. He'll tell my father like he told him about Dylan," I say.

"Maybe he had his reasons. He was freaking out when you disappeared. I don't even remember going back into the club, you know. It's like I blacked out for a few minutes and my body just kept going."

That explains why she and Evan went to find my father. I bet Zach did something to them.

Gah. Zach. I owe him a deal. I'm afraid to even think of what he'll want from me in return for shielding Dylan.

"That's strange," I say because I still can't manage to spit out any information about Zach.

She shrugs. "Not like it's the weirdest thing about my life."

As the words come out of her mouth, the door suddenly swings open. Raphael hovers in the doorway with a set of keys in his hands. Annoyance rushes over me as he steps out of the way so Malicevile can enter the room.

He turns to Cadence. "Please meet Evan in the living room. I need to speak with Camilla alone."

Cadence hesitates for a moment like she's considering standing up to my father, but I motion for her to go. I don't want Malicevile to think she's trying to turn me against him. Dylan swore she'd be safe, but I can't take the risk.

She exits the room and shuts the door behind her. Malicevile strides to me and stands in front of me so he looks down on me. I hate when we're not on the same level, but I'm too mentally exhausted to face him head on.

"You lied to me about the nephilim," he says, his voice calm. It's scarier than when he's yelling his head off. At least then I know what he's thinking. "And you let him get too close. Now look at you." He waves his hand over my dirty dress. "You're a mess."

I don't answer him. He speaks the truth.

"What? You have nothing to say? You always have something to say," he comments.

I still don't answer him.

He sighs. "You know, I thought you could take care of yourself, Camilla, but I was wrong. And I hate being wrong."

I brace myself for what he says next. I can already tell

where this conversation is leading. I don't like it one bit. I'm already forced to spend half of my day with Malicevile. I don't want much more than that.

"You leave me no choice. You are not to leave my side. If I need to do something alone, I'm going to lock you away. You can't be trusted, and I won't allow you to do anything that jeopardizes what I've fought so hard to accomplish," he says.

I laugh while shaking my head. He didn't fight for this. He got lucky. "So I'm a prisoner?"

"If that's how you want to put it, then yes."

"You can't control me forever, Mal." For the first time in weeks, I don't call him Dad. A glower crosses his face, and I know I got under his skin. If he wants to lock me away like some fairytale princess, I'm not going to make things easy on him. I'll make him want to toss me out the front door just to get away from me.

He leans forward slightly, getting into my face. "Oh, but I will try."

CAN'T SAVE HIM

MALICEVILE TALKS QUIETLY with Raphael near the back door as he watches me on the beach. He didn't try to stop me as I stepped into the crisp almost morning air, but he did follow behind me like a shadow.

Faith stands on the beach next to me, the waves drifting around our feet before sliding back into the calm ocean. Her blond hair falls loosely down her back, and she's wearing pajama shorts and a tank top despite the cold morning.

"I'm really sorry about tonight. You didn't deserve my anger. I know you're trying to help."

She rubs her hands up and down her arms. "Thanks. That

means a lot to me."

I press my lips together. "Do you think you can do something for me?" I whisper so quietly that I'm not even sure she can hear me.

She doesn't look at me but says, "Anything."

I shift closer. "Can you pass on a message to Dylan for me? Tell him that I need his help. That I need a miracle."

She subtly nods her head. "Does that mean you're..." Her voice trails off.

"I can't stay, Faith."

"What about Evan?"

I don't respond because I don't have the answer to that. I'm not ready to give up hope on us, but I can't stay and suffer through the torment of being with Malicevile. Maybe with some space, I'll be able to think more clearly, come up with a plan. As of now, the only way Evan's soul will ever be mine is if he dies. And then what? It wouldn't be any different than it is now. I'd still only hold a fraction of the boy I fell in love with. *God, why did he ever do this? How can I fix this?* My thoughts fade as fast as I think them. What's the point?

Finally after a long moment, when the sky starts to shift to purple, I say, "I can't save him if I can't save myself first, Faith. Right now, he's lost to me. As lost as he was the day he traded his soul for my life. I didn't want to believe it. I didn't believe it. But it's true." Tears leak down my face as I whisper the words. Saying them out loud to Faith makes them more real, more concrete. I can't deny them or bury the thoughts with the rest of my grief.

Faith reaches out and takes my hand, squeezing my fingers in hers. She doesn't say anything, doesn't try to make me feel better. Her silence is comforting enough for me to know that despite how horrible I feel, I'm doing the right thing in the end by contacting Dylan. The right thing has felt so wrong for so long that it's hard to accept. But I have to do it. I need to figure out my life and what it means for me to be a demon without being tainted by Malicevile. Because this life, this person that I am right in this moment, isn't me.

"Camilla, it's time to go back inside," Malicevile says from behind me.

I glance over my shoulder and spy Evan standing in the doorway behind him without Cadence. She must still be in her room. She's the only one apart from Faith who knows what I'm planning. And she's staying. If she tries to run, Malicevile will blame her. We've both decided to put our faith in Dylan's words. She promised to look after Evan.

When my eyes meet Evan's, he smiles his radiant smile, crinkling the corners of his aqua eyes. Even though he exudes warmth, exudes the flames that bind us, all his smile does in this moment is freeze my heart.

Turning back to the ocean, I don't reciprocate his smile. I don't listen to Malicevile, either. Instead, I drop Faith's hand and dash forward into the water. Steam sizzles from my hot skin as the freezing water encompasses me. It doesn't stop me. I take a deep breath before diving underwater, kicking my legs to propel myself from the shore.

My lungs burn for air after a minute, but I push myself to keep swimming, to put as much distance as I can between me and Malicevile before the sun rises. I only break the surface when I think I'm about to gulp in a mouthful of water.

"Camilla!" Malicevile yells.

I don't try to find where his voice is coming from. I doubt he'll swim after me and soak his suit this close to morning. I'm too deep that he wouldn't be able to levitate without still getting wet. He'll just wait until the world shimmers away and dispels us in the dead world of our daylight home. I just hope I'm fast enough to get away. I'll run all day if I have to. I can't spend another minute with him.

The density of the water shifts like thousands of tiny bubbles swirl around me. It helps me swim faster until my feet hit solid ground, and I bolt forward. The last ounce of darkness disappears as the white-hot sun glows from behind me, elongating my shadow.

Shaking my wet hair from my face, I push myself to keep moving. I dodge around dozens of trees, occasionally hitting my shoulder against the dead, white trunks as I squeeze through the narrow passageways.

"Camilla, you can never hide from me," Malicevile says from somewhere behind me. He can't be far. I'm not that good of a swimmer, but I knew that once I ended up here, my chances of staying away were a lot better with trees for coverage.

I force myself to move faster. My heavy breathing is the only thing I hear in this desolate world. Its quiet comfort is enough to keep my head clear. When I'm here, my heart doesn't feel like it's been crushed into a million pieces. I can think without all the sadness and grief that constantly clung to me the last day. I can just focus on running. Life feels simple.

A figure appears in my peripheral vision, startling me, and I jerk left to run in another direction. He's found me too quickly. I haven't had enough time.

A hand grabs the back of my shirt, yanking me off my feet. Air whooshes from my lungs when I collide with a hard chest. I gasp, the scent of jasmine filling my lungs, and for the first time since I've smelled the scent, I actually feel relief.

I don't struggle or fight. Instead, I just let Zach hold me against him. "I'm ready to make a deal, princess," he says into my ear.

I can only nod as I peer at him from over my shoulder. In one quick motion, he bends his knees while his huge black wings unfurl from his back. He launches us into the sky, the air heating the higher we ascend, and then everything below us disappears.

⁂

Zach stands at the end of the same pond he brought me to before. The inky water bubbles, smelling of sulfur, and I watch as a few animalistic demons hide in its depths. Resting my back against a twisted tree, I hold myself. I still don't trust the mysterious demon, but he's the lesser threat at the moment. I'd be lying if I said I wasn't glad he swooped in to save me from my father.

"Why do you always look like you're afraid of me?" Zach says, shoving his hands into his jeans. He's wearing a different shirt than the last one I saw him in, but it's no better with a picture of a pug wearing neon green sunglasses. "I'm starting to get offended. I've given you no reason to fear me."

"I'm sorry if I have trouble trusting any demon. Have you ever seen my father? You can thank him for that." My voice echoes louder than I want it to, but I can't help it.

"Oh, I'd like to," Zach says. "But, that's not on my agenda today."

But I am. Awesome. "Of course you have an agenda."

"And you don't?" he asks.

"My only agenda is to survive." I lean my head back and stare at the hot sun through the gnarled, leafless branches.

"That's pathetic," he says, surprising me. He waltzes away from the pond to take a seat next to me. He wraps his arms around his knees and rests his chin on them. The gesture seems ridiculous on a demon like Zach, but he looks so natural doing it. Malicevile—even I—could take a lesson in how to relax from him.

"Whatever." I don't know what else to say.

"No, I mean it, Cami. Surviving is so beneath you. There's so much more out there. You just have to want it."

"What are you, my guidance counselor? Didn't you want to make a deal or something?" I pull my own legs up to my chest to mirror his position. I consider getting up to pace, but the way Zach peers at the side of my face stops me from moving. "Isn't that why you brought me here?" I add when he doesn't respond right away.

"Oh, that."

"Yeah, that."

"Since I helped you and hid that half-breed you love to hate...or is it hate to love?" He bumps his shoulder against mine with a laugh.

"That's none of your business," I snap.

He bumps my shoulder again with a smile. "Since I helped you out with the nephilim, I thought that you could help me get something I need. A soul, to be more specific."

"I don't deal in souls," I say curtly. Why would I think any better of a demon? This is why I don't make deals.

"But the one I'm interested in belongs to you," he says.

My brows furrow. "You mean...you want my soul?"

He wags his eyebrows. "Exactly."

I launch to my feet, nearly tripping and falling into the bubbling pond. Levitating, I propel myself a foot back and find the strength in my legs. "I said I'd make a deal within reason."

He laughs so loudly that I startle. With a slap to the ground, he says, "I'm only kidding, princess. Jeez, lighten up."

"You're such a liar. You're only saying that because I didn't agree." He doesn't disagree with me, and I know that what I say is true.

He shrugs. "You seemed like the type to give up your soul to save another, or do you only allow others to do that for you?"

I blink at his remark. "Excuse me? Dylan's soul wasn't in jeopardy." We both know he isn't talking about Dylan, though. This has everything to do with me and Evan. "How do you even know about my boyfriend?"

"Remember when I relocated you the other day?" he asks.

"You mean kidnapped me," I say bluntly.

"I overheard your conversation and how Malicevile promised to return your boyfriend's soul when his mortal life ended. Which is totally messed up."

I swallow the lump in my throat. My father will surely take back his gift when he realizes I'm no longer going to be loyal to him.

"What are you supposed to do with someone else's soul for the rest of eternity?" he asks when I don't comment.

I lick my lips. "Set it free and ask for divine intervention." It's what I did with my mom's soul. If I ever find my dead sister's soul, I'll do that for her as well. Dylan would help me again. I know it.

He snorts, mocking me. It's like the thought never even crossed Zach's mind. "Then why didn't you just kill him yourself? That seems like the best and easiest way."

Kill Evan? Oh, no. Nope. At one point I thought I could do that. I thought I could kill him to save him. But the moment David—I cringe at the thought of Evan's dead partner's name—decided to try to save me, I knew I could never do it. It'd turn me into the people that destroyed everything. Like with saving the broken werewolves, I'm holding hope that there's another way.

"You try saying that after being stabbed in the name of redemption." I turn my back on him so I don't have to continue this conversation. What's the point of talking about it? It's not going to change anything, not come nightfall at least.

A shadow crawls across the ground next to me as Zach comes to stand by my side. "I'm really sorry that happened to you, Cami."

I frown. "You're sorry? God, Zach. You're so weird."

He chuckles. "I could say the same thing."

I push my curly hair from my eyes. "So, now that you know I'm not giving you my soul—or anyone else's—is there something else I can do for you? I don't like owing people." It's my way of ending the conversation. I've already shared too much with Zach.

"Yes, actually." He pauses for a moment, pressing his lips into a straight line. "I want you to reconsider leaving your father."

I swallow my surprise. "What? How did you know?"

He raises a single eyebrow. "You were running from him when I found you."

"I—" I snap my mouth shut for a second as I collect myself. I've never felt flustered in the daylight realm before, and suddenly, it's like not even this world can protect me from myself. "I can't go back to him. Please, think of something else."

"I'm sorry, princess," he says.

Fear slides down my back, but I'm too slow to move when

he reaches out his hand. A second later, he covers my eyes, and the world around me vanishes.

SELFISH

DAMP AIR CLINGS to my skin as I open my eyes to stare up at the almost dark sky. The scent of the ocean washes over me as I orient myself. Time flew by in a split second. I had to have been out for hours, long enough to return to the earth realm.

I shift onto my elbows and glance around. I'm on the shore just outside Raphael's beach fortress. Sighing, I sit up all the way. A folded piece of paper rests in the sand right near my hand, and I scoop it up to look at it.

Princess,

I apologize that you're about to face a wrath equivalent to that of Lucifer's, but I think you're plenty capable of taking care of your-self. All you have to do is get him to listen, and I think you'll man-age to figure it out. Good luck, Cami. I'll be around.

The note isn't signed, but it smells like Zach. And I'm fu-rious. How dare he do this to me? How dare he think an apolo-gy will make up for dropping me right back into the arms of Malicevile? I swear, if I ever see him around, he's going to feel everything that I have to go through. *You can still run...*

I hop to my feet as the thought comes to me and turn to run down the beach, down to where I can access the stairs that'll lead to the parking lot. I'll steal a car. I'll get far enough away that I can call Dylan myself. He should be expecting me. It isn't over.

The scent of cinnamon and clove catches on the breeze as it drifts from behind me. Malicevile didn't go very far. Maybe he just gave up after Zach rescued me with his devilish wings— ones that I can actually look at, unlike Dylan's ethereal ones that only cause me pain.

A burst of power hits me in the back, shocking me. I cringe as tiny sparks crackle from my skin. Electricity clings to my hair, but I pound my boots harder into the sand. I can still make it. I haven't lost yet.

"Do you honestly think that you're going to escape me?" Malicevile's voice rings through the quiet night.

I don't answer him. Escaping is the only way I won't face his fury.

A burst of bright flames hits the sand next to my feet, startling me. I didn't smell Evan over the scent of my father, but he's with him. He's trying to slow me down as well.

"Camilla," Malicevile says.

"I'm not going to let you lock me up all the time!" I yell.

"I wouldn't have to if you wouldn't keep disappearing," he responds. When Zach swept me away as I was running, he used his shielding power to protect and hide us. So it was like I disappeared. I glare at the world in front of me because I can't glare at the demon who put me in this position.

Another bout of electricity hits me, and I stumble forward. As I steady myself, my jeans catch fire. It distracts me long enough that another electric shock knocks the wind from me, and I fall face first onto the beach.

I spit out a mouthful of sand. Malicevile was right. There is no escaping him. Not when he's using my boyfriend against me. I can't concentrate on running as fast as I can and absorbing both their powers. It's hard to do if I'm not facing them.

Malicevile grins as he strides forward. He shoots another energy orb at me for good measure, but I'm prepared. Catching it in my hands, I snuff out the orb instead of absorbing it. I have enough of his power. I don't want anymore.

I dig my hand into the ground and toss a handful of sand into his face when he towers over me, ready to lift me from my feet.

Using his sleeve, he wipes his face and sneers. "You're going to regret that." He turns to Evan. "Give me the restraints."

My eyes widen as Evan pulls a pair of handcuffs from his jacket pocket. Malicevile tugs his handkerchief from his breast pocket and gently takes them from Evan. Smoke sizzles through the fabric, and I realize that they've been blessed. Malicevile is about to slap blessed handcuffs on me. He doesn't just want to bind me, he wants to make it hurt. It's all part of his plan to get me to comply.

Tears sting my eyes just at the thought. "I'm sorry," I say. I'm not against begging. "I promise I won't be any trouble. I'll come home. Please."

Malicevile motions to Evan. He grabs me by the back of my jacket and lifts me from the beach before locking his fingers around my wrist to hold it out for Malicevile. My heart aches, threatening to implode on itself in my chest.

"I'm sor-sorry, Cami." Evan's voice cracks as he whispers the words.

"Don't do this," I beg. "Don't help him."

"You know I have to," he says, breathing into my hair.

I thrash, kicking my legs up as Malicevile tries to grab me. The blow was hard enough to push him away. Jerking my head back, I head-butt Evan, but he only holds me tighter as Malicevile composes himself.

"Please, Evan. Fight for me. You don't have to do this. Fight for me." His fingers loosen for a split second. It's enough to yank my hand free to elbow Evan in the stomach. He releases me, and I dash a few feet away.

Malicevile's forehead creases with anger. "This is your last warning, Camilla."

"Please," I beg again. "Don't do this." *Remember what Zach said. Make him listen.*

"You've already proved to me that I can't trust you."

Strong hands grip me from behind as Evan yanks me back to him. His body trembles as he holds me against him and forces my arm out. Malicevile raises the blessed handcuffs to latch them onto my wrist.

I scream before they even touch my skin. In a quick jerk of my fingers, I summon power into my hand. It's neither Malicevile's nor Evan's. It belongs to the demon woman Zach killed. Translucent fog swirls in my palm, and I flick my fingers, pushing it forward.

Malicevile doesn't even see it coming. The shockwave knocks him off his feet, sending him sprawling to the sand. When he tries to jump to his feet, I send another small wave toward him. I only have enough to knock him down once more, and then this is it. He'll win.

"Just stop and listen to me," I say from Evan's tight hold. "I didn't turn against you. I haven't been purposely sneaking around. And as for disappearing, that's a nifty power I collected from that demon you saw splattered on the side of the road." The lie comes so easily, I almost believe it.

A look crosses Malicevile's face—he almost looks impressed.

"I swear I'll explain everything as best as I can, but you have to stop this. If you dare put those handcuffs on me, you'll lose me forever. I'll not be treated like a prisoner." My voice comes out surprisingly confident. "You will not treat me the way the alliance did."

"So tell me, why were you meeting with the nephilim, Camilla? Why did you run? Why disappear?" he asks.

I tug away from Evan, and he lets me go. "Are you sure you want to know?"

"Go on, enlighten me."

I rub my lips together for a second. "Because I'm in love with Dylan, Dad." I don't know why I say it. I could've made up a million different things—like I wanted my freedom or I wanted to prove that I could be on my own. I could've said anything. But a part of me wanted to say this out loud. I couldn't just leave it unsaid.

Turning to peer over my shoulder, I meet Evan's dark gaze. He doesn't return mine, just stares off at the dark ocean, his back stick-straight, his mouth tight. Jealousy is a common emotion for him, anger too, but this is different. I don't see either in his expression.

All I see is pain and heartache. All I see is how those little words just devastated his world. It's not until this very moment that I realize what I've done. I had begged Evan to fight for me. I begged him to do something, anything. And he fought for me. In doing so he released his humanity. He turned it back on for me. I know that look. I feel everything he does.

"Evan," I whisper.

But it's too late. Because a moment later, he composes

himself. He shuts it all off.

He shuts me out.

I was wrong when I said I had lost him before. Because he was still here. But now, I feel it deep into my soul. I've not only lost him in this world. I've lost him for all eternity.

<hr>

As much as I hoped I wouldn't be, I'm still a prisoner. Except now, Malicevile doesn't want me by his side. He locked me in a guest room near the back of the house with a view of the ocean. He said he needed time to figure things out—more likely to figure out how he's going to destroy Dylan.

Gazing out the window, I peer at Evan sitting on the sand near the water. He's been there since I walked back by Malicevile's side with my head bowed and defeat in my heart. I'm a horrible person. Not because I'm a demon—that excuse can't apply here—but because I saved myself by hurting someone I love. My relationships and feelings are so twisted, they threaten to strangle me. What makes it worse is that Evan tried. He allowed himself to feel for me, to try to fight against Malicevile's commands, and I basically stabbed him through the heart. *Maybe this is for the best. You were going to leave.*

Breaking someone's heart is never for the best, yet I managed to break several, including my own.

A knock sounds on the door, and I turn away from the window to hear the slide of the lock. Raphael hovers in the doorway, and I expect Malicevile to stroll in, but Faith peeks at me from behind her father. I can't stop the jealousy from sneaking into my mind. I never thought either of us was lucky to have demonic dads, but she clearly got the better one.

"What do you want?" I ask, my voice flat.

"I thought you should know that I don't agree with your father," Raphael says. "I don't think you're purposely trying to sabotage him, especially since you clearly have no idea what's going on." Raphael steps a foot in the room. "He's just reacting to your untimely confession. You might not think we're capable of fear, but he's afraid that you're going to give everything up for a boy, and an angelic one at that."

"And you're here to convince me I'm being ridiculous?" I fold my arms over my chest.

He shrugs. "I can't say I'll ever understand what goes on in your head, but no. I'm not here for that."

"Then why are you here?"

"Because Faith asked to see you, and your father's out. She shouldn't be punished because you made Malicevile uncomfortable." He smirks as he says it, and the world doesn't feel like it's going to end at any second. Maybe I was overreacting with my thoughts. *But Evan...*

"That's an understatement," I mutter.

He motions Faith into the room. Looking down at her, he says, "Make it quick, sweetheart."

He exits the room a moment later and closes the door, surprising me. Unlike Malicevile, Raphael gives me more credit, enough to trust me alone with Faith. Maybe he'd think differently if he knew what I had asked her to do, or if he knew that the same boy I unwittingly professed my love for was her De-mon Watcher.

Faith slides her dainty hand into the front pocket of her jeans and pulls out a folded piece of paper. "I did what you asked. This is from Dylan."

I take the paper in my hands and bring it up to my nose, catching traces of his angelic scent through the sweet vanilla of Faith's fragrance. She watches me with a curious gaze, her mouth twisted to the side and questions crinkling the corners of her blue eyes.

"Thanks," I say without opening the letter. "How was eve-rything today?"

Lifting and dropping her shoulders, she says, "My dad cor-nered me to have The Talk about boys, like I'd ever get a chance to meet any." She rolls her eyes.

I snicker. "Sorry about that. None of this was part of my plan."

"So you love Dylan, huh?" she asks, finally summoning the courage to say what's on her mind. I was sort of with Dylan when I met Faith, before we had a chance to define our rela-tionship. It was the same day of my transformation so I never really got into the complexities involving the boys in my life.

"Yes." The answer comes simply enough.

"Is that why you want to leave? You've chosen him over Evan?"

My cheeks warm. "I'm not choosing either of them. I'm choosing me." That's right. Once again, I'm going to be selfish.

Because how dare my heart ever put me in this position in the first place. When I met Evan, I was so certain he was the one. We were perfect together. Things weren't complicated. Life was easy.

But then Malicevile ruined it. He ruined us.

It was after that Dylan picked up my broken pieces and carefully put them back together the best he could. He followed me deeper into the madness of my life. He protected me and understood me. He fought for me and still fights. But everything that we had was lost before we even had a chance to hold on tight to it. Once again, everything was ruined. All because I'm a demon's daughter.

Faith touches my arm after a moment. I realize that I'm crying, clutching the note while peering at Evan's back through the window. Using my sleeve, I dry my eyes. Because I know what I need to do. I've been unfair for too long. This was never about me and Evan or me and Dylan. It's always been about me and my demonic father. It's how all this started, and will surely be how this all ends.

"I'm sorry I asked," Faith says. "I didn't mean to upset you."

I sniffle. "It's not your fault. Promise."

She nods. "I should return to my dad before he checks on us. Anything you need?"

A miracle? An escape? A time machine? Some magic to repair all the broken hearts? I let the thoughts disappear before shaking my head. Faith hugs me once before turning and leaving. I train my focus back on the window and catch Evan's gaze.

Fire shines in his eyes as his stare refuses to let me go. It's enough to force me to turn away first. I can't stand to see him like this. When I sneak a glance back to the window, he's gone.

Releasing a breath, I move and sit on the edge of the bed to read Dylan's note. Might as well get my mind off Evan.

Love,

I know that what I'm about to say isn't what you're going to want to hear, but I can't take you away from your father. Not yet. Know that I haven't abandoned you. If I knew you weren't safe, I'd be there in an instant. Please, just hang tight. We'll get this figured out.

Your Guardian Angel

My brows furrow as I read and reread the letter from Dylan. How could he do this to me? Now, I'm alone. I have to figure this out on my own, because I'm not staying. I only agreed to return with Malicevile because I thought it wouldn't be for long. This blows.

Fire bursts in my fingers as I set Dylan's letter on fire. Smoke hazes the room in front of me, stinging my eyes. I smile as I watch the paper disintegrate. It seems that watching things turn to ash is the only constant in my life. I'd burn this whole place down if I knew Cadence and Faith would be safe, but I refuse to bring any more people down with me.

"What are you doing?" Evan's voice reaches me before his

scent does. I didn't even hear him open the door.

I let the ashes of the letter fall to the pristine floor. "I'm burning evidence. And no, I'm not going to tell you any more."

His eyebrows peak on his forehead. "Is this because I told Malicevile about Dylan in the first place? I didn't do it to hurt you, you know. I just—" He pauses with a sigh. Balling his fingers into fists, he mutters. "You drive me crazy."

"That seems to be the consensus with everyone," I say. "And for the record, I never meant to hurt you, Evan. What I said—"

"Was true. I'm not stupid, Cami. I don't even blame you. I knew what I was getting into when I joined Malicevile. I knew that a future together would be impossible. I knew that Dylan would take care of you. I just—I never expected you to ever return—because I didn't think you'd throw away what I did for you so easily. I'm not even angry about it though, because this is where you belong, whether or not you want to be with me."

I grimace. It's not like I purposely threw it all away. "You know I love you, right?"

His jaw twitches. "Does it really matter?"

I reach out and grab his hand. "It does to me, even if you can't feel it. Even if you don't believe in it anymore. I do love you, Evan. And this is why being here kills me so much. When I needed you, you weren't there for me. You were there for *him*."

"You say that like I have a choice, Cami," he says, anger lining his words.

"Because you do! You don't even try."

"I'm not doing this right now. This isn't why I came here." He pulls me closer, spinning me on my feet. With a soft nudge, he pushes me toward the open door.

"Where are we going?" I ask.

"Where do you think?"

I close my eyes for a second. "I don't want to see him. Please, just leave me here."

"Don't make me carry you," Evan says softly. "Please." The new gentleness in his voice grips at my chest, leaving me breathless. It reminds me of a time that feels like an eternity ago.

"Then don't make me go," I whisper, the fight gone from my voice. "You have a choice."

With serious eyes, he scoops me into his arms and strides toward the door. "Don't you get it, Cami? None of us has a choice."

And he's right.

# VALUABLE DEALS

MALICEVILE NAVIGATES DOWN the dark road without uttering a single word to me. The headlights cut through the night, flashing across the lifeless, rundown neighborhood of a town a few miles inland from Moonlight Shores.

When I can't take the silence any longer, I say, "Where are you taking me?"

Malicevile watches me in his peripheral vision. "We're going on a hunt."

"A hunt?"

He grins at the empty road. "You know, it's not only full-blooded angels who fall."

Dread flourishes in my stomach, sliding up my chest to steal the breath right from my lungs. Shadows haze my vision. I knew that Malicevile wouldn't wait long before trying to find Dylan. But what he says, about falling, that's my worst nightmare. Dylan is too pure to be demon-tainted. How Malicevile will make him fall from grace, I'm afraid to ask.

"You don't have to do this," I say.

"Clearly, I do. Because I will do everything in my power to see that you don't mess up things for yourself. If you want the nephilim, you will have him. But only under my terms." He pulls to the curb. "Because if the nephilim loves you like you love him, he'd do anything for you."

Like Evan. He doesn't say it, but I know that's what he's thinking.

"If I've learned anything about humans over my existence, it's that they do a lot of ridiculous things for the sake of love, and it gets them nowhere. Look where it got E—"

I shake my head. "Don't say it."

"I'm just saying that you shouldn't put so much effort into something so temporary, especially when you already have someone who could end up just like us. Someone I approve of." Malicevile pushes his door open. "Hasn't the thought ever crossed your mind, Camilla?"

I blink the surprise away. "What are you saying?"

"If you can make the complete transformation, then why can't Evan?"

I dig my fingernails into my palms. "He'd have to die. It's

not even guaranteed."

"Well, it's a good thing that I'm not going to make him try first then, isn't it?"

What? I've known that Malicevile and other demons were interested in expanding their demonic army, but it didn't really cross my mind much. I know Raphael wants Faith to turn into a demon like me. But I just assumed they wouldn't try until I told them how—and now that I can somewhat feel again, I wasn't planning on it.

"I don't understand."

"Or maybe I should so you'll guarantee it works..."

Ice cold dread slides over me, freezing my fiery heart. If Malicevile wanted Evan to try, Evan would do it, and there'd be nothing I could do about it. But, he'd never survive. Because Dylan would never, and I mean never, go to Hell for him to intercept his fate. I'd never let Evan make it there in the first place.

The heavenly scent of rain and apples trickles through the air, cutting off our conversation. Malicevile inhales a long breath, crinkling his nose in disgust, and then he hops from the driver's seat. I scramble to follow him. I'm not allowing my father to get to him first.

"How did you even know he was here?" I ask, doing nothing to quiet my voice. I want Dylan to know we're coming.

Malicevile beams a dazzling smile, one charming enough to entrance anyone who happens upon us. "I've made a few valuable deals."

"With who?"

"Hunters within the alliance."

My eyes widen.

"Don't look so surprised, Camilla. Not everyone can resist a deal like you, especially those desperate to live." He laughs as he says it, like it's the funniest thing ever. "It helps that your transformation shook the alliance's foundation, and the hunters are turning against each other."

It's how he and Raphael have been able to kidnap demi-demons. It's how they got their hands on Jacie. She was betrayed and probably by her own partner. It all makes perfect sense. Malicevile is kidnapping demi-demons because he knows what's possible now. He knows that they could turn into full-blooded demons, just like I did. And just imagine if he bargained with them for their souls. He'd rule them all. He'd truly have his own army without worrying about being betrayed by another demon with the same idea.

The hushed murmur of voices sounds through the air from the side of the last house on the block. Malicevile jets out his arm, knocking me in the chest to make me stop in my tracks. If he thinks I'm going to let him sneak up on anyone, including Dylan, he's seriously out of his mind.

I place my hands on my hips. "What? I thought you liked a game of chase!" I yell out the words, letting them echo through the air. There's no way whoever is on the side of the house didn't hear me. I'm sure people heard me from a few blocks over. "Hello! We've come to collect Dylan. He's going to be on our side now."

Malicevile smacks his forehead. "Really, Camilla?"

"Yes, really," I mutter. When no one appears to greet us, I yell, "Dylan! We know you're here. I can smell you. It's time that I introduced you to my father. He thinks that because we're in love that you'll join us. And he says I'm the ridiculous one!"

The voices hush as I stride closer. Malicevile doesn't stay on my heels.

"Come on, Dylan! I'm pretty sure if you don't fall, my dad's going to push you."

As I approach the house, I suck in a deep breath. Unfortunately, to my horror, Dylan's apple scent still perfumes the air. I expected him to fly away, run, do something. But he's still here. For the first time ever, he's choosing to face a demon that isn't me. Maybe he has too much faith in me, thinking I can protect him when that's clearly not the case. I can't even manage to escape Malicevile.

"Seriously, Dylan! Can't you take a warning? I'm trying to sa—" As the words escape my mouth, I turn the corner of the house and freeze.

I don't even have time to react when the dagger sinks into my chest close enough to my heart that I swear I can feel it beating against the blessed metal before my skin sears and starts smoking.

Opening and closing my mouth, I stare in horror as Alana stands in front of Dylan in a fighting stance. My whole body screams in agony as reality sets in and burning pain radiates down my stomach, forcing me to drop to my knees.

A scream rips from my mouth as I wrap my fingers around the hilt but the pain is too much. I can't pull the knife from me. I can't do anything except fold in on myself and hope that Dylan stops Alana from finishing me off.

"Cami!" Dylan's voice echoes through the air as he pushes Alana out of the way to come to me. He touches the bloody skin around the dagger but doesn't pull it out. His brows furrow as he thinks about what to do.

I grip the front of his shirt in my fingers. "You have to run. Take Alana and run." I expect my father to round the corner at any second. If he does and sees me like this, they're both dead. I'm in no condition to fight for their lives. They'll just be over.

"I'm not leaving you," Dylan says.

"Malicevile's here."

"I don't care!" He peers over his shoulder. "How could you do this to her!"

"I—" Alana snaps her mouth shut without another word. I can't see her face from this position on the ground. My eyes are too watery to even try.

I groan as I try to stretch my sleeve over my hand, but it shifts the blade, causing another wave of fire through me—a heat unlike anything I can ordinarily ever feel. The dagger needs to be pulled out. I'm going to black out if it's not removed soon.

"Tell me what to do, Cami," Dylan whispers.

I can't find my words through the pain so I motion at the dagger. Dylan grimaces as he wraps his hand around the hilt and slides it from my chest. Blood pours from my wound, and he presses his hands over my heart. If I were human, I'd be dead for sure. But I'm not human. Even if I bleed out, I won't die. Alana's aim was off.

"Oh, God," Dylan says, his fingers sliding as he tries to put pressure on my wound.

Alana stands quietly in her place and doesn't move. Clutched in her hand is a flask of holy water. She knows if I'm here that Malicevile can't be far. She's preparing to fight. *What's taking him so long anyway?*

Maybe he wants me to suffer.

Darkness edges my vision, and my chest heaves through the burning agony. Deep convulsions erupt in my stomach and quake through my body so much that the world jerks. Closing my eyes, I imagine what a relief it would be if I just blacked out. Died even. Hell couldn't be much worse than this torture. Alana's wish can come true. She can send me where I belong.

"Cami. Cami." Dylan's cool, sticky fingers brush up my neck until he's holding my face in his hands. "Cami, hold on. I'm not going to let you suffer like this. Just keep your eyes closed and hold on."

For once, I listen to him. I don't have a choice.

Through my closed eyelids, I see a flash of red as something lights up in front of me. The wind whooshes from my chest, fire exploding over my heart. Another scream rips from my throat, and I thrash as Dylan holds me down.

A moment later, the scent of jasmine wafts into my nostrils, and then I pass out.

⁂

The pain isn't so unbearable, but it nags at me, wanting me to devote all my attention to it. I sit on a stone bench in a half dead garden. Dylan sits next to me without saying a word. He just rests his hand on my knee and stares at the lavender roses that magically bloom from the black, dead rose bush.

"Alana's dead if Malicevile finds her," I say. "You should've run with her when I told you to."

"She's fine. I'm fine," he says quietly. "You don't look so good though."

I peer down and stare at my ripped shirt. Though this is only a dream, I know it reflects what I look like in reality. Blood soaks the light blue fabric of my shirt and beneath the hole is blackened skin over my heart. The wound no longer bleeds, but only because Dylan branded me once more with his heavenly wings. This imprint will take longer to fade than the last time, judging from how deep and dark the branded feather imprints are.

"I would've survived regardless," I say.

"But you were in so much pain."

I shrug. "Yeah, well, it wasn't like Alana threw a pillow at me. You know I can't handle sacred things. I can't even handle you most days."

"You scared her," Dylan says. "She had no idea that I was

in communication with you."

I blow out a long breath. "Hell must be freezing over with all the demonic activity on earth because I never thought in a million years that I'd see Alana protect you."

He chuckles. "What can I say? I'm pretty special."

I roll my eyes. "Apparently so. I wasn't kidding when I said my father wanted you. You were right when you told me he was afraid. But it's not for the reason you think. He's afraid that I'm in love with you and will blow it all away."

Dylan smirks, flashing his dimples. "And why would he think that?"

I lift and drop one shoulder, staring at the sky. "I told him that."

"So, you still love me?"

I drop my gaze to the ground. "I never stopped. But it doesn't change anything."

"Because of Evan," he says flatly.

I shake my head. "Because of me. I just can't do this anymore. Not now." I link my fingers together. "With either of you."

"Oh."

I reach out and rest my hand on his. "I'm sorry, Dylan. It's just better this way."

He doesn't agree with me. Instead, he leans back on the bench and tilts his head toward the sky. The bright sun shines overhead, and it almost makes me feel half human again. Like the sun hasn't forsaken me, forcing me into another realm.

"I understand if you no longer want to help me. I get it," I say. "I'll figure out some other way to escape Malicevile."

He pouts his bottom lip, looking ever so sexy. The taste of his sweet kiss shoots to the front of my mind, and I have to remind myself that he's off limits now. I can't keep drawing him to me just to push him away. It isn't fair. He deserves better because he is better.

"Of course I'm going to help you, love. I just—I can't yet." He glares at the puffy clouds like they're about to turn dark to rain on us.

"Why not? I'm not sure I can survive another day. I'm a prisoner. Being here now is only going to make it worse. Malicevile's been planning something huge so there's no way he's going to risk me leaving him. It might be now or never, Dylan." My words fly from my mouth as desperation settles in my soul. I can't be responsible for transforming demi-demons into monsters like me.

"Cami, what do you mean?" he asks.

I hesitate telling him. I don't know why. It's just an automatic response. I still feel like I'm on the opposing side—like I still must remain loyal to Malicevile.

"Malicevile isn't taking demi-demons to weaken the Hunter's Alliance. He's going to try to transform them. He's going to make me try to do it."

"Oh, love. It'll never work."

"They're all going to die, Dylan. All of them. Jacie and even Faith. He might force Evan into it. He thinks I'll guarantee he doesn't die."

"This is bad."

"I can't let them die."

"But I can't help you either."

So now what?

I don't have time to think about it because the ground splits open under our feet, swallowing me into darkness before spitting me out to face the jasmine-scented night.

DAMSEL IN DISTRESS

"WELCOME BACK, PRINCESS." Zach stands over me, looking me up and down. "You need to stop being such a damsel in distress."

I groan as I prop myself up on my elbows. A dull ache grips my heart, but it's not unbearable. It takes me a moment to remember where I am, but when I do, I scramble to my feet and peer around the dark night. Dylan hugs Alana near the side of the house, but my father is nowhere in sight.

"Malicevile?" I ask.

Zach grins. "Pretty sure he regrets bringing you here."

I sigh. "He thinks I ran away?"

"Possibly."

I turn to Alana. "You stabbed me, but it doesn't even look like you raised your hand at this guy. Do you seriously hate me that much?"

Alana opens and closes her mouth but doesn't respond.

"She doesn't hate you, Cami," Dylan says softly.

"Oh, princess. Haven't you learned yet? I'm not one to be messed with. Plus, you don't usually attack the guy trying to help," Zach adds, lightly punching me in the arm. Oh, my God. This demon. He's seriously the bane of my existence. He's so cool and casual, but underneath his chill demeanor has to lie something as horrible as my father. He's weaseling his way into my life for a reason I haven't figured out. I want nothing more than to smack the answer out of him, but he's capable of knocking me out with the wave of his stupid hand.

I swivel toward him and glare. "Are you kidding me? I *was* trying to help. It's not my fault that I have a psychotic father who you happen to be able to hide from. What are you even doing here? Don't you have better things to do than stalk me?"

"I'll just take that as a thank you." Zach's grin annoys me so much that I roll my eyes and turn my back on everyone.

I can't deal with this right now. Maybe I should take the opportunity to put some space between me and Malicevile—that is, if anyone lets me do it. It's like no one wants me with him, yet they keep forcing me back to his side.

A soft hand touches my warm shoulder. I spin, expecting to face Dylan, but it's Alana. She stands a foot away, clutching the flask of holy water in one hand. She wouldn't hesitate to use it if she thought I was a threat to her.

I haven't talked to her since the day after my transformation—the day after David's death—and I'm not sure what to say now. I've already apologized. I tried to be there for her. But she turned her back on me, leaving me alone when I needed her the most. I can't stop the hatred that courses through my veins.

"I'm sorry, Cami," she finally says after a moment.

"For what? For stabbing me or for abandoning me when I needed you?"

"You have to understand where I'm coming from," she says quietly.

"That's the thing. I don't. We were like sisters, Alana. We have history. Yet it's like none of that mattered to you. All you saw was Hell in my eyes and just assumed the worst. Cadence was there, you know. Someone I had known for only months." I wave my hand toward Dylan. "And Dylan. He was there even when I shut off my humanity. He didn't give up on me. But you did. Why?"

She balls her hands into fists. "Because you remind me that I failed. You remind me of what I've lost."

A tear slips onto my cheek. "We've all lost. That's why we're supposed to cling onto what we can salvage."

I can't look at her anymore. Forgiving isn't exactly the easiest thing for a demon to do. And I'm not ready to forgive her. Not when she despises me for what I am and thinks I'm a reminder of all the bad things that happened in her life.

Turning to Zach again, I stare at the demon for a long moment. His chestnut hair looks like he just ran his hands through it once with some hair wax, letting it stick wherever it stood. He's wearing slim fitting jeans with a gray T-shirt with what looks like paint splatter in the form of black wings. How appropriate.

"You have your car?" I ask.

"You still trying to run away?"

I clench my teeth. "Why does that matter?"

"We had a deal."

"Come on!" I scream. "I'll even put up with you at this point if it means I don't have to go back there." I think for a moment. Why on earth would he want me to return to Malicevile? What does he get out of it? Then it dawns on me. "Wait a minute. You have a kid, don't you? That's why you want me to go back. You're waiting for information on how demi-demons can make the complete transformation like me."

He laughs. "Seriously, Cami? Hanging around you has turned me off to children. You're just a lot of trouble."

I cover the tender skin over my heart with my hand. "I should be offended, but thank God. I'd feel sorry for your demonic spawn."

He snorts. "Though conversations like these might be worth it."

Dylan clears his throat from behind me. He and Alana listen to us without saying a word, and I wonder what they're thinking. If I were still half-human, this entire conversation would unsettle me. We're joking about demons having kids. I used to cringe knowing that I was the spawn of a demon.

My eyes light up as I take in Dylan with his messy black hair, his now-stained shirt, and soft eyes. I raise my hand and point at him. "I don't need a car with you."

"Love, I told you I can't."

I shift my gaze to Alana. "Can I borrow yours? You can pick it up at sunrise."

An arm hangs over my shoulder as the strong scent of jasmine wafts into my nose. "Tell you what, princess. Go home, get on good terms with your dad so he trusts you, find out where the next collection will take place, and I'll see to it that you get what you want."

"Why does that matter to you?"

"Is it a deal or not? I think we'd make a great team."

Another deal. Great. I ignore his quip about being on a team. Not happening.

I look to Dylan for an answer, but his expression is unreadable as he stares between us. It's enough to make me reconsider agreeing. Zach might seem easy-going, but demons are excellent actors. He could easily be waiting for me to mess up. Or worse, what if he uses me to get to Malicevile and then turns against me. I can't put my life on the line in hopes that he's good on his word to give me what I want. Too much is at risk.

After a long minute, I say, "I'm sorry. I can't make a deal with you. The last one—that was a one-time thing out of desperation."

Zach's lips tilt downward. "Seriously? You seem pretty desperate now."

"I said I don't make deals, okay?" I shift on my feet before I turn to Dylan. "Drop me off back in Moonlight Shores? I can walk from there."

Reaching into his pocket, Zach pulls out a set of keys. He dangles them in front of me. "I'd be happy to give you a ride, princess. Wouldn't want something to happen to your precious boyfriend."

"He's not my boyfriend," I snap. I don't know why I need to say it, but I do.

With the sullen look Dylan gives me, I'm sure he wonders why I have the need as well. Everything in me tells me not to get in the car again with Zach. He did park on a dark, dangerous road last time to interrogate me. He put me in danger. He's the reason Malicevile wants to lock me away.

But he's right about Dylan. Malicevile could be waiting to discover us, and the moment Zach stops shielding me, he'll be able to find me. With Malicevile's power, even if Dylan stayed in the air, he might not be safe.

"Just come with me," Zach says after a minute. "We'll stop for food or something. Take our time."

I grimace. "Fine, but you're buying, and we eat in the car."

He sighs. "Whatever, princess."

"And stop calling me that."

"Why? It's fitting."

I ignore him as I focus on Dylan. He closes the space between us but keeps his hands safely tucked in his pockets. Peering into his dark eyes, I study him for a moment. I wish I could read his mind—then again, it's probably a good thing that I can't. Not now at least.

"I don't know when I'll see you again, so be safe, okay?" I stand on my tiptoes and give him a hug.

It takes him a few seconds before he hugs me back. "I will, love. I'll check in with Faith tomorrow to make sure you're okay, too."

I nod, squeezing him once more before I smile at Alana who has been quietly watching and listening to us. She's always been so closed off that I have no idea what she's thinking. Maybe seeing me now might have changed her heart. But she doesn't offer me a goodbye. Just turns and walks away with Dylan when he motions that they're leaving.

My bottom lip pouts when I force myself to face Zach.

He offers his hand, but I don't take it. "You can't expect to win her over so easily. She's only human after all. She'll never understand the world like we do."

Maybe he's right. Maybe it's best that she doesn't.

⌒⌒⌒

Zach grabs a handful of fries from the large container I prop on my leg. I agreed to share dinner with him since I'm not really hungry, and I kind of felt guilty for making him pay, especially since he scrounged for change in his center console. It reminded me of the dozens of times Alana and I had to drop everything to escape. We'd be on the run with barely enough money to pay for a place to stay until she could find another job.

"What? Not hungry?" Zach asks when I don't touch the fries. I'd already let him have my burger.

I hold up the container so he can finish off the fries. "Not really. I feel like I could throw up."

"Scared of going home?"

"Demons don't get scared," I mutter.

He laughs. "I'm sorry, Cami. You're barely even a demon to me. Sure, you occasionally have fire in your eyes and look like you're going to drag me to Hell with you, but you don't make deals, you don't mess with souls, you hang out with a nephilim and human. You're empathetic. You're—"

I raise my hand, cutting him off. "Okay, I get it. I'm not as powerful as Malicevile or as awesome as you."

"Are you kidding? You're both. But that still doesn't make you a very good demon."

I roll my eyes. "Then I guess I'll never be a very good demon."

"But you make a good Cami."

Scrunching my eyebrows, I swivel in my seat, stretching the seatbelt to peer at the side of Zach's head. He doesn't attempt to look at me as he exits the highway near the Moonlight Shores city limit. I know he knows I'm studying him, but still, he doesn't return my gaze.

"Don't think too much into that," he adds. "I'd hate for you to fall in love with me."

Heat crawls up my neck as my cheeks burn crimson.

"You'll never have to worry about that."

"I don't know..."

I smack his arm. "You're not even my type."

He smirks.

"Shut up."

He pulls to the side of the road. "I wasn't going to say any-thing."

"Whatever." I go to open the door but remember there's no door handle on the inside. "Just let me out."

He chuckles while opening his door. He smiles at me the entire time he moseys around the hood of the car to stand outside the passenger's side door. After a long, unnerving moment where we just stare at each other through the glass, he finally opens the door. I don't like being under his heavy scrutiny disguised as the need to annoy me. I'm not blind. I can see that the wheels in his mind are spinning and he's trying to catch a glimpse of my soul through my cracked armor. He's like a puppy, so not threatening, but then he'll nip you with his razor sharp teeth. He'll make you bleed all the same.

I take his proffered hand and let him help me out. I won't let him intimidate me. He already sees me as weak. If another demon saw me as he sees me, they'd try to send me to Hell like the woman at the club did. Why he doesn't means that I have something, or can do something, that he really, really wants. It's why I can't ever make another deal with him.

"I'd still like you to reconsider our deal," he says, dropping my hand the moment I'm standing on my two feet.

I sigh. "That's not going to happen."

"Why not?"

"Because I don't trust you!" I throw my hands into the air. I don't know how much clearer I can be. "You've been showing up out of nowhere, acting all mysterious, pretending to be some nice guy. But I see through you, Zach. You've done nothing but cause me trouble, and for some stupid reason, I can't even tell Malicevile about you. You're the reason I need to leave. You put me in an awful situation. I was fine until you showed up."

He scowls, his face distorting, but he doesn't show off his true body like I expect. Instead, he kicks the tire of his car. "You're forgetting how I saved your life and protected your friends."

I summon a burst of energy in my palms. "Sure, you saved my life. Thanks for that," I say with a hint of sarcasm in my voice. "But you can't count my friends. That was your fault to begin with."

He shakes his head. "No way. Your little demi-demon boy-friend was the reason for that."

I yell as I pitch the energy orb at the ground. Spinning on my heels, I rush away before I start a fight with a demon I'm not sure I could beat. Thankfully, Zach doesn't chase after me. He lets me go.

When I reach the end of the street, I stop and peer around the dark night. Anger swells in my mind as I consider all my options. I don't have to go back to Raphael's. I'm still far enough away that I have enough of a head start. No one can make me go back.

I hear the thud of footsteps before the sticky sweet smell of honey and rose drifts into my nostrils. Summoning another energy orb, I straighten my shoulders and turn to face the oncoming demon who thinks it's stealthily sneaking up on me.

A bald man with vibrant blue eyes leers at me from in front of an empty lot. Without hesitating, I chuck the energy orb at him. He releases a long breath, the air strong enough to push my energy ball away from him and back to me. He jets forward in my direction, dodging everything I have to throw at him.

I brace for an impact that never comes. He swivels around me, forcing me to spin with him, nearly blowing me over with his fiery hot breath. It's like he can create wind. It's not until I'm facing the opposite direction that I realize he's not alone.

In another quick motion, he charges me again, blowing me off my feet. The air whooshes from my lungs as I hit the ground. I didn't have time to levitate because he smashes his hand into the wound over my heart.

A string of curse words erupt in the night as he shakes out his smoking hand. I guess no one can touch the brand marks left by a nephilim. It gives me some comfort that maybe I'll not die here on this dark sidewalk.

Another figure appears over me. The woman, with long silver hair and black eyes, smiles down at me. "Camilla Hellshire," she says, baring her yellowing teeth at me. "We've been looking for you everywhere."

"Touch me and you'll regret it," I say, my voice low.

She laughs as she kicks me in the side with her pointy heel, forcing me over. She has to be ten times stronger than me with how easily she does it. As I try to push up to fight back, something hard hits my back, pushing me to the pavement with a thud. I jerk my neck up to peer in front of me.

At the end of the block, Zach stands and watches without doing anything. He's the last thing I see before the woman slides a bag over my head.

I guess I should've taken his deal after all.

SHIFTED

THE FOUL SCENT of rotting meat and vinegar permeates the air, sneaking into the cloth bag over my head, nearly suffocating me. If I wasn't so used to the stench of lower and mid-level demons, I'd have thrown up a few times already.

My wrists and ankles burn against the hot metal of blessed chains. Where these demons got such a thing, I have no idea. They must've been studying Malicevile. I always thought using sacred things was unthinkable to a demon, but I guess since they're not using the chains as a weapon, it must be okay for them.

Maybe they just want to humiliate me. Who knows? No

one has said a single word to me this whole time. I'm not even sure how much time has passed, but I know the sun will rise soon, and they'll take me with them into the sunlight prison.

I should be more afraid than I am, but I know Malicevile will find them and punish them for taking me. I just have to wait it out.

Something brushes up my leg, slowly moving from my shin to my knee to stop before my thigh. The smell grows stronger than ever, making my eyes water. What makes it worse is that I can't see who is brave enough to put their repulsive fingers on me.

A strange clicking sound, like the constant quick tap of a pen on a table, sounds close to my ear. The bag shifts slightly as something else, another limb maybe, touches my shoulder and plays with my hair.

Tugging my wrists against the searing chains, I struggle to get some slack from them. I wonder how long I can pull against them before they burn right through my wrists to slice my hands off. I'm not sure I'm willing to risk it.

"So pretty," a soft voice whispers into my ear. The clicks continue, and I tremble when yet another limb touches my other shoulder to slide up and down my arm in gentle, yet creepy strokes. "Just one peek." The demon isn't talking to me but to itself.

Swallowing my now uncontrollable shudders, I allow my fury to get the best of me. No demon gets to lay a finger on me without my permission. Ever.

I hold utterly still as the bag on my head shifts and a flash of light filters in below my chin. With it comes the most potent stink ever. The bag was actually saving my senses. Now, the stench is so bad that my stomach churns. I can taste it with every small breath. It sinks deep into my pores, promising to linger with me forever.

Click-click-click-click. The sound continues. The pressure of another hand touches my other leg, gripping just above my knee. It's strong enough to make me wince. I don't speak or cry out as much as I want to. I suppress the fear threatening to surface. Demons love fear. I hate to admit it, but I find the scent of a human's fear pretty intoxicating now. I wonder what my own fear would smell like. Probably good enough to send any demon into a frenzy.

Click-click-click-click. "One. Little. Peek."

My hair shifts on my shoulder as the other side of the bag gently lifts. Slowly, so slow it's almost painful, the bag eases up my face. Cool air caresses my neck, and then my chin. I hold my breath as the bag slides over my nose.

As it reaches my eyes, I blink at the sudden change in light.

Hovering not even an inch from my face is a mid-level demon. Beady eyes peer into mine, sunken deep into a round head that sits on top of broad shoulders without a neck. This demon's attempt to look human has seriously failed in the most terrifying way possible. Slightly gray skin hangs in loose folds on the demon's cheeks, and I see what might be pus lining each flap of skin.

I don't give the demon another second to stare at me. Jerking my head forward, I bash my head against his. When my head connects, it's like I've smacked into an inflated ball. Milky green blood squirts from the demon's forehead where I got him with one of my dainty horns. I wouldn't usually show off my true body, but there's no way I'm letting any demon mistake my normal form as a sign of weakness. I earned these horns.

A wail erupts from the demon as he flies back. His four hands, with fingers that look like lumpy sausages, smack against his forehead as he hits himself. With each blow of his hand, his milky blood splatters around the room, peppering over my jeans and shirt. A few spots land on my face, and I cringe.

Without a word, the demon suddenly stops and lurches closer, his feet shuffling in a quick motion, the footsteps sounding like someone sweeping a broom. He stops just short of me, glaring at me with his beady eyes that are much too small for his basketball-like head.

His nostrils flare within his fat, flat nose and then he makes the clicking sound again. I realize after a moment that it's the sound of his puffy lips quivering together as he sucks in a breath of my own scent. *Gross!*

Holding up one of his hands, he reaches for the bag hanging off my head before failing to put it back on me.

I soundlessly thrash my head back and forth until it falls on the ground. When his eyes avert to it, I levitate, pulling against the blessed chains until my metal chair flies from the ground. I launch into him, knocking him off his feet. Landing on top of him, I plant my boots on each side of his round head.

His thick fingers latch around my ankles before he jerks them away, his hands searing against the blessed metal. In one swift motion I stop levitating, pushing all my weight into my feet, tightening the chains in the spot where his neck should go.

His soft skin smolders as the chain burns into him. He flails beneath me, but it's no use. I ease off just enough to give me a foot of height over him. He's in too much pain to realize I'm no longer pressing on him, which was what I was hoping for.

In another quick motion, I stop levitating and drop down as hard as I can, the weight of my body and the burning of the chains too much for him. His head rips free with the motion, and as he deflates, his milky green blood fountains across the floor in front of me. Unlike upper-level demons, mid and lower-level demons are easier to send to Hell. If my chains weren't blessed it would've been a lot harder.

I stare at the disgusting dead demon for a moment before I levitate, using my feet to push me toward the only door. Whoever my captors are seriously underestimated me. It gives me enough hope to know that I'm not as weak as I thought I was. I still carry the hunter instinct within me. I'm a predator. If Malicevile taught me anything, it was that these demons are beneath me, and I'm going to prove it.

It only takes me a moment to reach the rickety door. This isn't some impenetrable fortress like Raphael's. It appears to be just another rundown, abandoned house—the type of place that demons just love.

Spinning around, I back up to the door and lock my fingers around the cold knob. My hands scream as I twist it because the chains shift up to grate against the sides of my thumbs before sliding farther up my arms when I release it. The only thing that stops me from screaming out is the sickeningly sweet honey scent. It wafts from the hallway, and I don't even have to look to know that the woman is waiting in the living room—I can hear her having a one-sided conversation, probably talking on the phone.

The chains jingle as I creep forward, half-levitating, half-hopping. I don't need my hands to do any damage. If I can get in the right position, I can attack her with an energy orb. When I reach the end of the short hallway, I stop and wait a second to make sure she's still on the phone.

"We had a deal," the demonic woman says into the phone. She listens intently with her back to me. She places a hand on her hip. "I don't care. *You're* the one who got your information wrong. She was alone."

I was set up.

A voice hums from the phone as someone yells through the line, but it's muffled and I can't make it out.

The woman paces for a second. "You're lucky I don't keep her for myself."

The voice on the line gets even louder.

"Fine. It's a deal. But she's mine until you come to collect her, and I promise you I'm not going to be very nice," the woman says.

As she presses the phone to her ear to listen for a response, I propel forward and knock into the woman's back to send her sprawling forward. The phone flies from her hands, clattering against the wall. She roars as reaches her hands up and locks them into my hair. Yanking me forward, she flips me off her, and I land hard on the bare concrete floor, smashing my hands. The chains sting my back as they graze the skin peeking from my rolled up shirt.

The woman scrambles to her feet, her heels sliding on the floor as she tries to find her footing. She reminds me of a toddler in a pair of her mother's heels. It's the most ungraceful move I've ever seen from a demon of her status.

I laugh, peering up from my awkward position on the floor. "If I didn't know any better, I'd think you were with the alliance. Blessed chains? Come on."

My words strike a nerve because one second she looks like she's about to leave me to suffer on the floor and then the next she clomps forward, hands fisted in front of her. She bends down and locks her fingers into my hair before tugging me upright. Thank God for levitation. I'm sure she'd have ripped my hair out if she could've.

She glowers, flashing firelight in her eyes. Without saying a word, she reaches out and backhands me hard enough that I topple sideways. The ache in my shoulder is nothing compared to the sting she left on my cheek. I'm sure there's a hand print across my face. My nose starts running, and it takes me a minute to realize I'm bleeding dark crimson, almost black blood, from my nose. It pools in front of me in a perfect circle.

I reach up and automatically cup my face, my wrists still smoking from the chains. The fall must've been enough to loosen my bindings, freeing me. The woman's eyes widen when it dawns on her that I'm free.

From my position on the floor, I summon the deep red lava bomb I've been holding onto for a while. While Malicevile's power is enough to fry this woman, she'd be expecting it. I love the element of surprise. In one quick motion, I reel my hand back before throwing the power at the woman. It hits her in the stomach, sending her shirt smoldering as the sticky power clings to her, eating away everything it touches.

While she's busy stripping out of her top, I reach down and unwind the chains from my feet. My hands blister and burn, but I don't care at this point. I just need to get out of here.

The front door bangs open, startling me, and the bald man who was with the woman earlier charges in. His whole appearance contorts when he shows off his true body. His arms turn into two long whips with what looks like giant rose thorns sticking out of them. His flowery scent merges with the honey smell of the woman. She regains focus on me, now standing in a bra and skirt with liquid-filled blisters decorating her stomach.

I expect them to attack me at once, but they stand still assessing the situation. They don't have surprise on their side now.

I straighten my shoulders and face them. "I'm giving you

one chance to leave. Unlike my father, I don't think you're my kin, and I'll add you to the list of demons I've sent home."

The man opens his mouth while releasing a gust of rose-scented air. This time, I absorb his power, feeling it rush through my veins, lifting my hair from my shoulders. When he realizes he's done nothing to me, he lashes out his whip arm. It cuts across my forearm, ripping my sleeve. A small trickle of blood seeps into the remaining fabric, and my vision turns the same shade of crimson. He doesn't get the opportunity to lash out at me again because I send a fireball right at his face. He hollers as the flames lick across his skin, singeing his eyebrows off. A faint pink color stains his cheeks.

As the man raises his whip arm again, the woman holds up both her arms. "Wait," she says. "I think we can work something out."

"And why do you think I should listen to you?" I ask, summoning the last bit of power I stole from Enviana at The Morningstar. It's invisible so neither demon can see it. I feel quite powerful in this moment with so many tricks up my sleeve. If only they weren't all so temporary.

"Because we weren't planning to kill you. We were just doing a job. You know how that goes," she says.

"And what did you get out of this?"

"Dibs."

"On what?"

"Two demi-demon souls." She must be desperate if she's willing to tell me all this.

I run my tongue over my dry lips, tasting the sticky blood from my bloody nose. I don't say anything for a moment as I think about what she's said. There's only two demons I know who have access to demi-demons—Malicevile and Raphael. They've been collecting them together.

Is it possible that Raphael turned on my father? Is he that desperate to transform Faith that he'd risk his hard work? Risk losing the one person who knows how to do it? I don't think so. Raphael isn't stupid. This has to be the work of my father. But why? To get revenge? To show me how tough it'll be without him? A deal gone wrong, maybe? No matter what, it's enough to make me want to murder him the next time I see him. He should only hope I never make it home.

"So Malicevile put you up to this," I say. "And you failed to hold up your end of the bargain."

"You were supposed to be with the nephilim," the bald man says.

This wasn't about me. It was about Dylan. Of course it's about him. My father thought I ran away with him using some random shielding ability. He probably offered the deal to everyone willing to try. That jerk.

I glance at the floor once to compose myself, to stop the anger from making me do something irrational. "Here's the deal." I look at the woman, an icky feeling settling in me as I speak. "I want you to spread the word that the hunt for the nephilim is off. Do that, and I won't send you to Hell."

She nods. "Done."

The bald man shifts on his feet. "And me?"

"I'm using you to set an example."

With a flick of my hand, I send the shockwave through the room, knocking both demons off their feet. I saunter across the room, stepping on the man's whip-like arm as I stand over him. He opens his mouth to try to blow me away, but I just absorb his ability.

His eyes widen as I blast him with an energy orb, sending his clothes smoking. But I don't stop there. I send one wave of electricity after another directly to his heart, burning a hole right through his chest until his heart's no longer there.

A second before his body slumps over, a tingling sensation crawls through me to my very soul, sending the air swirling around me before it enters me. I stumble back with the impact in time to cover my face when the demon explodes, cascading blood and guts over my legs, the floor, and the demonic woman who watches in utter silence.

Whoa. That was new. He was my first upper-level kill as a demon and it felt better than I could expect. It's like something has shifted within me. His power feels just as prominent as Malicevile's.

With a smile, I cross the room to the door and glance at the woman. "Just so you know, I'm nothing like my father."

I'm worse.

FORGIVEN

THE WALK BACK to the beach fortress takes longer than I expect it to. My ankles ache with every step, and I feel terrible. To my surprise, a mile back, an elderly man tried to get me to get into his car so he could take me to the hospital. Most humans wouldn't stop for a demon because we exude evil, but he was so set on helping me that I had to flash my true body to get him to leave me alone. I've probably ruined him for life but whatever. The last thing I need is to drag some innocent guy into the Veiled Realm.

The purpling sky indicates that the sun will be rising shortly. The crisp ocean air plays with my tangled curls as I stroll into the breeze. The flash of a fiery hellhound darts in the corner of my vision, and I stop when I spot Greg barreling toward me from the sandy hillside that leads down to the beach. He traveled pretty far to find me, but I'm glad he did. I could use someone on my side.

I release a low whistle, and the hellhound bounds my way, black tongue lolling from his open mouth. It's the first time I've seen the broken wolf since Dylan cracked the wall protecting my humanity. And I feel so many emotions—regret, grief, rage, admiration—because I did this. It was my first true act as a demon. It's the reason I shut off my humanity in the first place. But now, after being numb for so long, it doesn't seem as bad. It wasn't my fault. I didn't ask Greg to stand up to his pack for me. *You stole his life. You ruined his eternity. He was so young.*

Yeah, and my life was stolen, my eternity ruined, all before my eighteenth birthday. Greg and I—we're a lot alike. *No, you're not.*

As I run my fingers through his fiery, slimy fur, the scent of patchouli and amber cuts over the smell of burning flesh. I draw my gaze away from Greg to peer at the porch where Evan stands in the shadows watching me.

I bet Malicevile told him I ran away with Dylan—my father would say anything to torment another person just for the fun of it. In fact, I know he basically told the entire demon world. I don't know what he got out of telling other demons that his daughter was in love with someone of good grace, but he had his reasons. I'm sure I'll find them out soon enough.

"Where's my father?" I ask as I stroll forward with Greg heeling next to me, waiting for my command.

"He went to save you," Evan says evenly. "But apparently you didn't need rescuing after all."

"That's crap and you know it. He's the one who set me up." I pull my sleeves up to reveal the burns around my wrist. "Look what those demons did to me, Evan. I didn't deserve this because I didn't run away with Dylan. Hell, even if I did, I still don't think I deserved to be treated like this."

He steps from the shadows and trails his gaze up and down my body, his eyebrows furrowing the more damage he sees done to me. His eyes fall on my chest where my black skin peeks out from my V-neck. He'd have to be blind to miss the angelic branding, and his concern shifts to fury in seconds before I can even explain what happened.

"Damn it, Cami. You know I'd never hurt you by my own freewill and look what that bastard did to you! How can you love someone like that? How could you even let him get away with it?"

His voice rumbles as he questions me. I don't blame him for assuming the worst. I look awful.

I close my eyes for a second. "Oh, don't blame Dylan. He wouldn't have felt he had to if my father would've just left well enough alone. When my father took me to hunt him down, Alana was there. She stabbed me in the chest. Dylan was only trying to help me."

"By marking you?" He doesn't even mention Alana, the

one who was responsible for nearly cutting my heart out in the first place. It's how I know that nothing I say will ever make Evan okay with Dylan. It'll all come down to being his fault.

My shoulders slump. I give up. I'm done fighting and defending myself. I'm done trying to make people understand. I feel like I'm back in Purgatory as Heaven and Hell each take a part of my soul, threatening to rip me apart because neither wants to share and would rather see me dead than in the other's hands. Not that I'm okay with being shared. Or owned by either one, for that matter.

"You know what? I'm not having this conversation." I push past him. "And so you know, I didn't choose him."

"Cami," he whispers.

"I'm not choosing you either. It wasn't my intention to ever hurt you. It wasn't my intention to fall in love with him. But you were gone, Evan. You left me."

"I was saving you!"

Tears blur my vision. "I know! I know that! I think about that every day. If I could do something to change things, I would. I've tried. I've offered my father everything I could to get your soul back. But he's relentless. You have to die first. I won't lose you like that, but I can't have you like this. I just—I can't."

Evan steps forward and pulls me against him. "But you can. You can shut your humanity off again. It can go back to how it was."

I shake my head, my hair whipping against my face as I

pull away. "But that wasn't really living. I need to feel everything. I need to feel every sharp piece of my broken soul. I need it to feel human again."

"But you're not a human. You're a demon, Cami."

I suck in my bottom lip as it quivers. "No, I'm more than that."

As the words escape my lips, a bright flash cuts through the air. The world shimmers around me as the sun rises, stealing me for another day. Sweet relief washes over me as I stand in the forest of gnarled trees, alone, but with more hope than ever.

<hr>

I lie on my back, staring into the brownish sky as the sun journeys across it at a faster pace than it does in the earth realm. A few hours have passed, but it feels like time is crawling since nothing or no one has bothered me. Being alone with only my thoughts has given me time to think things through without my emotions muddling my thoughts.

But the plans I've tried to devise all end badly.

My first thought was to kill Malicevile the moment I returned to the human world. That would solve at least a dozen of my problems. He wouldn't be able to hold things over my head or make me miserable. I could have a nice eternity alone. I could take up a hobby—not collecting souls though.

The problem with that idea is I'm not sure I could successfully kill him. And then, there's all the messiness of controlling the demonic world. Someone will replace him, and it sure as Hell wouldn't be me. Not to mention the fact that all the souls he has in his possession would probably follow him, including Evan's. It'd void our deal. You can't have a deal with a dead demon.

My second thought was to take Zach up on his deal. Help him in exchange for a new start at life. This deal is the most tempting, because it would free me from my father and allow me to figure out things on my own. The problem? I'd be forced to leave Evan behind, and I'm not so sure I can live a guilt-free life knowing I'm just giving up and letting Malicevile win. Plus, I don't even know if Zach could guarantee such a thing. He doesn't even have money, which is necessary in a fresh start.

And my last thought, which is the most reasonable one, is to suck it up and play nice with Malicevile. Be a good little daughter and demon and just wait until things get better. He'll eventually give up on Dylan, and maybe give me what I want with Evan one day. The issue? None of that would ever happen. I'd be seriously dreaming to think things would ever change.

So now, I'm stuck.

"Hey, princess," a familiar, masculine voice says through the trees. Zach's jasmine scent reaches me before I lay my eyes on him.

When I do, I scowl. In a quick motion, I swing my arm out and blast him with a baseball-sized energy orb. It collides with his chest, burning through his shirt, but he only laughs. I can't really hurt him here. Though I did mess up his obnoxious T-shirt with a penguin high fiving a snowman with the slogan *Stay Cool* printed below it. Now, the snow man looks melted.

He steps behind a tree when I send another ball of power at him. Slowly peeking out, he glares. "You owe me a shirt."

"I was doing you a favor."

"What? I thought it was funny." He steps back out from the tree when I don't try to blast him again.

I sit up on my elbows. "You shouldn't be here. I'm mad at you, and I can't be held responsible for what I do come sundown."

"So, you want Malicevile to find you?" he quips, strolling closer to take a seat a few feet away, resting his back against a tree trunk.

I should've known this peace and quiet wasn't because my father was too far to find me or too annoyed to spend the day with me. It was because of Zach all along.

"You're a creep," I say.

"You're welcome."

I sigh and spin around without getting up to face the other direction. "You know, you could've done something tonight about those demons. I had to kill two of them because you didn't intervene."

"And that's a bad thing?"

I sigh. "When the lot of them starts challenging me it is."

"Then send them all to Hell for trying."

I spin around to face him again. I can't help it. "Whose side are you on anyway?"

He smirks. "Your side."

I puff my cheeks out as I push air through my lips. "Not

only are you a creep, but you're cheesy as well. And so you know, the position for my right-hand demon is closed."

"Then it's a good thing I'm not applying." He grins, showing off his straight teeth.

I can't help watching him, taking in his hazel eyes and the light brown scruff around his strong jaw. If Cadence were here, she'd appreciate the view with me. She'd say it was okay to appreciate him and still hate him. When he raises an eyebrow at me, I shift my gaze away.

Silence falls between us, and I don't do anything to break it. I'm going to try my best to pretend he isn't here invading my space—space I really did need to think things through. If only he didn't make it so impossible for me to ignore him. Zach has one of those presences that beg for attention without even having to do anything.

"So," he says after a long while. "I've been thinking about our deal."

"We don't have a deal," I say with a little too much annoyance in my voice.

He raises his hand. "Just hear me out."

I roll my eyes but don't say anything.

"I've had some time to think about it, and I think you're right not to make a deal with me."

"Really?" I question. Now that's surprising.

"Yeah. I just assumed it was easier to make deals since it'd be something you were familiar with. But how will you ever trust me if you think that I'm only ever doing things for you out of obligation?"

"And why do you want me to trust you?"

"Because I trust you."

I press my lips into a thin line and wait for him to start laughing, like this is the funniest joke ever. But he doesn't. He's totally serious.

I giggle—actually giggle—like the few times I've embarrassed myself in front of Evan when we first met. Heat crawls up my neck and the nervous giggles turn into laughter, and I snort.

He blinks a few times. "Really, princess? Is that so hard to believe?"

I answer him with another bout of uncontrollable laughter. It takes him getting to his feet, unfurling his scary black wings, and bending his knees to prepare to launch into the air to get me to stop laughing.

I jump to my feet and reach out, running my hand across the soft, inky feathers. Pain bursts in my fingertips as my skin sizzles from the touch. Jerking my hand back, I cradle it against me and take an instinctive step back.

He freezes, the vein in his neck bulging as he swallows. "Cami," he says quietly. "I can explain."

Fear slices through me, fighting against the world that numbs everything in me. His wings shouldn't have hurt me like they did. My hand shouldn't be blistering from the simple touch of his black feathers.

The puzzle pieces that make up Zach start shifting and sliding into place the more I look at him. Every conversation we've had plays through my mind—how he interrogated me about my life. How he told me I was special. How he asked for my soul. He told me I didn't act like a demon. He didn't even act like a demon. I just assumed. No wonder I was incapable of telling Malicevile about him—anyone for that matter. *Except Dylan...*

Anger rushes through me. All this time Dylan knew as well, and he didn't tell me. Why should I be surprised? He never tells me anything.

A scream burns in my throat, but I don't unleash it.

Zach takes a step closer to me, his wings disappearing with the motion. "It's not what you think."

I scramble backward. "You don't know what I'm thinking. How could you lie to me? How could you make me think we were on the same side?"

"Because we are!" His voice echoes through the air.

I shake my head, using my hair to veil my face, like the dark locks will somehow protect me from the full-blooded angel that stands in front of me. The angel who has intruded my entire world and messed up everything. The angel, who I know in this very moment, wants nothing more than to save me. Malicevile was right all along. But it was never Dylan he should've worried about.

Zach wraps his fingers around my arm, stopping me from running. With my free hand, I swing my arm around and punch him in the face. When he releases me, I shove both my hands into his chest and knock him down.

Without waiting another moment, I break out in a sprint, weaving in and out of the trees. An utter silence falls around me, sending a shiver down my back. It's like the first time I discovered that I wasn't human, that I was half-demon, and my entire world starts to split at the seams. Once again, I know nothing. I'm left swimming in dark waters that threaten to drag me under.

"Camilla." Malicevile's voice rings out through the quiet forest.

I spin to face him as he stands a dozen feet away with his arms folded across his chest. He doesn't look like the monster I've created in my mind the last few hours. If anything, he looks exhausted.

I stop in place, digging my nails into my blistering palm, thinking about what I'm going to do now.

Taking a deep breath, I run as fast as I can, arms wide. Malicevile reciprocates my hug, squeezing me against him. His clove and cinnamon scent washes away the scent of jasmine, clearing the fear from my mind.

I don't know why I hug him after everything, but in this moment, the thought of an angel stealing my soul has me wanting to fall at my father's feet, begging for him to protect me, to keep me safe, even if it means I'm his prisoner. Because with Malicevile, I'll still have a life. I'll still get my chance at eternity here.

Who knows what the angelic army wants to do with me or

my soul? It's something I'm unwilling to find out.

I peer over my shoulder for signs of Zach, but he's nowhere in sight. Malicevile pulls away, inspecting me like he's unsure of how to handle me as I start crying. "You were right all along. The angels—they got to me. I didn't even know what was happening until—" The words finally escape my mouth, though Zach's name remains lodged in my throat.

He drops his arms from my shoulders and searches the area like he can see something I can't. After a second, he turns his gaze on me. "I warned you, Camilla. They think you're unfit for this eternity. They'll obliterate your soul from existence."

Fear slices through me at the thought. "I didn't know. Dylan, he—" I suck in a ragged breath. I drop my thought. Deep down, I still can't drag Dylan through this. Instead I rub my temples. "Everything is so messed up. Look what they've done to us. To me. They're getting into my head, trying to turn me against you. God, how could I be so stupid?"

Malicevile straightens his shoulders. "I'm partly to blame. I've been so absorbed in my demonic affairs that I had assumed the worst from you. It's not like you've ever made our lives easy."

"I know," I say with a sigh. "You don't make life easy either, you know."

He nods. "I suppose that's something we can both agree on in regards to each other. But you have to know, even though your attitude and actions are sometimes downright maddening, I'll never let them have you. Understood?"

"Understood."

"Good, now we can focus on what's important."

"What's that?"

"Taking what is ours."

CHOICES

CADENCE IS THE first one to greet me on the porch of Raphael's beach fortress. She rushes forward, slinging her arms around my neck, and rocks me back and forth as she hugs me. We cling to each other for a long while, and Malicevile strolls past us to greet Evan in the foyer. They share a few words as I watch them from over Cadence's shoulder, but I do my best to not let myself fall into existing habits. I might be home, but my mind is still set on being alone.

"Are you okay?" she asks. "Evan cornered me and told me about Dylan. He wanted me to talk some sense into you."

I hook my arm through hers and pull her away from the

doorway so no one can eavesdrop. "I'm sorry he tried to put you in the middle. I kind of officially broke up with him last night."

"Because of Dylan?"

"There's nothing going on between us."

She studies me for a minute. "Boys are exhausting anyway."

I pout my bottom lip. "Tell me about it."

"Camilla," Malicevile says from the doorway, interrupting my conversation with Cadence. He studies me for a moment, like he's reconsidering whatever it is he wants to say, but then he tightens his jaw. "I have an errand I need done, but I'm still concerned about your erratic behavior. I know what the angelic army is capable of, especially for someone susceptible like you."

I straighten my shoulders. I wouldn't exactly trust me either. "It's fine if you send Evan. He's capable of handling anything."

"Not this."

"Oh. Well, I don't know how to get you to trust me again. I told you everything." As much as I could at least. With my inability to talk about Zach and how he's been stalking me, I was forced to tell him about Dylan instead, even though it hurt with every word I said. I told him how Dylan works for the angelic army and how he wants to save me. Dylan had to take most of the blame. "It's not like you're exactly trustworthy either. I didn't appreciate killing two demons last night."

When I think he's about to smirk, he rubs his chin instead, wiping away whatever expression he was going to offer me.

"You handled that well. If I didn't know any better, I'd say you surpassed my reputation for most unforgiving and powerful demon."

A backhanded compliment? I'll take it. "That's my goal."

He doesn't make a snarky comment like I expect him to. Instead, he reaches his hand into his suit pocket and pulls out a slip of folded paper. He holds it out for me to take, and I trail my eyes over an address not too far from here. It must be a soul collection.

"I have to warn you," Malicevile says. "This is an alliance member. Think you can handle it? She's very important to me, so don't make any mistakes. If you do, I'm holding you responsible. But I won't take it out on you." He lifts his finger to Cadence. "I'll take it out on her. Because I'm serious, Camilla. I need this member alive." Spoken like my demonic father. Threatening the people I care about is worse than threatening me. He knows this. He'll use it against me. I wish I didn't need him.

Cadence stiffens next to me, and I offer her a half smile.

"Understand?" Malicevile asks.

Oh, jeez. I'm not sure I'm up for this, but I can't admit to that now. I don't want to sit back and act useless. Doing something will keep my mind off everything else, especially the angel my mouth won't even let me mention out loud.

"Yes, but I'm taking my human with me. She can help assure that I don't screw up her fate." With Cadence by my side, I know we can handle things. Dealing with alliance members is more her specialty. She won't kill anyone.

Malicevile peers at my best friend who stands quietly behind me. I should've probably asked first if she wanted to go. It can't be easy on her knowing that we're about to collect someone who works for the organization she grew up in.

"Fine, but I also want you to take Evan," he says.

"Seriously? I thought we could give this whole trust thing a try. I don't need a babysitter, and Cadence can help me if I need it. I'll even take Evan's cell phone so you can track me." I'm not ready to face Evan. I need space. Because my heart can't take the constant struggle, and I refuse to shut it all off. I'm positive I couldn't even if I wanted to. My protective wall is now a sieve.

"Is this about the neph—"

I raise my hand. "No. I just—never mind. You would never understand in a million years." I'm not discussing my love life with a demon who thinks everything is just a phase. "Evan can come."

"Good," Malicevile says. "I want you back by nine. We have dinner reservations."

I open my mouth to reject the idea of dinner but think better of it. If Malicevile wants to treat me like the last few nights didn't happen, then I'm going to do the same. At least he doesn't hold a grudge like I do.

Evan saunters up next to me and touches his fingers to my lower back. I'm still wearing the nasty shirt from yesterday, so his heat trickles over my skin. He watches me, but I refuse to look at him. If Evan is one thing, he's determined.

I step away from him and say, "I need a few minutes to change. Why don't you give the keys to Cadence? She's driving tonight."

Evan smirks without a word. "Anything else?"

I shift on my feet. "Yeah, quit acting like this is a game."

He smiles wider. "Whatever you say, babe."

⁂

At first I was wary jumping right back into the swing of things after a night and day away from everyone, but things aren't as awkward as I expected. Evan hasn't said a word since we climbed in my Mustang, and I wouldn't even know he was here if it weren't for his—comforting? No. Familiar? Yeah, familiar scent, permeating the car every time we stop. Having the top down helps with that.

As Cadence flies down the freeway, I peer around the night. I hate to admit that I'm slightly nervous about the distance between me and Malicevile now, because I fear that at any minute, Zach will return, wings blazing behind him, to steal my soul away. He claims that it wasn't what I thought, but why would he even get close to me if that weren't the case? As far as I know, Demon Watchers do only that—watch demons. He's much more involved. He purposely deceived me. What kind of angel does that? What kind of angel stalks me and teases and kills for me if it didn't mean his ultimate goal was to claim my soul? All I know is I don't want to find out.

A flash of light cuts through the windshield, and I jump in

my seat, nearly levitating from the car in the middle of the freeway. Warm hands lock onto my shoulders and push me back into my seat. The light wasn't caused by ethereal wings but another car flicking their brights on and off from across the median.

"Maybe you should put your seatbelt on before you blow away," Evan says into my ear.

I shift in the seat, knocking his hands away. "I'm fine."

"Sure you are," he says, his warm scent washing over me as he leans between the seats to talk into my ear. It does more to me than I want it to. I need him to lean back before I accidentally get caught in his gaze. "You shouldn't have agreed to do this job. Your head isn't in it."

I narrow my eyes before flicking a small bolt of electricity toward Evan, just enough to make him wince and fall back into his seat. "I said I'm *fine*. Just drop it."

"You are kind of jumpy, Cami." Cadence glances at me once before training her eyes back on the road.

"Whose side are you on anyway?" I snap, though I don't mean to. I wasn't nervous until they started telling me I was nervous. So what if a beam of light scared me? They don't know what it's like to be a demon with an angel stalking them.

"Hello? Obviously your side if I'm here. Kill a girl for being concerned. You still kind of look like Hell." Cadence switches lanes to fly past a slow moving SUV.

I roll my eyes. "Like you would know."

Evan erupts in deep laughter from the backseat. I smile as I flick my gaze in his direction, immediately regretting the action. It's been a while since he wasn't moody and brooding at me. I forgot what it was like to joke around and just be together without the world weighing down on us. *Stop it, Cami.*

The smile melts from my face, and I turn back in my seat as Cadence exits the freeway. She comes to a stop at the stop sign, something neither Evan nor I would've done, but she isn't a reckless driver. At least she drives faster than Zach did.

The moment his name comes to my mind, goose bumps prickle up my arms. It makes the dark intersection scary—which is strange because I've never been afraid of the dark since turning into a demon. I just don't like how the shadows could hide anything.

Before Cadence lurches forward, I reach out and press the convertible top control to close the roof. I'm suddenly okay with Evan's scent taking up all my air because I keep imagining someone flying from the sky to steal me away.

"Cold?" Cadence asks while closing the latch.

I lean back in my seat. "Uneasy."

Her brows lower on her forehead as she squints, her full lips pouting. I know she wants to ask why, but I shift my eyes to the backseat without looking at Evan so she knows I'm not about to talk about my feelings in front of the boy who'll bring it to Malicevile's attention.

Cadence eases off the brakes and turns right onto another dark road. The sprawling hills lack streetlights, and if it weren't for the headlights, I would think we were driving into a void.

Even the stars don't shine tonight.

After an eerie mile, small lights pepper the tops of the hills as we head inland into a ritzy community. It's easy to forget that hunters don't live in slums like a lot of demons do. They have the backing of the alliance. They have no need to hide in rundown houses. And whoever lives at this address is definitely taking advantage of the alliance's payroll.

Cadence navigates a winding road that leads to a small suburban community filled with cookie-cutter houses, all in the same tan color, with the same perfect lawns, young trees, stone pathways, and two car garages.

"How'd you like to live here?" Evan asks, tapping his finger on my shoulder.

I shrug. "It's better than some of the places I've lived. I wouldn't complain."

Before Evan can comment, Cadence pulls the Mustang into the empty driveway of the last house at the end of a cul-de-sac. If there wasn't a light shining from within, I would assume that whoever lived here wasn't home. It's not like most hunters hang out indoors at night. They have better things to do. But Malicevile didn't say this was a hunter. He only said it was an alliance member, which means whoever she is isn't actively hunting. I wonder what her importance is and how she got involved with my father.

Cadence cuts the engine. "You know the place has probably been blessed."

I twist my lips to the side. She's definitely right about that.

We're close enough that I can sense the annoying barrier that'll make things more complicated. If I can't get this woman out, I'll have to take drastic measures like burning the place down unless Evan or Cadence can drag her out for me. Minions are useful. *They're not your minions.*

"Well, I'll figure it out. You two stay here."

I climb from the car and search around the neighborhood for signs of any threats. The last thing I need is to have to face a team of hunters who happen upon me in this neighborhood. If one alliance member lives here, then I can only assume more do.

Taking a deep breath, I glide forward up the driveway toward the stone path that leads to a simple porch with a swing chair, small table, and a few pots with robust marigolds blooming in bright yellows and oranges. As I take a step onto the path, a shock zaps through me as I smack into an invisible blessed barrier.

Stinging pain erupts in my face as the tip of my nose burns along with my hands. Thankfully, my jacket protected the rest of me from the shock. I wasn't expecting a barrier this far back, but whoever lives here really doesn't want demons knocking on their door.

The car doors slam as both Cadence and Evan hop out. With watery eyes, I glance at them before turning away so they don't see what an idiot mistake I made. I hate the small reminders like this—the reminders that tell the world I've been forsaken and Hell-bound.

Evan spins me back to face him. He grimaces as he touches my chin to hold me still while he looks at the burn on the tip of my nose. He leans closer, too close, and my heart forgets to beat for a moment as I remember the hundreds of kisses we've shared. The way he sucks in his bottom lip tells me he remembers them, too. It takes all my willpower to distance myself, hardening my heart against his charms.

"I'll knock," he says, messing with the zipper on his jacket.

Shaking my head, I turn to Cadence. "Will you knock? You're the least threatening out of us. It might make the summons easier."

Cadence huffs. "Did you just say I'm the least threatening?"

I smirk. "Like a kitten with the heart of a lion."

She grimaces as she runs her fingers through her purple hair, tying it out of her face. Without another word, she strolls up the path where I can't follow and bangs on the door a few times without even a second thought. Cadence has always had this carefree fearlessness about her that I've always envied. If our roles were reversed, I'm not so sure I'd be as together.

When no one answers, Cadence bangs another few times. If I didn't know any better, I'd assume they were asleep, but alliance members outside of huge protective compounds don't follow a mundane schedule.

After banging once more, the front door finally whines open, but a security screen protects our mark from Cadence. I stay just out of view near my Mustang and listen.

"What are you doing here, Cadence?" a familiar voice asks. "Do you need help?"

When Cadence doesn't respond, I step from the shadows and into view. My old teacher, Hunter Garcia, hides behind her security door in the safety of her house. Surprise is enough to make me inch forward, but Evan's strong hand pulls me away before I run into the barrier again.

"Are you kidding me?" I ask, my voice echoing through the air. I turn to glance at Evan, who's staring at me intently, probably gauging my reaction to give Malicevile the full report.

The security door clicks open, and I wish that my old instructor would remain locked safely away from me. This is nearly as bad as it would've been had I discovered Alana on the other side of the door. How can I knowingly drag my old instructor away without guilt? *She made a deal with your father. This is your job. You can't just forgive her mistake. You can't save them all.*

"You're dealing with my father?" I ask when no one says a word.

"It's n—"

"Stop," I say. "Don't say anything more. I'm not here as your friend. I'm here on behalf of my father. You made a deal and now it's your turn to hold up your end of the bargain. As long as you cooperate, I won't hurt you." This is where the fun used to happen—when the mark realized that they've made a huge mistake in making a deal. A lot of times there are tears and begging, almost always running, and the few brave who fight.

I expect Hunter Garcia—Jazmin—to do the latter. I can't imagine her crying or groveling, not to me at least. I'm her former student. She's never known me as a demon or seen my true body. She's probably only heard the rumors. She'll underestimate me.

With a quick nod, Jazmin says, "Give me a minute to grab a bag."

Surprise washes over me. I almost let her go back in but think better of it. She could try to stock up on weapons. Grab some holy water. Anything that she can use against me, though I don't think she'd risk it. She's outnumbered. She'd have a better chance running.

"No, come forward with your hands where I can see them. Evan will check you for weapons. I'll allow Cadence to grab you a bag though, because unlike what you've probably heard, I'm not really a monster."

"But you're a demon," she says as she steps forward with her hands linked on her head.

"And you're dealing with them. Doesn't look good on you. What did you want so desperately that you made a deal with my father anyway? Did he threaten to kill you?"

Jazmin presses her lips together for a second like she's deciding whether or not to tell me. Her fingers grip her red-streaked hair, the color blazing against her warm complexion. Her hazel eyes look more brown in the night as she holds my gaze, showing me she's not afraid of me. She should be though.

"That's none of your business, Cami," Evan reminds me

from behind me.

He's right, but I still want to hear it from Jazmin. Spinning with anger, I face Evan with narrowed eyes. "Go wait in the car, Evan. If I want to talk to my old instructor, I'm going to. If you have a problem with that, then you can take it up with my dad after you walk home."

Evan's lips tilt down for a split second, but he doesn't argue. He heads to the car and gets in, respecting my status as a demon. He could get away with bossing me around before, because it didn't bother me and I knew his intentions were good, but he's not reminding me it's not my business for my sake. He's loyal to Malicevile. This is for his sake.

As Jazmin stops next to me, I tense. Sending Evan to the car means that he didn't get to check her for weapons. I'm failing all over the place. Cadence had already stepped inside to grab a bag without waiting for my command, too. Now it's just me and my old instructor facing off.

She doesn't try anything though. It makes me worry even more. With a quick flick of my hand, I tug up the hem of her jacket, spotting her weaponry belt around her waist. I don't think she's wearing it because I'm here but out of habit.

Pulling my sleeve over my fingers, I quickly unsnap it, burning my fingers for a quick second before I kick it a dozen feet away. I tug up her pant legs next and clench my teeth as I rip a dagger free from her ankle before chucking it in the grass. She could try to use her demi-demon ability on me—though I've never seen her use it at all—but even if she did, I could absorb it.

I hold my face emotionless as Jazmin studies me, noting the faint smoke drifting from my now pink hands. Unlike Alana's reaction to me being a demon, Jazmin's much more controlled. Maybe because she knew.

"What?" I ask after a minute.

"It's just hard to believe," she says.

"Why? The alliance treated me like a demon. Might as well fit the part. And in all honesty, I'm surprised they don't treat you like that as well. Aren't they afraid of what can happen?"

"Shaking," Jazmin says. "It's why they haven't done anything about—" She snaps her mouth shut like she remembers who she's talking to.

"The kidnapped demi-demons?" I ask, filling in what I know is on her mind.

She nods once without a word.

Silence pushes around us as we both hold back what we want to say. It's not until this moment that I realize why Jazmin's here. Why she made a deal with my father. And I want to scream at her and tell her how crazy she is. She's one person. There's nothing she can do about those Malicevile has taken already. She's just going to end up another demi-demon on his army.

I scowl. "I can't believe you, Jazmin. You seriously made a deal with my dad because of them. What do you plan to do? Kill my father? Rescue the others? That's impossible. You'll end up dead."

"I can't just do nothing. It's not like I traded my soul," she says. Her response catches her off guard, and she turns away. She let our association with each other ruin her cover. Now I know what she's planning.

I grab her arm, turning her toward me. Leaning in, I whisper, "I won't tell my dad, but you can't trust anyone else. Don't even trust me again."

Her jaw twitches as she clenches it. "Why won't you tell your dad?"

I flick my gaze to Evan. He's staring at me intensely, probably trying to read my lips. I don't let him though. Turning my face away, I whisper, "Because I wouldn't wish this life on anyone. Not even my worst enemy. I just wish there was something I could do to get you out of this mess. My hands are tied though. Malicevile already doesn't trust me. If I don't bring you in, he'll go after Cadence. I can't let that happen."

There is something I could do—let Jazmin go and run with Cadence, but am I willing to risk the outcome of getting caught? No. I'm not. The old Cami would've. The old Cami would've done so in an instant even for a stranger. But that Cami died and went to Hell.

"I don't need your help, Cami. We all make choices, and we all have to live with the outcome."

No one has ever been more right. I just hope Jazmin has a chance to live with the outcome of her decision.

DON'T BELONG TO HELL

I FLOOR THE gas pedal as I fly down the I-5 freeway fast enough to make Cadence squeal every time I switch lanes to pass up another slow—slow to me—vehicle. My eyes flick to the time on the stereo, and I have less than twenty minutes to get back to Malicevile with Jazmin. I've thought of a dozen excuses not to show up or to show up empty handed, but they all ended badly, not only for me, but also for both Cadence and Evan. It's not my fault she put herself in this situation. She knew better.

The green exit sign for Moonlight Shores reflects in the distance, and I jerk the wheel to cross four lanes, cutting off a semi in the slow lane who blasts his horn when I speed even faster to exit the quickly approaching off-ramp.

Cadence yells out a string of curse words as I race down the dark road without slowing down at the red light. I can see the beam of headlights from a car from the nearly nonexistent cross traffic and slam the brakes to slow us down enough to narrowly miss the back bumper of a white sedan.

Grinning, I meet Evan's eyes in the rearview mirror when I was meaning to check Jazmin's reaction. He wags his eyebrows a few times as I fly down the road along the ocean. In the heat and excitement of the moment, it's easy to forget that he's not on my side. God, if only he'd stop looking at me like that. He's so dang sexy, and there's nothing wrong with a little flirt—

A flash of light erupts in my vision, and I stomp the brake pedal as an ethereal figure blocks the road in front of me. Cadence screams, Evan swears, and Jazmin remains utterly silent as the tires squeal, sending the smell of burned rubber into the air.

The Mustang stops a few feet away from Dylan, who stands in the middle of the street, his bright wings unfurled and flapping behind him.

Without thinking, I slam the car into park and launch from the driver's seat. Rage darkens my vision as I rush toward Dylan with an energy orb glowing between my fingers. He bends his knees and launches into the air as I throw the electricity at him. It flies through the air before exploding on the hillside.

"Get back here and face me!" I scream.

A car door slams, and I twist to watch Evan climb from the backseat, pushing past Cadence as she remains by the open door.

Evan bolts in my direction at the same time Dylan dives toward me. As fast as Evan runs, he's still not faster than Dylan, who swoops down and grabs me by the shoulders. Angry tears trickle down my cheeks as I'm lifted a few feet into the air. Swinging my arms up, I lock my fingers around his wrists and shock him. It's enough for him to drop a few feet, but he still doesn't let go of me.

A blazing fireball zooms right past my face, colliding with Dylan's arm, and he yells out while dropping me. I hit the ground with a thud, too surprised to levitate, and Evan lifts me off my feet before tossing me over his shoulder.

Another flash of light blinds me as he spins back toward the car, and I watch in horror as two figures land near Cadence. She hesitates, her hands remaining by her sides, just gaping at the two angels, one with familiar, scary black wings and the other I've never seen before, another angel of the angelic army.

"Cadence, run!" I yell from my upside down position on Evan's shoulder.

But she doesn't move. She doesn't do anything, mesmerized by their heavenly grace that threatens to burn my corneas and leave me blind. With his free hand, Evan chucks a fireball right at the angels. It doesn't even get within a dozen feet of them as Zach flaps his giant wings, double the size of Dylan's, creating enough wind to knock the power off course.

"Don't you touch her!" I scream, still unable to say Zach's name out loud. "I swear if you even touch her, you'll regret it!"

Still ignoring me, the unfamiliar angel with Zach reaches his hand out to Cadence. Her eyes dart to me as they share a quiet conversation, but she doesn't move from her spot. Her arms move to cross over her chest. This isn't about her choosing between an angel and a demon now. She's choosing between a life with her best friend or one without.

Evan launches another fireball as we race closer. It skids across the ground and thumps into the tire of the Mustang before disappearing. Zach flaps his wings again, sending a gust of wind strong enough to make Evan stumble. With me on his shoulder, he can't keep his balance and we both crash backward. I somersault across the pavement in time to watch as my Demon Watcher reaches into my Mustang to help Jazmin out from the backseat.

I don't even have time to scream before warm hands lock under my arms and pull me back. Dylan drags me away from Evan toward the cliffs that overlook the ocean. If he can get me there, Evan can't follow.

Evan glances between me and the angels with Cadence and Jazmin, determining who's more important. I half expect him to pick Jazmin, since Malicevile will surely show his true body for this, but instead, Evan rushes toward me.

I thrash in Dylan's hold, squeezing my eyes shut every time his wings get a little too close as he struggles to take flight. "Why are you doing this? How could you do this to me?"

"I'm trying to save you, Cami," Dylan says, digging his fingers harder into my ribcage. "You don't belong to Hell."

"You lied to me. You betrayed me. You should've told me about—"

Strong hands grip my ankles, ripping me away from Dylan once more. Evan hits Dylan with another fireball, knocking him a few feet away. As Evan goes to launch another burst of power at Dylan, Dylan sweeps his wings forward, their light nearly knocking me out. A wail rips from my mouth as they come an inch from touching me. Evan yanks me back, blocking me with his body. His need to protect me outweighs his need to fight, and Dylan takes the opportunity to ascend high into the air.

A whistle sounds out, and I jerk my attention back toward my car where the unfamiliar angel launches into the air, holding Jazmin. Cadence and Zach wave their arms at each other, arguing, and it only takes one glance from Zach for me to know that he's not going to give Cadence a choice.

In one swift motion, he charges her, gripping her by the waist before launching into the air. Evan's weight presses me hard into the pavement as he breathes heavily into my ear, like he can somehow protect me from Heaven and Hell—from the universe.

Dylan disappears a moment later, leaving us alone on the ground. I push Evan off me, scrambling to my feet. Kicking the ground, I yell out in frustration. I can't believe this just happened. I can't believe a task so simple could have fallen apart. And now, my best friend is gone.

"You should've gone after them," I say, launching an energy orb into the air for no other reason than I want to blast something. "Now Cadence is gone."

"Are you kidding me, Cami?" Evan says, gripping my wrist. He pulls me closer to look into my eyes. "You're more important than they are. You're my world." His words hang heavy in the air.

"Please," I whisper. "You can't say things like that anymore."

"Why?"

"You're just making things harder for me."

"Like this is easy for me? Heaven's army is after you, Cami. Dylan is one of them. If they get to you, it's over for us. Forever. I can't follow you there. I'm not losing you." The desperation in his voice slices deep into my soul, opening me up even though I want nothing more than to remain cold and distant.

"Evan," I whisper.

He slides his arms around my shoulders. "Don't. I don't care if you don't want to be with me. I don't care if I can never kiss you again. I don't even care that you love Dylan. I need you here. You're the only thing that makes this all worth it."

I rest my head on his shoulder, breathing in his warm scent without saying a word. It's so easy to just be with him—always has been—and I wish the world would melt away so I don't have to think about all the wrongs going on in my life.

Zach isn't playing games anymore. He's not going to try to win my trust. He's gone full on battle mode, and now I'm really going to have to fight for my place in this twisted world. I'm going to have to stand up and be what I was transformed into if I'm ever to survive.

I've given up too much already.

I'm not giving up my life on earth.

WAIT FOREVER

"WHAT THE HELL do you mean you were ambushed?" Malicevile roars, his hot cinnamon breath blowing the messy curls from my face. "You're a demon, for Lucifer's sake!"

"It's not Cami's fault," Evan says from behind me. "They were heavenly, and we were outnumbered."

"Shut up!" he hollers at Evan. "I'm speaking to my daughter." Malicevile raises his hand and flicks a bout of electricity at Evan, causing him to stumble back into the wall.

Flying forward, I smash my hands into Malicevile's chest, pushing him back. "Don't touch him!" My voice cuts high through the air. "We tried our best. You think I wanted them to kidnap my best friend?"

"But how did they even know? Did Cadence tell them? I'll kill her, Camilla. I needed that demi-demon. Do you even know what her power is? Do you know how many connections she had?" Malicevile spins and sends a blast of power at the wall, setting one of Raphael's bookcases on fire.

I'm tempted to ask him what exactly is Jazmin's power, but I doubt now's the time to do so, not with the fire that's basically spewing from his intense glower.

None of us moves as we all watch the bookcase burn. It's not until the curtains on the window catch on fire next to it that Evan grabs a fire extinguisher to put out the mesmerizing flames.

Malicevile's question lingers in the air. He has no idea that I know Jazmin. He has no idea that she was the one who was helping me find him when he disappeared with Evan after saving my life. Every lead I had was because of her. She knows the Veiled Realm and everyone in it better than anyone.

I open my mouth to tell him that I do in fact know how many connections Jazmin has, but something deep down tells me not to. It's the doubt that prevents me from telling my father the real reason she made a deal with him—to find the missing demi-demons. She would've ended up in a terrible place had it not been for divine intervention, but I'm still pissed off because it happened on my watch, making it *my* fault. The punishment falls on me. And Zach, he stole my best friend. He didn't have to do that. Now it looks bad on Cadence.

"...the perfect addition to my army. The alliance is already floundering. Once they're gone, there's no stopping us." Malicevile grins with a spark in his emerald eyes.

I stare at my hands. "From what? I thought that was the goal? We punish the souls that need to be punished. We can do that when there aren't any more hunters."

Malicevile pauses, tilting his head to the side. "Camilla, this is only the beginning. With you, we'll start our own army here on earth with a new breed of demons under my command. The balance will forever shift to earth, so that even Lucifer will cower before me." He steps forward and gets into my face. "This is why collecting souls is so important."

He's told me that with collecting souls comes power, but I had no idea at what price. My father is crazy. He's not only trying to control earth. He's trying to control all of existence. "That's a pretty crazy plan. I didn't realize that your collection upsets the balance."

"It doesn't upset anything. They tilt the balance in our favor. Have you not listened to anything I've ever told you?"

I drop my gaze to the floor. I hate admitting that I haven't. I didn't really care about what Malicevile did while I was cut off from my humanity. All I cared about was being reckless, having fun, and being with Evan. I was an idiot.

"Of course I have," I say, lying. "I guess I should've started my own collection, huh?"

He grins. "That's the beauty of having me as your father. You get your strength and power from me. It runs in our blood.

Without me, you'd be nothing, Camilla."

Sure. Of course he takes all the credit for my occasional badassness. It annoys me more than it should. For being such an intelligent, calculated demon, he is delusional. It's like how he takes credit for my transformation. I don't argue otherwise. I don't have his needs. But, there is something I can take credit for. One he won't deny. "And you wouldn't have humanity without me," I quip, to remind him why he chose to pass on his evil genes in the first place.

He presses his lips into a thin line. "Which helps make all this possible. Without it, I'd never be able to work with Raphael. I wouldn't see reason. Demonic charm can go only so far. Humanity levels the playing field. Understand how humans work and you can control them without a problem."

And here I thought it was making him a more bearable dad.

"This is why it's so important that you're with me, Camilla. I know this is hard on you. I understand the allure of gallivanting around town with the boys you desire and of having what you must not. But there comes a time where you must stop acting like a child. This is our future. Do you really want to be responsible for messing up our eternity?"

"Of course not!" I throw my hands into the air. "It's not like I do any of this on purpose. If only I hadn't let Dylan—" I snap my mouth shut. I wasn't going to mention him because Evan hadn't yet.

"The nephilim?" Malicevile's expression turns hard.

I run my hands down my face. "Yes. He used my emotions to get to me. He doesn't think I belong to Hell. He thinks I'm *good.*"

He scoffs. "How insulting. So it's really over between you two?"

"There was never really an us, Dad," I say. "I wouldn't be here if there was."

The smile he gives me is enough to freeze my fiery heart. "Then you wouldn't mind if we show him how bad you really are?"

"What do you mean?"

"You'll see."

My heart hangs heavy in my chest, threatening to slip to the ground at any second. Spending the day in the light prison realm has done nothing to ease my fears and trepidation. If I didn't know any better, I'd think my transformation into a demon was only temporary. The place that used to numb it all did nothing for my emotions, though it didn't help that Malicevile kept his hand on my arm almost the entire day. If I wouldn't protest, he'd have probably tied me to him.

After my disappearing the last few times, he wasn't going to take any chances. As far as he's concerned, the entire universe is out to get me. I'm pretty sure that's all in his head. I'm not even that great of a demon. I don't have the charisma or leadership skills he does. I honestly think that Heaven wouldn't even be after me if Dylan weren't so entangled in my life. I've never heard about a demon being saved before. Seems silly. *You're unlike any demon...* Zach did say that himself.

"You're not coming inside?" Evan asks, strolling up next to me.

I've been standing on this spot on the beach, watching the twilight turn into night since the moment I returned from the daylight realm. If Malicevile knew that Dylan had swooped in and picked me up right off this beach before, he'd have never allowed me to watch the lapping waves while he makes a few phone calls.

"No, I don't think so." I step closer to the water, shoving my hands into the pockets of my leather jacket.

Evan casually hangs his arm over my shoulders. "You know, you might not believe me, but you can talk to me. I know something's bothering you."

I press my lips together. I consider making a snarky comment about his lie, because he has done nothing to show me he can keep a secret from Malicevile, but I don't. I've chosen to stay here. I've chosen my side. Evan is the only one I have left connecting me to my past. It's just hard to think that all the rest of the people who were in my life are on the opposite side. If Evan had never traded his soul to Malicevile, he'd be on that side, too. In this moment, eternity is feeling so lonely.

"How did you deal with it? Giving it all up." Because really, Evan and I aren't that different. Malicevile might be the reason he's here, but he chose this side, too. For me. It was like we were destined to follow our bloodlines to the side of Hell.

"Honestly?"

"You better not say I make it easy," I say.

He chuckles. "I wish that were true. You make it incredibly hard. When I first chose to trade my soul, I was prepared to suffer. It didn't take me long to turn off my humanity. To stop feeling. Your father is quite the bastard."

"Don't I know it?" I rest my head against him as we stare at the water.

"But it was still easier before you called in need of help. I honestly never dreamed you would call. I never saw you by your father's side. Ever." He doesn't answer my original question, but I decide not to ask again. Somehow, he manages, and I know I'll manage, too.

My bottom lip trembles with his words. "I've wasted everything."

I expect him to agree, but instead, he shifts to step in front of me so I have to look at him instead of the ocean. His blue eyes shine brightly, even in the fading light, and I yearn to see them in the sunshine again. I'd give anything for it, to drown in the blue of his eyes, to burn under their intensity.

"Don't say that, Cami. Our time now is not a waste. You're not a waste. Things are just different and unexpected. If David had succeeded in killing you, then that would've been a waste." He sucks in a shivering breath as he loses himself in the memory. "That moment, watching the light leave your eyes—it still haunts me."

I don't know what to say. I was in too much shock to ever

ask him what it was like for him. It's another reminder of how selfish I am. Maybe Malicevile isn't the delusional one after all. Maybe it's me.

"Watching you struggle every minute of the night, that haunts me, too. Because I know you're not happy. I hate that there's nothing I can do to make you happy either. I miss your smile."

"I still smile."

He shakes his head. "It's not the same thing."

"I'm not the same person."

Slowly lifting his hand, he brushes strands of my hair behind my ear. The heat of his touch awakens the desire I have for him in my soul, and I catch myself leaning forward, wondering if I could ever find what we had lost, what we both discarded. Because love isn't enough. Love is like a veil that hides all the missing pieces, the pieces we tore away from each other, the pieces the world dug free, the pieces that just couldn't stay in place any longer. It takes much more—like trust and understanding, hope and determination. Things we're—*I'm*—currently lacking.

Evan holds my gaze, waiting for me to make the next move.

I swallow and step back. As much as I want to kiss him, to feel him against me, to remember what it was like before the world turned dark, I can't. Kisses don't actually take away the pain. Evan's arms can't actually hold me together. Memories can't change the present.

"I'm sorry," I whisper. "I need time."

Evan nods. "I'll wait forever, you know."

I don't answer. How can I? He doesn't have forever. We'll never have our always.

"You don't believe me," he says. It's not a question.

"I'm immortal, Evan."

He reaches out and takes my hand. "And I will be one day, too."

My breath catches. I've been afraid of this ever since Malicevile threatened me. I was afraid Evan would want to try to go through the transformation. And how can I argue? How can I tell him that it's impossible? Heaven would never allow it. No angel will go to Hell to pull him away.

"Camilla, it's time." Malicevile's voice erupts over the ocean before giving me a chance to try to convince Evan to change his mind without having to tell him the truth about the matter—the truth he'd take directly to my father.

I don't drop my hand from Evan's. "Are you coming?"

He squeezes my fingers. "If you want me to."

"I do."

<hr>

"Are you on speaker phone, love?" Dylan asks, sending a long breath into the line. Voices hum in the background, and he sounds like he's somewhere public—a restaurant maybe? I don't know. I pray he doesn't tell me.

"Of course not." Glancing over my shoulder, I watch as Evan talks with Malicevile next to my Mustang. We're parked on an empty street just a few blocks away from downtown Moonlight Shores. Malicevile keeps his eyes trained on me, like I might suddenly disappear. It took a lot of convincing for him to let me call Dylan on my own. If he'd had his way, Dylan would be on speaker phone. But I can't say what I want with Malicevile listening.

"Your father doesn't give me much credit. If he thinks I'm going to fall for his games, he's going to be severely disappointed. I should hang up on you now for even agreeing to try to lure me to you." The line goes quiet, and if I hadn't heard him take another breath, I'd think he had hung up.

I clench my hand at my side. "You have a lot of nerve. You promised you wouldn't try to get to my soul, and then you show up with an angelic army. I wanted to leave, not be acquired like a piece of property, and that was before I found out about—damn it. Why can't I say his name?"

"For both of your safety. Talking to me on the phone isn't the same as being in person," he says. "And I think you overreacted."

"He lied to me. *You* lied to me!"

"I did not. I told you that you were reassigned."

"Why didn't you tell me it was the guy I thought was a demon?"

"Wasn't my place."

"But your place is trying to kidnap—"

Dylan groans into the phone, cutting me off. "I'm not doing this, love. You're all over the place, and I can't risk everything for you anymore."

Ouch. "Whatever, Dylan. I never asked you to. I wanted to be left alone. But then you came flying back into my life to ruin the only thing that made sense, and you went and stole my best friend. You said she'd be safe with me. You tell whoever you're working for that we aren't your little dolls to play with. I want Cadence back."

"It was no longer safe for her to be with you, Cami. Malicevile would've killed her, and you know it. She serves a different purpose now. If you want her back that badly, if you want to risk her life, then fine. You can have her back."

What? That was too easy. "What's the deal?"

"Just walk to the end of the block."

I've made a huge mistake. I was supposed to send Dylan a message before we started burning this town to the ground, before I did what my father told me to do. This was meant to be a warning that my being—my soul—is not up for negotiation and I've chosen my place in the world. If only it were that simple. But Dylan reminds me of who I was. He drags my humanity out of me—and I don't even kick and scream while he does it. Maybe he was right about my goodness all along—but that doesn't change things. I'm not losing my soul or my will to stay on earth no matter the consequences.

My fiery veins suddenly go cold as I process his words. I knew he was close by. Malicevile tracked down nearby angel activity through one of his contacts. I just didn't know how close he really was. Or that he was prepared for me to contact him.

Malicevile stops talking to Evan when I glance at him. He witnesses the wave of emotions that cross my face. I don't even have to tell him something's wrong. The angels are already a step ahead of us.

"I can't do that, Dylan," I whisper. "Please. You have to do something. You have to call them off. I don't want to fight."

"It's out of my hands."

Malicevile strides to me, ripping the phone from my hand. As he puts it to his ear, he snarls into the line, his face contorting as black horns cut through the skin of his forehead. A bright light flashes in my peripheral vision the same time I hear a thud as something lands on the roof of my car.

A strong body collides into me, pushing me to the ground as another flash of light cuts through the darkness. Evan's patchouli scent drifts into my nose as I peer through the hazy air at a figure standing on my Mustang.

An angel I don't recognize, a woman with honey tresses flowing in the wind of her blinding wings, jumps from the roof of my car to the hood. She opens her glowing hands and tosses a golden ball of light right at Malicevile.

The light doesn't get within feet of him before he launches his own energy orb at the angel. The orb hits my Mustang and a shower of sparks explodes, charring its pristine paint.

"Get her out of here!" Malicevile yells.

I'm already on my feet running as another ball of light hits the wall to my right. Another angel, the same one who was with

Zach before, flies overhead, circling like a hawk after his prey—but I'm no mouse. I'm a deadly snake. I'm not afraid to bite.

I launch an energy orb into the sky, but I don't stop to see if I hit my mark. Instead, I take Evan's hand and we run.

NOT OVER

"FASTER, CAMI!" EVAN yells, launching a fireball in an arc over his head.

I force myself to run as fast as I can, my feet pounding against the pavement. My heart slams into my ribcage, my lungs protesting with every gasp of breath. I don't think I ever ran this fast from Malicevile. He loves to play games. These angels, they mean business.

Evan weaves around parked cars, checking handles as we go. I'd hide in a building if it didn't mean we'd be trapped. If we could find protection from their attempts at torching me with their holiness, I could focus on attacking instead of fending them off.

A half a block ahead, a woman clicks her key fob, turning off the alarm on her SUV. As we dash toward her, she freezes in place, like an animal caught in the headlights of a car. Terror crosses her face, and she drops her purse on the sidewalk in her haste to get into her car.

Without hesitating, I send a small bolt of electricity at her as she touches the driver's side door. She yelps, jumping back. I can't let her get into the car. I need it more than she does.

"Keys!" I yell at her. "Now!"

Without protesting, she throws the keys in our direction, and Evan snatches them out of the air. The woman screeches as she turns on her heels and runs back inside the building she came out of. The rest of the street is utterly still—lifeless—like the world knows a demon is on the run.

Before Evan can reach the driver's door, a figure smashes into him, knocking him away from the SUV. A flash of light and fire burst in the air as Evan and his attacker tumble across the street. Evan quickly propels to his feet, hands flaming, prepared to attack.

My eyes shift from Evan to the figure, aglow in firelight, and my heart jerks. Dylan lies on the ground, sneering, his ethereal wings flapping forward against Evan. But Evan is a million times more skilled at fighting. He's trained all his life to fight and trained with the most powerful demon on earth.

Without thinking, I bend my knees and launch forward, grabbing Evan's shirt to yank him back. The fireball hits the ground next to Dylan. With a jerk of his arm, Evan elbows me in the ribs and flips me off him. He bares his teeth, his hands ablaze again, and then he stops mid-attack.

When our eyes meet, recognition lights his face. A wave of mixed emotions crosses his stern expression. Not only is he angry, he's afraid. Quickly pulling himself together, he lifts me to my feet, glancing once more at Dylan, who's standing again.

"I spared you, Angel Boy. Now don't follow us," I say. "I'm not making a habit of protecting you."

Before I can run, a blast of light hits the ground near my feet. As the heavenly light seeps through my jeans, my legs burn, but it's not enough to stop me. I push through the pain, letting Evan drag me away.

We barely make it to the end of the block before Dylan lands in front of us. Evan's about to plow through him when I tug him to turn around to dash in the other direction. As much as my mind tells me that Dylan and I aren't on the same side, that he wants nothing more than to destroy my chance at eternity, I can't hurt him. My heart won't allow it. I don't know what will happen to me if they take my soul. I'm too impure for Heaven, probably too good for Hell. Maybe I just won't exist. If that happens, how could I even care? The thought is enough to freak me out. I like existing, like it a lot.

A thud resonates as another figure lands in front of us, blocking our path. When Zach stretches out his magnificent black wings, the scent of jasmine hits me before they disappear again. If touching his wings wouldn't cause me a massive amount of pain, I'd force him to show them again so I could pluck each and every black feather free—the pain might even be worth it. It wouldn't be the first time a demon ripped off an angel's wings. My father kept a pair of his own Demon Watcher's on the wall at our estate down in the valley.

"Princess," he says. "I thought I had you all figured out, but you keep surprising me."

I glower as an energy orb erupts in my fingers. I don't give Zach time to brace himself before I chuck it in his direction, hitting him in the chest. Smoke billows from his burned T-shirt, displaying the tight muscles of his chest and abs. Stupid attractive angel showing off his glorious body, one not unlike... *Pull yourself together!*

"Hopefully in a bad way, you jerk." A whole slew of curse words stream through my mind. If I thought I could sully his purity with my demon-tainted mouth, I would.

"Princess."

"Suck it, poser." I flip him off for good measure.

His brows furrow as heavenly light erupts in his hands. He's trying to scare me, but I'm not backing down. Actually, he looks pathetic in his teal T-shirt with the design burned off. Lifting his hand, he shoots his ethereal light at me faster than I expect. Evan shoves me out of the way before it can plow into me, but the light knocks him off his feet. Groaning, he slumps onto the pavement. Fear blazes through me.

As I watch the boy I love suffering from the burst of heavenly power, anger wells within me. Crimson edges my vision, and I feel my true body breaking free from my human form. My skin stings with each pop of black bone that juts out, showing off the true demon I am. How dare Zach come into my life to try to change my destiny? How dare this angel think he can get away with touching Evan?

Rushing toward Zach, I ram my shoulder into his chest, knocking him backward. He catches himself on the side of a car. I close the distance again and pop him in the jaw with a right hook hard enough to jerk his head to the side, and then knee him in the stomach to knock the wind from him. He doesn't even try to fight back, which pisses me off more.

Shaking out my hand, I meet Zach's annoying gaze. "Why won't you fight back?"

He raises his hands in surrender. "Princess, please. I don't want to hurt you."

"Are you kidding me? You want to rip my soul away! Isn't that why you're here? Because in your mind a demon doesn't deserve a soul. I don't deserve any of this."

His jaw tightens. "You're right, Cami. You don't deserve any of this."

It's enough to send me over the edge. "I'll destroy you, Zach!" I turn to glance at Dylan. "I'll destroy you both!"

With my words comes a huge gust of wind, the power I had absorbed from my demonic kidnapper. Except now that I've had a chance to use it, it doesn't feel foreign to me. Not like Malicevile's or Evan's. It feels like it's my own power, and it feels unlimited. Killing the upper-level demon not only sent him to Hell, it left him powerless. His power is now mine.

Zach stumbles in the wind, trying to launch into the air. As I watch him, I summon Malicevile's power, swirling it in my fingers. When Zach jumps into the air and expands his wings, I throw my hands out, blasting the energy orb at him. It hits his leg, sending him reeling through the dark night. He crashes into the side of a building with a loud thud before toppling to the ground.

I inhale a deep breath, my chest heaving, but it does nothing to suppress the animosity coursing through my veins and burning in my soul.

I turn to Dylan, fire raging within me. He stares at me with the saddest eyes I've ever seen but says nothing. Tears burn in my eyes. Dylan betrayed me more than anyone. He was the only person on Heaven's side that I could trust. I thought he was incapable of turning against me, but then again, I'm responsible for breaking his heart. For turning my back on him and pushing him away. My thoughts hurt so much I can't look at him. His presence alone is enough to send me sobbing to my knees, begging for someone—anyone—to make this all stop. But I can't give up. I was never one to give up, even if the world felt against me.

I glance around the area for more threats. Zach remains on the ground in a heap of smoldering clothes, yet Dylan only watches me. It's not until I know I'm not going to have to fight for my life that I turn my eyes to the body lying on the ground.

My heart splinters as I rush toward Evan and kneel next to

him. He lies on his back, his skin pink from the burst of angelic light. His chest rises and falls, and it's the only thing that keeps me from falling apart completely.

Cupping his face, I lean over him. "Evan? Evan, wake up. Please." He doesn't respond to my voice. Moving my hands to his shoulders, I give him a few good shakes, feeling the intensity of Heaven's power as it clings to his skin. Dragging him away from here seems an impossible task, but I refuse to leave him behind. "Evan, please."

Tears blurring my vision, I continue to shake him. Footsteps echo behind me, and I jerk my head up to see Dylan freeze in his spot. I glare through my wet eyelashes at him while raising my hand, motioning him to stay back.

"Don't come near me. This is your fault." My voice deepens with anger. "I *hate* you."

"Cami..."

I shake my head. "Don't. You know I'd never dream of hurting you and look what you've done to me. Evan was right. If you had ever loved me, you'd have never hurt me. You wouldn't even be here. You'd have just left me alone."

"That's not fair, love." He rubs his hands down his face.

"Like this is fair?"

Evan shifts under me, drawing my attention back to him. He blinks a few times and turns his gaze to me. Combing my fingers through his golden locks, I brush strands from his forehead. He quirks a smile, one that sends my heart racing, and I bend down and kiss him. I can't help it. I don't even resist. It wasn't until I thought I lost him that I realized how stupid I was being for trying to distance myself from him. Evan's always been on my side even when we weren't even on the same team. He's been here for me even when I hurt him, even when I didn't want him to be with me.

"You scared the Hell out of me," I say, laughing through my kisses.

Evan leans his head back to look at me. Reaching up, he rubs his finger across the dainty crown of horns on my head. "I can see that."

Tears burst from my eyes as a flood of emotions threatens to drown me. Evan wraps his arms around my shoulders, hugging me against him for a long moment before I pull away.

As Dylan launches into the air, his wings create a stiff breeze. A flash of light blinds me, and I cover my eyes for a second. The scent of apple and rain wafts toward me on the wind before he disappears into the dark night.

I take Evan's hand. "Come on. We need to go. It's not over."

"You're right, princess." The sound of Zach's voice slices straight through my body to cut deep into my soul.

Strong hands wrap around my waist, and Zach tries to yank me away from Evan. I scream, my voice echoing through the air. My fingers remain locked on Evan as Zach pulls me. Evan is strong, but Zach is stronger. If Evan tries to launch a fireball at him, he'd break our hold.

Zach yanks me hard, and my shoulder screams. I'm pretty

sure it's been dislocated. Evan swears, losing his grip on me, but it's no use. Zach launches into the air, and I'm forced to let go of Evan as freezing air wraps around me, sending steam from my burning skin.

A fireball careens through the air in our direction, but Zach quickly maneuvers out of the way. There's no stopping him. Zach's grip is too tight, and we're flying too high.

I scream once more, thrashing as hard as I can to break free. I don't care if I'll freefall back to the ground. I'll accept breaking all of my bones as long as it means I'm no longer in the strong arms of this stupid angel.

"I swear to God you're going to pay," I say, digging my sharp nails into his wrists.

"Those are some tough words, princess," Zach says in my ear. "Now relax. This is going to be a long ride."

I scream again.

In a quick motion, he covers my eyes with his hand. The last thing I see is Evan launch one last fireball into the air before the world disappears.

SCORNED

UGH. NOT NOW. Why can't this traitor, life destroyer, son of a fallen angel bastard take a hint and leave me the Hell alone. The last thing I need now is his vomit-inducing angelic company. I'd rather stay lost in the darkness my own soul creates. Maybe if I concentrate hard enough, that darkness will grow some teeth and devour Dylan's soul whole so he'll leave me alone.

I can sense him hovering over me, his dewy apple scent demanding that I know he's here to bother me, though I won't allow myself to open my eyes. I can't disappear from my own mind, but I sure as heck can pretend that none of this exists.

I'm stubborn, and I'll not let him try to seduce me into his arms again, especially while the edges of my broken soul cut deeply enough to hurt me even in this dream state.

"Cami."

Nope. Not going to happen. *Don't do it, Cami. You're a powerful demon. He's beneath you. He's garbage. He's worse than garbage. He's crap. A big pile of hellhound crap.*

"I'm not going away." Dylan's soft voice caresses my ears, but it doesn't send my heart beating wildly. His voice only makes it hurt, like my soul is squeezing it so tightly that it'll turn into an unbreakable stone. "I know you're angry right now, but—"

I swing my leg out in the direction where the scent of apples is the strongest and kick as hard as I can. My boot connects with what I think is Dylan's knee, and I hear a satisfying thump landing near me.

"Angry doesn't describe how I'm feeling!" I scream before shutting my mouth. *Don't interact. Don't fall for his antics. He's trying to get you to talk.*

I roll over and rest my head on my arms, sniffing the imaginary ground that smells like nothing. Dylan's fingers wrap around my calf, and I shake my leg to make him let go. No way in Hell am I going to let him touch me.

"I'm sorry," he says after a moment.

I considering making him tell me why, but I hold strong.

"I just—I don't understand you, Cami. And the harder I try to, the more lost I feel."

Okay, I can't resist him. "I'd never expect you to understand, Dylan. You've always thought you knew what was best for me, but have you ever considered that you don't know me at all?"

His hand rests on my back, and I reach up and flick it away. He's unrelenting. "I know you are torn between what you think you are and who you are. I can't say I know what it feels like being a demon, but I know that it's not all that you are. You're lost, and you feel that everyone is trying to control your life like you're some puppet. You care about the people you hold dearly. A demon wouldn't have spared my life. A demon wouldn't have cried over Evan."

"But I am a demon."

"You're so much more. Why can't you see that?"

Damn him and his deep conversations. Like any of it matters anyway. Who knows if I'm even still alive? Maybe this is Dylan's way to help me find peace with myself before he sends my soul wherever it is I'm going. Maybe this is it.

I turn my head to the side and peer at Dylan sitting next to me, his palms flat on the ground with legs outstretched. He doesn't even face me, his back inches away. He probably can't stand to look at me in this moment. All he thought he knew about me has been tossed to the wind, scattered in the universe. It's heartbreaking to think you know and love someone, only to discover you've been seeing them through a veil that has been suddenly ripped away. I should know. It's exactly how I feel about him.

"Even if I was more, even if I wasn't just a demon's daughter, it doesn't change anything. So what if I have a soul or my stupid humanity? All it does is make my life harder. I'm still a creature of Hell. I'm not *good*." I've done some unthinkable things. I tried to destroy an angel, and I'm not even sorry. That's pretty unforgivable.

Dylan doesn't respond. He just sits with his back facing me. I'd give anything to see the look on his face.

After a long moment of silence, I finally get the nerve to ask the question that's been on my mind. "So, what now? What happens to me now?"

He shrugs. "I don't know, love."

"Or do you just not want to tell me? Come on, Dylan. I deserve to know what's happening to me, don't you think?" If I'm about to die or disappear or whatever, I want the chance to figure out how to say goodbye to those I'm leaving in the rubble of the calamity that I call my existence. The thought burns me to my core—that I might not get to make amends with those I've hurt or face those who've scorned me with dignity. It can't end like this. I refuse to believe it.

"Of course I think you deserve more than what you've been given." Dylan taps his fingers on the ground. "Why do you think I'm here?"

"To rub salt in my wounds."

He laughs, but it's not lighthearted or funny. It's filled with something darker. "I'm here because I promised to always look after you."

I shift again to stare at the darkening sky. "My self-appointed guardian angel, always here to try to heal the broken pieces." There isn't any sarcasm in my voice. Sitting here reminds me of a time that feels like a million years ago. It's comforting to know that this hasn't changed.

"Do you remember what you told me at the academy? The day I took you to see Annabelle?"

I haven't thought about the forest nymph since the night I transformed. "No," I say quietly. "I don't like to think about those times."

Dylan finally shifts to look down at me. Sunlight halos his dark curls, and his eyes hold such intensity, I can't keep his gaze more than a few seconds. "You yelled at me for always trying to fix you. You said you were a demi-demon, not broken. And you were right. You're a demon, but that doesn't mean you're broken or need to be saved. You just need to figure out what it is you really want out of all this."

Hello, guidance counselor Dylan. I bite my tongue before I call him that. "What I want doesn't matter. Unless you know how to turn back time..." My voice trails off.

"If only I'd never gotten on that bus."

I blink a few times at his words. He's referring to the first time I saw him, the day that changed my entire life. He's responsible for dragging me deeper into the Veiled Realm, though if he hadn't I'm sure something else would have. Malicevile would not have waited forever. He just jumped at the opportunity Dylan had created.

"You regret meeting me that much?" I ask. This conversation has been a long time coming.

He sighs. "I regret a lot of things, but meeting you isn't one of them."

The world suddenly flashes in and out like someone is messing with a light switch. Dylan fades with the light and panic rushes through me for a brief moment when it takes him an extra few seconds to reappear.

"Whoa, what was that?" I can't stop myself from reaching out to him.

"I have to go."

I scramble to wrap my arms around him, burying my face in his chest. "Don't leave me. I'm scared."

He squeezes me. "Be brave, Cami."

Oh, my God. Is this it? Holy crap. *No. No. No.* "Dylan..." Tears spring from my eyes, and I start sobbing. "Please. I'm sorry."

I blink as he fades from existence without another word. The bright sun overhead slides across the sky, disappearing into the horizon, leaving me in darkness. For the first time in a long time, I bow my head. I don't know why I do it. I feel so utterly alone, and I doubt anyone can hear me.

But I can't stop myself.

I close my eyes, and I pray.

A mixture of scents assaults my nose as I'm pulled from the dark recesses of my own demented mind. Wet cement, mildew, charred fabric, and a hint of jasmine permeates the air, giving me a massive headache. My neck is stiff and aches when I try to lift my head. I couldn't see anything if I wanted to though, because my dark hair hangs across my face, shielding me from the world.

I can't move my hands either. At least they don't burn. I expected more from an army of angels. Surely the entire place is blessed, leaving me without an escape. But in this moment, I don't give a crap that I'm stuck in some smelly room. Because I'm alive. Waking up like this was the last thing I expected.

"Hello?" I call out. My voice falls flat. I'm somewhere enclosed and small.

A few minutes later, the air shifts as I hear what I assume is a door swinging open. A soft light cuts through my curly tresses, blinding me for a second before my vision adjusts. Sniffing the air, I inhale a long breath of a familiar yet terrifying scent: jasmine.

I scream. Thrashing in my chair, I buck back and forth, my voice bouncing off the cement walls. I levitate forward before my chair yanks back, toppling to the floor with me still in it. Air whooshes from my lungs, cutting off my screams, and pain bursts in my shoulder as it hits the hard ground.

"Princess, are you okay?"

I gaze through blurry eyes up at Zach. I close my eyes, swallowing my fear. Any sort of response stays lodged in my throat, and I wonder if I can choke and die on unsaid words.

He kneels next to me and prods his fingers against my aching shoulder. "I'm going to untie you, but you have to promise you won't try to hurt me. If you do, I'll just knock you out and keep knocking you out until you comply."

I remain frozen as he picks me and the chair off the floor and sets me upright like I'm as light as one of the inky black feathers of his wings. When he bends forward, his jasmine scent overpowers my senses, and I'm sure I'll never get the sweet fragrance off my skin.

My arms fall to my sides like two overcooked noodles. "Thank you," I whisper, my voice barely audible.

Zach unties my feet and remains kneeling at my side. "You're welcome."

I bow my head again without meeting his hazel eyes. What fight I had in me has fizzled out completely, and exhaustion threatens to send me sprawling to the floor. I'd consider trading my soul for a soft bed I could curl up on and sleep like a human. I doubt my mind would let me though.

Zach rests his hand on my knee. "I want to apologize for last night. I know you're scared."

Terrified is more like it.

"And I know you're thinking the worst," he continues, "but I want you to trust me. I care very much about what happens to you, and I'm not ready to give up on you, princess."

"Is Malicevile dead?" I ask instead of trying to decipher what he's saying. He's ridiculous if he thinks I'm going to trust him. Trust must be earned. And caring about me? He doesn't even know me. Why should he care?

Zach pulls his hand from my knee and crosses his arms. "Would it matter?"

I suck on my bottom lip to keep calm. I'm doing exceptionally well, if I do say so myself. "Of course it matters. He possesses a soul that's very important to me."

"Oh."

"What did you think I was going to say?"

"It doesn't matter. And to answer your question, if Malicevile could be killed so easily, we'd have taken care of him long ago."

Covering my face with my hands, I start to sob. And once I start sobbing, I can't stop. My chest heaves, and my aching shoulders shake. I gasp short breaths, while tears spill onto my dirty jeans, and hair clings to my wet cheeks.

Wrapping his strong arms around me, Zach hugs me and pats my back. He shushes me, holding me against his firm chest until I can't cry anymore.

"God, this is so stupid. I'm a freaking evil demon crying onto an angel's shoulder. What is going on in the world?" I wipe my runny nose on my sleeve before pulling away. Embarrassment heats my face even hotter than it already is. I'd walk away if I wasn't sitting in this dang chair with him blocking me.

He laughs, the melodious sound for once calming me. "It's pretty funny if you think about it."

"Stop trying to make me feel better. I'm still incredibly pissed off at you. If I weren't so drained, I wouldn't be so complacent."

"I'm sure. You're a little spitfire, Cami." Zach pushes my messy hair from my face.

I wish he wouldn't though. The calmer I become, the grosser I feel, and the more uncomfortable and self-conscious I get.

"And I don't think it's because you're a demon. That's all you."

"Okay." I don't know what else to say. I'm not a sucker for compliments. He can dance around the matter at hand all he wants, but my patience is wearing thin. "Not to be rude, but I'm tired and in pain, and I'm sure the sun's going to come up soon, so will you just get whatever it is you're going to do to me over with?"

"It's more complicated than that, princess. And the sun just set. We have all night."

My brows crinkle in confusion. "What? I don't under-stand."

"You can't tell me you actually like hanging out in the sun realm," he says. "That place is so boring. You know, most De-mon Watchers don't ever visit there. I did it because of you."

"Stop skipping around the subject, Zach. Either tell me why you felt the need to rip me from my life to imprison me in this dreadful room or just leave me alone."

He blows a breath through his lips. "You're not going to like it."

"Probably not, but I don't like most things anymore."

This gets a chuckle out of him, but he still doesn't answer.

I push him away. "Get out and come back when you're not so scared to talk to me."

He scoffs. "I'm not afraid of you or your power. I just happen to like the shirt I'm wearing. Either you really hate all my clothes, or you really enjoy seeing what's under them."

What. The. Hell. "Get out! I mean it."

He rises to his feet. "Fine, princess, but first things first."

"The reason you're here."

He nods. "I want you to let me into your soul."

I blink in surprise. I expect him to laugh and tell me he's joking, but he holds the most serious expression, all brooding with lowered brows and a tight jaw.

Narrowing my eyes, I yell, "Are you insane? You seriously think I'm going to just let you near the only thing I have left? Get out."

He reaches out and grips my shoulders. "Cami, listen. It's the only way any of this is going to work out. Just give me permission to check out your soul. I promise I'll be careful, and I won't hurt you."

Letting Zach near my soul is a little too intimate for my liking. It's like allowing him to see me naked, and I've only let one person see me so vulnerable. "You're not going to like what you see. It might ruin your purity."

I didn't think angels could blush. "I highly doubt that."

"I'm just warning you."

"So, are you giving me permission?"

"Will it get me out of here?"

He nods.

"Fine. I give you permission. But no funny business, and you have thirty seconds."

"I only need ten."

"Okay. Get it over with."

He slowly raises his hands and presses them to my chest above my heart. We lock eyes for a long moment but not in the get-lost-in-each-other's-eyes type of stare. This is a battle of wills, one I'm having a hard time giving up. But I have to.

After a long moment, I suck in a deep breath, opening my whole being up to the angel who sits in front of me. An uncomfortable pull yanks at my chest, stealing my breath away. Angelic light glows from Zach, burning my eyes, threatening to burn my soul.

A sudden, sharp pain radiates through my body. I scream and collapse into my Demon Watcher's arms.

Then all I see is light.

NEUTRAL

I BLINK IN and out of consciousness. Voices hum around me, though too softly for me to understand. The temperature shifts from warm to cold to warm again. An array of scents dance around my nose—the ever-present jasmine, juicy mango, dew-dampened grass, plump strawberries, zesty bergamot, sweet honeysuckle—a collection of light and airy fragrances I'm sure are attached to ethereal beings with achingly beautiful wings. Sucking in a deep breath, I hope to catch a whiff of rain and apple, but it's not here.

Strong arms hold me close as the world rocks with the squeak of sneakers on over-polished tiles. My dirty hair hangs in my face, blocking the world that flashes by as I'm moved from one fragrant room to the next.

I lose consciousness for another few seconds—disappearing into utter blackness and silence—before the world breaks through again, begging me to stay in it.

My cheek presses against a hard chest covered in soft cotton, and I rest my hands under my chin, folded in on myself. My entire body hurts with a pain I haven't felt in a while. It's enough to make me thrash about.

"Shhh, it's okay, princess," Zach whispers into my ear. "I got you."

I groan. "Put me down. I can walk." Now that my senses have finally returned, I realize that I'm being relocated within a place filled with angels. And I want to see where I'm going, even if I have to drag myself across the floor to get to our destination. Being carried like this makes me look weak when I need to look strong, even though I only have enough strength to mutter empty threats.

Zach sighs but doesn't argue. A second later, he sets me on my feet. I flick back my hair, tucking the maddening wild mane of curls behind my ears before I glance around an expansive room filled with unfamiliar people. The high, domed ceiling looks straight out of an art history book. Its mural is comparable to the ones that covered the walls of the academy's older buildings. A mixture of fire and light, the image depicts what I can only describe as a battle between Heaven and Hell with a whole bunch of anonymous bodies in between.

Shifting my gaze, I glance at the gold ornate fixtures glowing with soft light against large stained-glass windows. I'll never see the colorful glass as it was imagined since the sun will never shine through it for me. Maybe it's best I don't think about it.

When I shift my gaze once more, I finally find the bravery to look at the people in the room and meet the curious eyes of dozens of angels. Everyone is blatantly staring at me like I'm some wild animal brought in to be put on display. The annoyed part of me wants to give them the show they probably expect, but one look at Zach tells me that doing so is probably a terrible idea.

I stand on my tiptoes instead of levitating. "How am I here?" I whisper. This place is sacred. I can feel the sting in my bones yet I'm not blasted away.

"You get a free pass because of me. Not sure how long it'll last. Depends on you."

Right. Maybe that's why they're all staring at me, waiting to watch the outcome of a demon on sacred grounds. Fun. "Can you tell them it's rude to stare?"

"Maybe if you'd pull yourself together and put your horns away," Zach says back.

Oh, unholy Hell. Raising my hand to my head, I run my fingertips across the sharp points of my true body. I didn't even realize I was showing myself for the world to see.

Swallowing my embarrassment, I say, "Sorry. Must be instinctual. You could've said something sooner, jerk."

Zach smirks as he taps my now smooth forehead. "Sorry,

princess. It doesn't bother me any."

I roll my eyes. "Whatever. I always knew you were twisted."

Sliding his fingers around my elbow, he guides me down the center of the room that seems to have parted just for us. If everyone wasn't watching, I'd drag my feet and limp because my legs ache from being bound. Something dark nags at me, whispering that I shouldn't let them see me broken. It also urges me to run away, to get out of here. I don't belong.

Zach uses his free hand to push open a heavy wooden door that leads into a warm hallway that looks like something you'd find in a hotel. Wood framed paintings line the gray walls, and a dark blue floor runner extends the length of the tiled hallway. Numbers hang above the wooden doors; we stop in front of lucky number thirteen.

Zach raises his hand and knocks.

"What are you doing?"

"I thought you could use some familiar faces before I tell you what's going on," he says, pressing his lips together without meeting my gaze.

My heart clenches. "Is this about my soul? I failed whatever you were looking for, right? Is this you letting me say goodbye?"

Before Zach can answer, the door swings inward, and I steel myself for a second before I meet Cadence's honey-brown eyes. She squeals as she thrusts her arms around me and drags me into the room so fast that we both fall on the floor.

I half laugh and groan as I hit the carpet next to my best

friend. She tackles me again, rocking us back and forth on the floor as she talks too fast for me to understand. Tears prickle in my eyes because I didn't know if I'd ever see her again, but I'm so happy that she's here and not alone with Malicevile.

"Take it easy, Cadence," a masculine voice says from the corner of the room.

I was so caught up in my best friend's attention that I didn't even smell the apples. I stiffen in Cadence's arms, tilting my head back to draw my gaze to Dylan, who perches on the arm of a sleek, uncomfortable-looking upholstered chair. A whirlwind of emotions rushes over me, and I turn away without acknowledging him with even a second glance. I can't help it. It's even weirder being with him in person.

Someone else clears their throat from a small couch, and I meet Alana's steely gray eyes. She sits back on the couch with her knees pulled to her chest and her bare feet sliding between the cushions. I haven't seen her since she stabbed me through the heart. Quite frankly, I'm shocked she's even here.

Seeing what's left of my family sends a deep ache into my heart. The absence of Evan is like a gaping hole in the center of my chest. David's absence doesn't go unnoticed either, because I recognize his wedding band on a chain around Alana's neck.

Zach steps into the room and quietly closes the door. Instead of helping me off the floor, he plops down right next to me, stretching his long legs in front of him. His tan T-shirt with a screen-printed picture of a bacon-and-eggs smiley face is stained, and his jeans have seen better days, too, with singed bottoms and ripped knees. He lounges back while he watches me, and I wish someone would say something to ease the awkward silence.

But everyone's waiting on me.

I turn to Zach. "Is this where I say goodbye? That's why you brought me to see them, right?"

"What?" Cadence says, sitting up.

Dylan gets to his feet.

Alana sucks in a breath.

Zach palms his forehead. "No, you're fine, princess. Your soul is just as I suspected."

"What do you mean?"

"It's neutral."

Huh? What does that even mean? By the looks on everyone's faces, no one is sure what that means either, and if they do, they're sure hiding it well from me. Except Dylan. A smile pulls across his face, flashing his dimples. It's been a while since I've seen him smile like that, and it pulls at my heartstrings. *Stop looking at him.*

Zach flicks my arm. "Neither side has a claim on your soul."

Frowning, I hold my hand to my chest. "That can't be right. I'm Hell-bound. I know I am. I've *been* there. It was quite welcoming."

Zach rubs a hand on the back of his neck. "Things change, Cami."

"But she's still a demon...right?" Alana speaks for the first time since I've entered the room.

"Yeah," I answer for Zach. No denying those dainty horns I was sporting not long ago. Inhaling a deep breath, I summon power between my fingers. Flames dance in my palms. "Definitely still a demon." I ache just a little seeing Evan's power within my hands.

"I don't understand," Alana argues. "How does this change things? What difference does this make? Cami is still loyal to her father. She made that quite clear. Bringing her here was a huge risk."

Way to stab the knife in my chest even deeper, Alana. Go ahead, twist it around while you're at it. Anger coils in my mind as I glower at my old guardian. I thought maybe she could move past this, but she's clinging to her hatred so much that I can see the black streaks cutting through her soul. I don't mean to look at it, but it calls to me. I can't help it.

I sneer. "Why is she even here? She'll stab me in the back the moment she has the opportunity."

Alana leaps from the couch. "Are you kidding me?"

If I didn't think someone would tackle me, I'd jump to my feet to face her. It takes a good amount of concentration to ignore her mesmerizing soul. "You act like you're this perfect person, fighting the good fight and all that, but guess what, Alana? You're not even fighting on the team your soul wants to be on."

Her eyes widen.

I straighten my shoulders. "What? No one told you?" Shifting my eyes to Dylan, I catch his gaze. He subtly shakes his head. His response does nothing to stop me from uttering my next words. "You're the one who's now Hell-bound. You have been since the night of my transformation. I wanted to take your soul that moment, but I didn't. But you know what, I'm kind of in the mood for a deal now."

Fury flashes in Alana's eyes, and I expect her to fly across the room to attack me. Everyone else is utterly quiet. Zach's black wings unfurl on his back, and Cadence tenses next to me, like she's ready to grab me if I try to move.

But Alana only covers her face and cries a long, loud wail that rips right through me, knocking all thoughts of her soul from my mind. Dylan crosses the room to pull Alana against him. Unfurling his achingly beautiful wings, he flaps them forward to wrap around her.

Shading my eyes, I turn away from the blinding light. As I watch Dylan comfort Alana in a way I so desperately want to comfort her, my bottom lip trembles. I never wanted our relationship to turn out like this. I never wanted her to feel such extraordinary pain and loss. I never wanted her to fall to the side of Hell like I have...or had.

I press my hands into the soft carpet to push to my feet, but Zach locks his fingers around my wrist, holding me in place. His brows furrow as he gazes at me, speaking a thousand silent words. He knows as well as I do that anything I say will be wrong. Not to mention that getting anywhere near Dylan will leave me branded.

After a long moment, Alana's cries fall silent, and Dylan's

shining wings disappear. I blink the spots from my eyes. It feels so wrong for me to be here, in this place, that my skin crawls. The air grows thick, suffocating me, and an easy breath is suddenly hard to come by.

I lick my parched lips. "I shouldn't be here."

Zach doesn't let go of me. "You really shouldn't have done that, princess. Just take a breath. The residual effect of being so close to the nephilim is messing with you. Give it a second."

I cover my hands over my face. "Please, I need some fresh air. I'm going to be sick." Or burned from all the holiness.

"I can't let you leave. Not yet."

"Then when? I'm serious, Zach." My hands tremble as I dig my fingers into the carpet for something to grip onto. "You have to get me out of this place. I might not be going at Hell at the moment, but Heaven sure isn't calling my name either." Shadows crowd my vision as the world begins to spin. Whoa.

Cadence touches my face and says something I don't understand. I lean heavily against her, and Zach touches his cold fingers to my face. He cups my cheeks and looks deep into my eyes.

"Focus, princess. Stay with me." He blurs in and out of focus. "I can make this stop, but you have to give me your soul."

I blink. "Just get me out of here."

"I can't do that. Will you please just trust me with your soul?"

I lean back, staring at the ceiling as a golden haze dances around my vision. "What do I get out of it?"

"Princess, it can't be a deal. You have to give it to me willingly."

My whole body starts to burn. This isn't just from Dylan's wings. This is more. The whole place is turning against me. It's rejecting me because of who I am. Whatever Zach was doing to protect me from the blessed building before has suddenly worn off.

"What's happening to me?"

"Hell's trying to pull your soul back, and you're allowing it to."

No, I'm not. Am I? Is that what I want? The world blinks in and out. I'm getting really annoyed that I keep passing out. What kind of demon passes out?

"Princess, please. You have to trust me. I'm not letting Hell get you back. I need you. We all need you. Give me your soul."

Fear clenches my chest. Not because Zach is begging me to give him my soul, but because the thought of Hell trying to force me back into its fiery depths terrifies me. But willingly giving up the only thing left that's still me? This sucks.

My skin starts to smolder in reaction to the sacred place, and even the air burns when I gasp. "Why?" I manage to ask. "No more lies. I want the truth. Why am I so important to you?"

"There's no time to explain."

A scream rips from my mouth. "Tell me!"

"Malicevile," Zach says a second later. "We need you to destroy your father. Now, give me your soul."

Closing my eyes, I try to process his words. They're ridiculous, but the pain is too intense to laugh. I'm no match for my father. They'll learn their lesson though.

"Cami! Please!" It's Dylan. I've never heard him so scared before. It's enough to jolt my eyes open.

"Okay," I whisper, staring into Zach's eyes. "You can have it."

With heavenly light shining in his hazel eyes, Zach nods and wraps me in his wings.

And like that, the pain stops.

All of it.

I'm officially Heaven-bound.

FIGHT FOR HEAVEN

ALL I WANT is a moment alone to process everything. My head swims with the knowledge that both Heaven and Hell now officially have a part of me. It just couldn't be a simple switching of sides—oh, no. My mind and body still carry Hell with Malicevile's blood running through my veins. There's no getting around that. Not even a blood transfusion can take away my demonic birthright. I know because I've asked.

Zach and I remain on the carpet in Suite 13. Dylan, Cadence, and Alana left us shortly after Zach marked my soul for Heaven because I was caught on a dangerously emotional wave adjusting to the sudden change occurring within me. It's strange—my emotions don't run so hot and out of control anymore. I can think clearer.

"Can you tell me what happens now, or are you going to force me to do your bidding?" Annoyance lines my voice. I can't help it. Malicevile is a scary demon. He might've tortured me for years, but he never gave me an ultimatum like this. While I'm not as upset as I should be, this was a sneaky, manipulative move on Zach's part.

"It wasn't supposed to be like this, princess. I'm sorry. You just chose the wrong moment to bring out your demonic ways," Zach says, peering at his hands.

"So this is my fault now?"

"I didn't mean it like that." He draws his knees to his chest. "It's my fault if it's anyone's. This is a tricky, unheard of situation, and I'm flying blindly. I admit, I did handle things wrong, but I thought I was doing the right thing at the time."

"You mean by lying?"

He nods. "I couldn't exactly tell you who I was."

I rub my palms against my eyes. While it still pisses me off, I can't blame him. My guard would've flown up, and I'd have tried harder to tell Malicevile. "I hate secrets. Just when I thought I was getting the hang of things, thought I was learning, you had to go and make me feel clueless all over again."

"And I'm sorry. I'll try my best to be as honest as I can be."

"Because people don't trust me."

"Something like that."

I roll my eyes. "Well, I don't trust them either. In all honesty, there aren't many people I trust at the moment."

"I hope to change that."

"Sending me on a suicide mission to destroy my father isn't the way to do it. Don't expect me to put my eternity on the line a day after you ripped me away from my boy—" Boyfriend? Is Evan even that? I sort of broke up with him. Do titles matter now anyway? "I can't be your weapon from the goodness of my heart. I have people to think about. Plus, destroying Malicevile isn't going to solve your problems. There are other demons out there."

"I'm aware of that. We have to proceed with caution. Since the alliance has been weakened, we're all more susceptible to attacks. And there are a lot more demons than there are angels. It's why we rely on humans and half breeds. But Malicevile is taking that from us, too. He's already messed up the balance, and we're losing, princess. Not Heaven, but all of earth."

I know exactly what he's talking about. My father told me his plans. "I know," I finally say. "But you seem like you can handle yourself," I quip. "I bet you could take on Malicevile."

He grins. "I could give him a bad sunburn before he ripped my wings from my back and grounded me."

"Which he would. He has a pair on display."

Zach pales before he flushes. I wish I could take back my words, especially how they came out. The wings used to intrigue me, just hanging on the wall, but now I'm feeling sick as I think about it. Knowing they belonged to an angel didn't mean anything to me before. I hadn't met an angel apart from

Dylan, and he doesn't really count because he's half. It's different.

I reach out and touch his clenched fist. "I'm sorry. I shouldn't have said anything. Malicevile collects a lot of sickening things. You should see how many souls he has."

"Probably thousands."

I shrug. "Probably more."

Just when I was starting to get the answers I need, a silence falls between us. After watching Zach get sucked into his own thoughts, I say, "I can't promise much, Zach, but if I can help, I will. Just don't expect me to try to murder my father before dawn."

"I think I can work with that."

"So what now?"

"We send him a message. Let him know we're not giving up without a fight."

***

Sweat beads on my temples as I go over the plan in my mind for the millionth time. I've been standing in this spot at the edge of this cliff since Zach flew me away from the massive cathedral on an island that houses a small army of angels. According to Zach, Seraphim Rock is an impenetrable fortress untouchable by demons—well, except for me. A few hours off the coast of California by wing, the islet remains invisible to the world. It's like a little slice of Heaven, and one of the many headquarters for the angelic army.

I'd give anything to go back there right this second. I could use another few hours without the impending threat of demons.

I gaze at the expansive ocean that fades into the purpling horizon. Despite the coming dawn, stars still manage to pepper the sky like tiny sparks, reminding me that the dark doesn't only hold the ugly and damned. Beauty still remains even in the most dreadful nights.

"If we don't leave now we'll miss our window," Dylan says, coming up next to me.

"I'm just going over everything in my head one more time." A chill washes over me, and I shiver. Rubbing my hands over my arms, I brush it off like I'm cold. The last thing I need is for Dylan to realize that I'm not feeling so powerful. I'd never admit it, but missing the window of opportunity is exactly what I want to happen. I'm not ready to face my father, especially like this.

Dylan shrugs from his black hoodie and tugs it over my head before I have a chance to argue. His apple scent washes over me, stirring a bunch of mixed emotions within me. After a second, I slide my arms into the sleeves, which cover my hands.

"We're all set, princess," Zach says from behind me. "Remi and Dani don't have the patience for you that I do."

Standing fifty feet away are the two angels who assisted Zach last night in retrieving me from Malicevile. Neither of them has said a word to me, which I'm totally okay with. Silent and distant is exactly how I'd like them to stay. Pressure from one angel is enough.

I wave my sleeved hands. "Fine. Let's go before I lose my

nerve."

Zach turns to Dylan. "You sure you're up to this?"

I wish Dylan would change his mind. The last place I want him to be is in my father's line of sight. But I need him for this to work. I need him to help me draw out Malicevile.

"Yup," Dylan says. "I have faith that Cami will get me out of this alive."

I nod. "I promise. All of you."

"Then let the fun begin," Zach says.

He bends his legs, launching himself into the air. His two fellow angels quickly follow suit, leaving my head spinning in the fragrant air of heavenly scents. Dylan holds out his hand and pulls me to him before lifting me off my feet. As we fly through the dark night, my eyes burn. Now over the ocean, Dylan stays close behind Zach. While Dylan's ethereal wings still glow brightly, they no longer cause me pain. They look even more dazzling than they ever have before.

Dylan begins our descent toward an empty road that stretches out below. The plan is to drop me off and make it look like I've escaped, though Malicevile isn't stupid. He'll know it's a trap from a mile away, and he'll come fighting harder than ever. I wouldn't expect anything less.

Dylan slows his wings and swoops down, easing me onto the street before taking off again. Within seconds, Zach will drop his protective shield, and I'll be exposed for the demonic world to see.

Without hesitation, I sprint forward, glancing up only once

to see Dylan disappear. I run for a good mile. My boots thud as I pound down the empty street. Wind whips my messy hair from my face while cooling the sweat beading at my hairline. With each burning breath, I push myself to keep running. To keep going. I have to make this believable for it to work.

My senses on high alert, I shift my gaze around my surroundings. On one side is the vast ocean, and on the other, a hillside. I've been down this road so many times that I could probably run it blindfolded.

A flash of light brightens the dark sky, and I scream, making as much noise as I can even though Malicevile will find me regardless. I'm to draw him out and make him believe that I fear for my very existence.

The scent of cinnamon and clove wafts through the air. Perfect timing. We picked a place close enough to Raphael's so that Malicevile could get here before morning. And I'm glad, because I'm already tired of running. My life has been non-stop for days. I have a feeling I might start missing the spoiled life of being taken care of by a paranoid demon. I'll miss my Mustang, too.

And Evan. More than anything. But sacrifices must be made, because Zach was right. This is for something bigger than me. It's bigger than the tiny bubble I've found myself pressing against and yearning to pop, just to see what lies past the rainbow haze.

A burst of fire lights up the center of the road a half a mile away from me. I was expecting Evan to show up, but it doesn't make it any easier. Our last kiss still lingers in my mind, and I hold tightly onto that moment to help me get through what is to come.

"Cami, watch out!" Evan yells just as a burst of heavenly light hits the ground near my feet.

Stumbling, I fall forward, tucking my chin to my chest to somersault back to my feet. I charge forward in Evan's direction, throwing a ball of energy toward the sky as I do. He rushes toward me, lighting up the night with another burst of fire.

Another flash of light erupts in my vision. A gust of wind from flapping wings sends me sprawling to the pavement again. Strong hands grab my waist, lifting me a few dozen feet into the air. The world around me shakes as Dylan flies higher, dangling me like the puppet I've become in the war between Malicevile and Heaven.

Another fireball careens through the air, and Dylan jerks up a foot before it hits his chest. Instead, I absorb the flames, eager to take any and all power I can get my hands on.

Screaming out, I yell, "Let me go! You promised, Dylan!"

I thrash in Dylan's grip a little too hard, and I drop from his fingers, the world spinning around me. He grunts, diving to catch me, but only manages to slow me enough to find my levitation so I don't skin myself on the road. When another fireball heads his way, I yell and slap his leg and he ascends again.

Another strong pair of arms encircle me, but this time it's Evan as he yanks me from the ground. His heady patchouli scent invades my senses, making my heart explode with relief and love and happiness—it's the first time I'm not feeling utter hopelessness and despair around him. Heaven's changed me. It's enhanced all the feelings my demonic side tried to suppress. It's given me more than the ability to feel hatred, grief, and anger, or drown in desire. It's given me courage and hope and joy.

I find myself losing my focus the longer Evan holds onto me. This isn't the time to forget what I'm doing here.

"I never gave up hope, Cami. Your father thought they'd send you to Hell, but I knew. I knew you'd figure out things like you always do. He underestimates you—the universe underestimates you."

Oh, God. I wish he wouldn't talk. It makes it that much harder on me.

An angel shoots heavenly light and a flash erupts over us, causing Evan to jump into motion. He yanks me forward, not giving me a chance to respond to his words. Words that touch me so deeply I can feel their truth in my soul. The words stir something within me, and I realize just how true they are. No one, not even me, knows what I'm capable of.

My feet decide to stop working, so Evan nearly drags me down the road. Doubt crosses my mind. Can I really go through with the plan set in motion by Zach?

"Cami, keep up. We're almost there," Evan says, locking his fingers to my waist to try to carry me.

The strong scent of cinnamon cools my boiling blood as a figure comes into view. Malicevile stands tall, electricity flowing within the palms of his cupped hands, though he doesn't aim it toward the sky. He doesn't need to. There aren't any more angels flying above us.

Yanking away from Evan, I stop in the middle of the empty road. Malicevile gazes at me, his green eyes flashing in the darkness. I don't move to go to him. I can't. My feet won't let me. Fear paralyzes me as I face my demonic father.

"I can't do this," I say.

Evan stares at me with furrowed brows. "What do you mean?"

It takes everything in me to summon the courage I was so certain I had a moment ago. Heat swells from my core, working its way up my chest and down my legs. Steam radiates from my clammy skin as the cool air fights against the fire coursing through my blood. I release the demon I hide under my human façade, unleashing inky darkness from my heart and mind. My true body breaks through, slicing away at me as black horns jet from my forehead and a golden sheen slicks over my skin. My vision tints red, making the lightening sky turn midnight dark.

Pointing at the sky, I yell, "I can't do this! You were wrong about me! I'm not going to destroy my father."

Silence greets me as I unleash my demonic power, sending a bolt of energy into the air. My chest heaves, and I suck in a breath, turning my gaze toward Evan. His aqua eyes light up as he realizes what's going on.

Malicevile smiles, strolling closer, power still strong in his hands. "Camilla, my dear. I expected a trap the moment I felt your presence return into existence, but I never expected this."

"The angels, they tried to turn me against you. They brought me here to give you a message. They wanted me to break your heart by pledging myself to the fight of Heaven." The words tumble from me, leaving a bitter taste in my mouth.

"You've made the right decision, Camilla. You don't want to be on the losing side," Malicevile says, opening his arms out to me.

"I don't."

A ball of heavenly light explodes near our feet, knocking us apart. Evan jumps into action, blocking Malicevile as Zach and the two other angels land on the street behind us. Zach's black wings expand out as he faces me with a look so stern that my knees buckle.

"Princess," he says, "You're making a terrible mistake."

Forcing myself to my feet, I face the angels. Dylan lands behind them, watching me with his chocolaty eyes.

"Nothing I do is a mistake," I say, forcing my voice to remain even. "He's my father."

A ball of electricity zings past me as Malicevile attacks from behind. The angels hold strong as the guy on Zach's left takes the demonic power right in the gut.

"You stupid angels," Malicevile says, pushing past me. He throws another ball of energy, but Zach steps out of the way. "Did you really think you could turn my own blood against me?"

Zach meets my eyes for a split second before all three angels summon heavenly light in the palms of their hands. It's bright enough that Malicevile's steps falter.

"Dad, watch out!" I scream.

When the angels pitch their glowing balls in his direction, Evan rushes forward to my father, but he's not fast enough. The sudden action kicks me into motion, and I lunge forward, colliding into my father. My hands grip his shoulder, and I spin him around. Our eyes meet for a split second before heat explodes in my back.

His eyes widen, and he screams out my name as the heavenly light enters me, filling me to my core. It pushes against my very essence, filling me like a balloon. At any second, I'm bound to pop.

My ears hum with the sound of the ocean blocking our screams. I watch horror cross Malicevile's face for the first time ever in my life. In this moment, as he drowns in the humanity my existence created for him, I realize how twisted and cruel the world is—his world, not mine. In this second, my whole world is set ablaze in a light so pure, so full of goodness, I'd gladly let it consume me.

My back arches as every ounce of heavenly light the angels push at me fills my being, and my hands slip from Malicevile, leaving the shoulders of his suit jacket charred with his skin blistering and black where my hands had been.

Blinking through the haze, I watch the sky overhead lighten as the sun rises. The air shimmers around me, but something grounds me to the earth realm. Malicevile shades his eyes as he fades away, disappearing into the light prison realm.

Air whooshes from my lungs, and I hit the pavement hard, unable to keep upright. The blinding light stings my eyes, and it takes me a moment to realize that for the first time since my demonic transformation I'm seeing the sun.

"Cami?" Evan's voice is everywhere, wrapping me in his familiarity. His warm hands touch my face, his fingers run down my cheeks before brushing across my lips. He leans over me, his golden hair sparkling in the glorious light of day. Crying, he pulls me into his arms, his wet tears pelting my face.

He showers me with kisses like he can't get enough. It only takes someone clearing their throat behind us for him to pull away and revert to defense mode. Fire explodes in his palms, but I reach up and steal the power right from his fingers. As I absorb it, it churns with the rest of the power I store in my soul. Like oil and water, demonic power doesn't blend well with angelic light, and it makes my head spin.

"Evan, it's okay," I whisper. "They're not our enemies."

When my words sink in, he stiffens and brings his gaze back to me. "What are you saying?"

"I'm sorry." Tears burst from my eyes. He thinks I've betrayed him. Maybe I have. "I had to do this. It was the only way." Malicevile would've never truly accepted that I had given my soul to Zach. He'd have killed me himself had he known. Tricking him into thinking the angels destroyed me was the only way. Pretending to sacrifice myself for my father was my own twisted way of getting back at him. I hope watching the light he can't stand devour me caused him pain. Being Heaven-bound, it can't hurt me like it once did. My soul sucked it right in like it's been waiting all along.

"Way to what?"

"Escape Malicevile. If he knew I was alive, he'd never stop hunting me."

He swallows. "I don't understand. You're a demon. How are you even here?" His fingers brush against the smoking horns on my head before I compose myself and return to my human form, one now unaffected by the sun.

I nod toward Zach. "I gave my soul to an angel. I've agreed to fight on Heaven's side."

Confusion crosses his face. "But, Cami. What about me?"

I reach out and cup his face in my hands. "I'm not abandoning you. I'll never abandon you. I'm going to figure things out."

His blue eyes darken at my words. "How?"

"I swear I'll get your soul back from my father. I'll make sure you'll be saved from Hell. I'll never allow you to go there. I promise."

He scowls at me, causing me to drop my hands. "You know what I want, Cami."

My heart clenches. "Evan, please."

As he pulls away, I can feel my heart shattering. He looks at me with such hurt and disgust that you'd think I've done something unthinkable—something unforgivable.

In his eyes, I've given up our forever. In mine, I've saved his.

He gets to his feet and then turns his back on me. With a teary gaze, I turn toward the angels watching us. I beg with my eyes for Zach to intervene, to make Evan see something he obviously can't. I beg him to grant me a miracle.

No one says anything or moves.

I don't let Evan get far before I race to him, spinning him to face me. I can't let him go like this.

"Evan, I want you to know that I love you. I'll always love you no matter what side we're on. And I'm not giving up on us." Standing on my tiptoes, I kiss him, pulling him so close to me that he takes up my entire world. He relaxes under my touch, devouring my kisses, wrapping himself in all that I am.

Then he pulls away, a strange look on his face. "There's no us, Cami. As long as you're on Heaven's side, there can't be an us."

"Please, Evan."

"Cami, stop."

And just like that, it's over.

Evan turns on his heels and walks away without looking back. He doesn't even see Zach approach him before he's knocked out. When he awakens, he won't be able to speak the truth. Malicevile will still think I've perished by Heaven's power, and Evan won't be able to share a single detail of our plan. He'll be forced to quietly hang on to the information. He might think I've chosen Heaven over him, but I've chosen Heaven *because* of him. Because of all the people I love. But mostly for me.

I'll make him see.

A cool hand touches my shoulder as Dylan comes to my side. He slides his arm over me in a half hug, but I don't fall into him. I don't break down and cry.

Because this fight isn't over. No side has won. And I haven't lost yet.

Staring up at the bright sun, I let myself be filled with hope. Because with the rise of a new day comes a fresh start.

And this is mine. This is just the beginning.

EPILOGUE

SAVED

"ARE YOU SURE?" I ask, my heart beating so fast it hardly feels like it's beating at all.

"No, but he didn't attack me," Cadence says. "Just come look before one of the brave tries to put him down."

Hooking her arm through mine, Cadence drags me down the aisle of the small church past dozens of wooden pews. Zach hangs in front of the open door, blocking one of his angel sisters from exiting the building.

The scent of burning flesh wafts in at the same time a guttural howl sounds through the night. At the familiar sound, I tug my arm from Cadence and rush to the door, shoving Zach out of the way.

Running back and forth along the sidewalk, just on the outside of the invisible blessed barrier, is Greg. My hellhound releases a few excited barks before spinning in a circle to sit back on his haunches.

"Holy crap!" I yell as I rush to my demonic pet.

I can't believe he's here. I can't believe he found me. Malicevile said only the worthiest of hellhounds will always find their way back to their master's side, and the rest end up meeting hellish fates. I had just assumed the worst. He wouldn't have stayed by Malicevile's side without me, and I doubt Malicevile even noticed he was gone. Greg was always a roamer.

Kneeling, I wrap my arms around Greg and let him lick my face with his slimy black tongue. His fiery body singes my clothes, but I'm too excited to even care.

Turning back to the church, I say, "You were right, Cadence. It is Greg." He was commanded to never attack my best friend. "It's so cool he found me."

Well, I thought it was cool until I meet the gazes of two frowning angels. Zach steps from the church, earning a low growl from Greg. I squeeze the back of my hellhound's neck to stop him from trying to cross the blessed barrier to attack my Demon Watcher.

"Princess, he can't be here," Zach says, folding his arms over the illustrated sunset on his aqua-colored shirt.

I frown. "Well, duh, but I can't just send him away."

"That's not what I meant."

My eyes widen. "No way. I'm not killing him. He's not a threat. You know what happens when you kill a hellhound. I won't do it."

He shifts on his feet. "Then go wait inside. I'll be quick."

Summoning an energy ball in the palm of my hands, I hold it out at him. "You're not coming near him. I won't let you. I owe him as much. He saved me."

"Then save him."

Tears prickle my eyes as I hold Greg's fiery body against mine. Had it been any other hellhound, I'd have done what was right and taken it from this world. But this is different. Greg is my responsibility. Doing what's right feels so utterly wrong.

"He's right. The pack would thank you," Cadence says, stepping from the church. "I'll be right here. You don't have to do it alone. I knew Greg, too, remember?"

Oh, God. I'm going to be sick. "I'm sorry, Greg," I whisper into his ear. He whimpers against me, nudging my cheek with his muzzle. Black saliva sizzles on my sleeve. My heart feels so heavy that I think it might slide out through my feet. "You don't deserve any of this."

Holding out her dagger to me, Cadence's hand shakes. I don't take it though. I can't.

"Princess," Zach says.

"Shut up and let me say goodbye!" I yell.

Zach turns his back on me and walks inside.

Cadence drops to her knees next to me without a word, her presence alone enough to stop me from turning into a blubbering mess.

"I'm so sorry, Greg," I whisper again. "I wish you'd never tried to stand up for me. I didn't want to break you. I just want you to be free from this curse. I have to free you."

A sudden burst of light blinds me, causing Greg to wail, and it takes me a moment of blinking and yelling to realize that Zach didn't just betray me by hitting Greg with heavenly light. The light, so white and pure, radiates from my own hands, cutting through the fire. It encompasses Greg's large body, putting out the flames while seeping into his slimy coat and disappearing into his body.

"What's happening?" I yell, unable to contain the light in my hands. "I can't stop!"

Greg's body shivers and shakes, the sound of bones breaking and shifting loud in my ears. Another wail rips from his throat, sounding much more human as his muzzle shortens. Fur breaks through his slimy black skin before getting sucked back in. A moment later, a naked, hairless boy rests limply in my arms.

My mouth falls open in shock. "Greg?" Shifting his body, I tilt his head to look into the boy's face. "Oh, my God. He's alive. Zach, come here!"

Zach rushes from the church, surprise making his mouth hang open even wider than mine is. "Princess, what did you do?"

I throw my hands up. "I don't know! I told him I was going to free him and the angel power I absorbed from you came bursting out. It triggered the transformation back."

"Cami?" Greg whispers from my lap. "What's going on? Where am I?"

He doesn't remember a thing. Oh, unholy Hell. I'm so relieved. I'm embarrassed by how I treated him just like a pet.

I lean over and kiss his forehead. "It doesn't matter," I say against his cool skin. "But you're safe."

"Let's get him inside," Zach says.

Zach scoops him from my lap, and Cadence follows behind him. I can't move from my spot though. I'm so stunned and relieved. I feel like shouting it to the world. I saved a hellhound. I saved *my* hellhound.

Greg's transformation erases every doubt I had about giving my soul to Zach. Because even if Greg turns out to be the only person I'm ever able to save, it was totally worth it.

I suck in a breath to calm my excited nerves and regret it immediately. The scent of patchouli and golden amber fills my senses, sending both love and fear through me. I gulp in another breath, expecting to catch a hint of cinnamon, but it's not there. My father won't discover me. *Not unless you want him to. Zach makes sure of it.*

Footsteps sound in the suddenly quiet night, and I jerk my head up as Evan crosses the street. His hands are tucked into the pockets of his hoodie, and he meets me with eyes so lost that they nearly break me.

"How did you find me?" I ask, jumping to my feet. I close the distance between us but steel myself for a fight.

"I followed your pet," he says, motioning to the scorch marks on the sidewalk behind me.

"Does Malicevile know?"

His long pause does nothing to calm my fear. "No. It's not like I can tell him either, thanks to your angel."

"It's for my protection."

"Well, it kills me."

"And you don't think it doesn't kill me, too?"

He scrapes his boot across the pavement. "Sure looks like it with that smile you were wearing a moment ago."

"That isn't fair. Did you see what I did?"

"You mean losing the most devoted protector you had on your side? Don't you see, Cami? They're using you. They don't care about you—not like I do. Please, you have to come home. I thought I could handle this, but I can't. I'm losing control of my humanity. You messed me up." His low voice wraps around me, tugging me closer. He slides his hands from his pockets and opens his arms. "Please, we can work this all out."

Against my better judgment, I slide into his arms. I can't help it. He's intoxicating and makes me careless. "You know I can't," I whisper.

"I don't understand why you're giving up on our forever. All you have to do is tell me how. I know you're afraid it won't work, but I'm strong enough. I want to spend forever with you."

He wants the information the demon world thinks I died with. I bristle. I shouldn't have expected anything better. "As long as we're on the same side, right?"

"Cami."

I tug away from him. Relief washes over me when he doesn't try to grab me. I wish he would though. I wish I could fall into his arms and pretend he isn't under my father's influence. I want so badly to right things between us. My heart aches for him every day, the constant reminder of what I'm preparing for. What I need to fight for.

Seeing him like this, so desperate and angry at me, is as painful as the first time I lost him. It's not only Malicevile that stands between us now. It's all of Hell.

I don't answer him when he calls my name again. Instead, I turn toward the church. Zach stands a few feet away from me like my ever present shadow. He frowns at the tears streaming down my cheeks.

Zach takes me into his arms, and a second later, he bends his knees and launches us into the night. As Evan disappears on the ground below, I know in my whole heart that Heaven is right. I'm going to be the one to destroy my father.

Malicevile must die.

To be continued...

# ACKNOWLEDGMENTS

I'M FOREVER GRATEFUL to my editorial team, Jan, Jamie, and Katie, for all their hard work and dedication in making the Demon Within series something I'm extremely proud of. You three mean so much to me, and I'm happy to have you in my life.

I also want to thank those who have supported me in various ways through my writing journey. Thank you to Amanda for your enthusiasm over the series. Your thoughts always make my day. A special thanks to Nikki, my friend and confidant, for letting me talk your ear off, for your guidance and opinions on all my book stuff, and for keeping me entertained with all sorts of shenanigans. Jazmin and Malory, you two have been here through all of it, and I appreciate your constant love and support.

Thank you to my family, who are too many to name. You

all make my life amazing. I love you all.

Thanks to you, my readers, for following Cami's journey through all her ups and downs, good and evil, and through the complexities of all her different relationships. I love hearing whose team you're on and who your favorite characters are. Thanks again!

ABOUT GINNA MORAN

GINNA MORAN IS A WRITER from sunny Southern California. She started writing poetry as a teenager in a spiral notebook that she still has tucked away on her desk today. Her love of writing grew after she graduated high school, and she completed her first unpublished manuscript at age eighteen.

When she realized her love of writing was her life's passion, she studied literature at Mira Costa College in Northern San Diego. Besides writing novels, she was senior editor, content manager, and image coordinator for Crescent House Publishing Inc. for four years.

Aside from Ginna's professional life, she enjoys binge watching television shows, playing pretend with her daughter, and cuddling with her dogs. Some of her favorite things include chocolate, anything that glitters, cheesy jokes, and organizing her bookshelf.

Ginna Moran loves to hear from her readers so visit her online at www.GinnaMoran.com. You can also find her on her Facebook page or Group, Twitter, Instagram, and Snapchat. To stay up-to-date on new releases, sign up to her newsletter. You'll not only get a FREE book, but you'll be able to participate in monthly giveaways!

Ginna Moran is currently hard at work on her next novel.

MORE BY GINNA MORAN

PARANORMAL
Destined for Dreams Series
Demon Within Series
Finding Nate Series
Going Ghostly Series
Spark of Life Series
When Souls Collide Series
Demon Watcher Series
Call of the Ocean Series

CONTEMPORARY
Falling into Fame Series

STANDALONES
Life After Lila